Also by Catherine Cookson

KATIE MULHOLLAND
KATE HANNIGAN
THE ROUND TOWER
FENWICK HOUSES
THE FIFTEEN STREETS
MAGGIE ROWAN
THE LONG CORRIDOR
THE UNBAITED TRAP
COLOUR BLIND
THE MENAGERIE
THE BLIND MILLER
FANNY McBRIDE
ROONEY
THE NICE BLOKE
THE INVITATION
THE DWELLING PLACE
FEATHERS IN THE FIRE
THE MALLEN STREAK
OUR KATE

The 'Mary Ann' Series

A GRAND MAN
THE LORD AND MARY ANN
THE DEVIL AND MARY ANN
LOVE AND MARY ANN
MARRIAGE AND MARY ANN
MARY ANN'S ANGELS

and published by Corgi Books

Catherine Cookson

Life and Mary Ann

CORGI BOOKS
A DIVISION OF TRANSWORLD PUBLISHERS LTD
A NATIONAL GENERAL COMPANY

LIFE AND MARY ANN

A CORGI BOOK 0 552 09075 1

Originally published in Great Britain by
Macdonald & Co. (Publishers) Ltd.

PRINTING HISTORY

Macdonald edition published 1962
Macdonald edition reprinted 1963
Macdonald edition reprinted 1967
Corgi edition published 1972
Corgi edition reprinted 1973
Corgi edition reprinted 1973

This book is set in 10–10½ pt. Intertype Baskerville

Corgi Books are published by
Transworld Publishers Ltd.,
Cavendish House, 57–59 Uxbridge Road,
Ealing, London W.5
Made and printed in Great Britain by
Cox & Wyman Ltd., London, Reading and Fakenham

**NOTE: The Australian price appearing on the
back cover is the recommended retail price.**

Life and Mary Ann

PART ONE

Growing Pains

CHAPTER ONE

I WISH I'd never clapped eyes on him. I wish he had left us alone.

What! In Mulhattan's Hall?

Mary Ann hunched her shoulders as indication that she was ignoring the voice of gratitude that usually played no small part as a component of her character. Well, he made you sick, he did. Who did he think he was, anyway? Playing God. Directing all their lives. He certainly tried to live up to his name. . . . Mr. Lord, indeed! Well, he could think he was the Lord, and act like him, but he wasn't going to get the better of her in this latest fight. . . . But he had, he had already got the better of her, hadn't he?

Mary Ann unclenched her hands and rose slowly from the side of the bed and walked towards the window. There had been a black frost in the night, there would soon be snow. The cutting air came from the window-pane and chilled her nose and lips. So cold was her mouth that she did not feel her teeth biting into the flesh. But she felt the trembling of her chin in its fight, not against the cold, but against the rising storm of tears.

Although she was gazing across the farmyard towards the house on the hill, Mr. Lord's house, she was seeing none of these things. The width of the farmyard had taken on the shape of a face. The buildings at each side were cheeks, high-boned, prominent cheeks, and Mr. Lord's house on the hill was a deep brow, half covered with tumbled black hair. Somewhere, in the distance between the farm and the house on the hill, were the eyes of Corny. They were deep-set, and dark. She couldn't see if they were merry, or sad, or held that spark of fighting fire that made him stand up to people. . . . Stand up to Mr. Lord.

9

For over three years Corny had stood up to Mr. Lord. From the very day he had come to her thirteenth birthday party, a belated, awkward, aggressive, grotesquely dressed guest, he had stood up to him. His appearance on that day had thrown the whole party out of joint. But he had made an impression on Mr. Lord, for the old man had recognized in the gangling fifteen-year-old a worthy opponent, worthy to fight, worthy of many things . . . in fact, of anything in the world, but herself. Corny, in a subtle, even cunning way, had stood firm against all Mr. Lord's tactics, and had got the better of him time and time again where she herself was concerned. And in the end he would have won. She knew this, she felt it. But what does he do? What does Corny do? Of a startling sudden, he gives in to Mr. Lord. He accepts the offer that the old man has been dangling like a golden carrot under his nose for years.

When she had gone for him last night, almost reaching five feet in her wild indignation, he had remained utterly calm. The only time he had raised his voice was when he said, 'Look, I'm tellin' you, he's got nowt to do with it.'

She knew that he had used nowt to vex her, because he could speak as well as anybody now, even as good as their Michael. Had she not coached him month after month from that thirteenth birthday when she had given him his first lesson in English? Northern English, for although her grammar was correct, the inflexion of the dialect was still thick on her. But so convincing had been his denial that Mr. Lord had any hand in his decision to go to America, that she had asked, with pain-touched docility, 'Is it because they are always ragging you about me being so little?' He gave a scornful, hard laugh before saying quietly, 'Don't be daft.' And then he had added, with a touch of the quiet, sly humour that she loved, 'It's just as well you're no bigger, else you'd aim to wear the pants all the time. Not that you don't have a go, even now.'

She had not laughed for her mind was looking at the saying literally. The waist of his trousers would reach up to her bust, and her head came far below his thick shoulder. Over the last few years she had done everything possible to put on inches. During one period, she had measured herself every day for three months, until the disheartening result had begun to affect her. Her mother had said, 'If you worry, it will stop you growing.' Her da had said, comfortingly, 'You'll sprout all at once, you'll see. One of these mornings you'll wake up and find your feet sticking through the bed rails. Anyway,' he had added, with his arm about her shoulder, 'you've got more in your little finger than most people have got in their great boast bodies.' But that comfort did not make up for such silly remarks as, 'You two are like Mutt and Jeff,' or, 'Here comes the long and the short of it.'

She had tried wearing very high heels. The first pair of stiletto shoes she had worn had caused her da and Corny to fall against each other with laughing. Somehow she didn't suit high heels, and so she had been unable to take advantage of such helpful accessories. But what did it matter? High heels, the long and the short of it, Mutt and Jeff, that wasn't the reason he was going. He was going because Mr. Lord had won.

At this point in her thinking the bedroom door clicked and her mother came in. At thirty-eight Elizabeth Shaughnessy appeared like a woman bordering on thirty. Her face was without lines, her long blonde hair resting in a bun on the nape of her neck still retained its natural sheen. Her bearing was dignified. During the last three years, with the lessening of worry, life had seemed to stand still for her. Only during these last years had she taken the comfort of the farmhouse and the security of Mike's position as a natural sequence of events. Mike no longer drank – at least he no longer got drunk – and this fact alone would have spelt security no matter where they had lived. But in the comparative opulence of the farmhouse – comparative when thinking of their early beginnings, in the slum in Burton Street, known as Mulhattan's Hall – the fact that he was steady had paid dividends far surpassing anything she had ever dreamed of. Not that she had been entirely free from worry over the last three years; she experienced the usual worries of a mother concerning her son and daughter. But, as from the very beginning, it was the daughter who gave her cause for most concern. Somehow, Michael's life had always seemed cut and dried. Right from when he was a child, even before he ever saw a farm, he had wanted, like his father, to be a farmer. In times past she had thought this was the only thing father and son had in common. Now, all that was changed. But with Mary Ann it had been different. Perhaps it was the fact of Mr. Lord coming into her life that had made Mary Ann more of a trial. And yet she knew she shouldn't think of her daughter in that sense. Mary Ann had been the saviour of them all. But for Mary Ann they would be rotting in Mulhattan's Hall at this moment. She had no illusion about the strength of her husband. Without this environment, brought about by his daughter's strategy, Mike would still be fighting a losing battle with the drink and the shipyard.

Lizzie knew that everything in life must be paid for, and Mary Ann was expected to pay Mr. Lord in the kind of payment he most desired. By becoming the wife of his grandson she would be tied to him for life. He would then have claims on her far outreaching those of the present. And it was a glorious prospect, Lizzie knew, when looked at unemotionally: Mary Ann Shaughnessy, a child from the slums of Jarrow, lifted into the family, the élite family of the Lords, where money and power went hand in hand.

Three years ago, when the old man's plans had been made known to her, Lizzie's first reaction had been one of shock and disgust. Mary Ann was only a child, a child of thirteen . . . not thirteen. And Mr. Lord was actually voicing his plans to marry her to Tony his grandson. Tony was then twenty-four and seemed already a very adult man. But the shock and disgust had not lasted long, for when Lizzie thought about it calmly she became excited, even elated, almost overcome with the idea of this wonderful future for her child. That was until she realized that Mary Ann's interest in Corny Boyle was no passing childish fancy. Her daughter, she knew, took strong likes and dislikes, and where she liked she almost nearly loved. She loved her father more than she did God. She loved, yes, she loved the old man, there was no doubt about that. She loved him, she stood up to him, she fought with him but she loved him. And she also loved Corny Boyle. That was the trouble, that was the worry now in Lizzie's life. Or it had been up till yesterday when Corny had sprung his decision on them all. He had walked into the kitchen unannounced, and with a coolness that set Lizzie wondering, he had told them he was going to America. She wondered if this big, raw-boned fellow was calculating the benefits to be derived from submitting to Mr. Lord, or if he was being super-humanly unselfish and leaving the road clear for her daughter. Whichever way it was, she thanked God from the bottom of her heart that Corny Boyle had decided to go to America. But now before her lay the task of comforting Mary Ann.

'Come on downstairs, lass, you're froze up here.'

Mary Ann remained gazing out of the window. And her voice was flat-sounding as she replied, 'I'm all right. I'm not cold.' Her mother had called her 'lass'. She only called her that when she was deeply touched. She usually called her Mary Ann or 'My dear', and she had insisted some time ago that she be called 'Mother' and not 'Ma'. Mary Ann's lips moved tightly over one another. That was Mr. Lord again. She could hear his voice now, saying to her mother, 'You must make her drop this "Ma" way of addressing you, Mrs. Shaughnessy. Make her adopt Mother. It is a much nicer term, don't you think?' When her da had found out about this – and he had found out, because her mother kept insisting that she did not call her 'Ma' – he had cried indignantly, 'To hell! If you are Ma to her, then you are Ma to her. .... And let me tell you this. You'll lose something by being more Mother than Ma. I'm tellin' you! As for the old boy. If he approaches me with the idea of turning me into Father, I'll spit in his eye. So help me God, I will.'

Her mother had had to do a lot of talking to calm her father down that time.

'Come on down.' Lizzie's voice was soft and coaxing. 'The tea's all set, and Michael and Sarah will be here any minute. Come on.'

Mary Ann turned and looked at her mother, and her voice held no bitterness as she said, 'You're glad he's going, aren't you?'

'Oh no, I'm not. What makes you say that? Oh no, I'm not.' Lizzie's reply was too quick. There was too much emphasis on her words. Mary Ann lowered her lids, covering

13

her great brown eyes from her mother's gaze. Her mother couldn't lie very well. She turned her head away and looked out of the window again before saying, 'Why is it you don't mind our Michael going with Sarah, but you have always minded me and Corny?'

Lizzie could find no words, no false words with which to answer this statement. If she had spoken the truth she would have said, 'It's a man's position that matters. Michael's future is set. At the end of this year, when he finishes his probation on the farm, he will go to the Agricultural College. His future is mapped out. He'll be a farmer. If there wasn't a job waiting for him here, he could get set on anywhere. Perhaps I would have liked someone better than Sarah Flannagan for him, because, as you know, none of us can stand her mother. But I must admit that Sarah's turned out to be a nice lass. And moreover she's Michael's choice.' Perhaps her son had one more thing in common with his father. There'd only ever be one woman for him. There were men like that. They were few and far between, God knew, but there were still some left; and she had the feeling in her heart that Sarah Flannagan was the only one for Michael and he for her, strange as it seemed, for only a few years ago Sarah hated the sight of Mary Ann, and Michael into the bargain. But then, like a child, she was taking the pattern from her mother.

Mary Ann said into the silence, 'You're supposed to like Mrs. McBride, and she's his grandmother.'

'Of course, I like Fanny. I could almost say I love her. But there's a great difference between a woman and her grandson. Not that I don't like Corny. I've told you, I do like Corny. Why do you keep on?'

Mary Ann nodded to the icy window-pane. 'But you don't like him for me, because there's Tony, isn't there? And Mr. Lord. Mr. Lord's little plan. Oh, I know all about it. But listen to me, Mother.' She pulled herself away from Lizzie's side. She even stepped back a pace to widen the distance between them, before saying, 'I'll never marry Tony. Not to please you, or him, or anybody else.'

'Who's talking about Tony?'

'You are. You're thinking about him all the time. That's

why you've never been able to take to Corny. Corny hadn't a big house. He hadn't a splendid job. He hadn't a grandfather rolling in the money. But let me tell you, Mother, Corny will make his name with either one thing or the other. With either cars or his cornet. Oh, yes. That's been a laugh in the house for a long time now. Corny, with his cars and his cornet. The three C's. Well! You wait and see. . . .'

As Mary Ann's head drooped forward and the tears began to roll down her cheeks, Lizzie cried, 'Aw! lass, lass. Aw! don't cry like that.' And she enfolded her daughter in her arms and rocked her gently back and forwards as if she were still the little elfin-faced child. The endearing, maddening, precocious, beguiling child. And she was still a child. She would always remain a child to Lizzie. And she wanted her child to be looked after; and like every mother, she felt that half the battle would be won if there was money at hand to help with the looking after.

Saturday tea was still a function, a time when Lizzie had her family all around her. It was usually a meal of leisure with no one dashing to catch a bus to the secretarial school in Newcastle – that was Mary Ann; or golloping the meal to attend to this, that, or the other on the farm – that was Mike; or, if not following his father's pattern and dashing outside, reading, reading, reading – that was Michael, always reading, and not eating. There were more books in the house concerning the diseases that animals were prone to than in the Public Library, so Lizzie thought. But Saturday was different.

All Saturday morning Lizzie baked for the tea. Besides the old standbys, egg-and-bacon pie, fruit tarts and scones, there was always something new. She liked to try a new recipe each week. On Tuesday she would look forward to the coming of her magazine. Not for the stories, but for the recipes, and each Saturday they would tease her, 'What's it, the day, another stomach binder? By! I'll sue that paper afore long.' Mike would generally start in this way, and the others would follow suit. However, they nearly always ate the last crumb of her new recipe. But today things hadn't gone according to plan. Mike made no reference whatever to the table. His large, heavy, handsome face looked dark as he took his seat at the head, and immediately he gave signs of his inward mood by running his hands through his thick red hair, and this after combing it only a few minutes earlier.

Lizzie felt a rising irritation in her as she gauged her husband's mood. He wasn't going to start and take up the cudgels again. Talk about like father, like son. It had never been like that in this family, it had always been like father, like daughter. Mike was also, she knew, blaming Mr. Lord for Corny's decision. Although the boy had stated flatly that no one had influenced him, Mike was as furious at this moment against the old man as Mary Ann herself. It was quite some time now since any major issue had occurred to make Mike take sides against Mr. Lord. As Lizzie looked sharply between her husband and her daughter, she thought she could almost feel the emotions flowing between them, as if they were linked by actual blood vessels. Talk about Siamese twins. As was her wont when worried, she muttered a little prayer to herself. It was, as usual, in the nature of a demanding plea, and in this particular case she asked that Mike might not lose his temper with the old man. 'Let him go for anyone else, but not for Mr. Lord, dear God.'

Trying to bring normality into the proceedings, Lizzie now addressed herself to Sarah. 'How's business been this week, Sarah?' she asked with a smile.

'Oh, not too good at all. The roads have been so slippery. It's been hard enough to exercise them. And nobody seems inclined to ride. I don't blame them. I nearly stuck to the saddle yesterday morning.'

'I don't know how you do it. I think you're wonderful.'

Sarah Flannagan remained smiling across the table at Lizzie. But she made no answer. She would have been glad had this woman thought she was wonderful, but she felt it was merely a phase. She knew there was tension in the house and that Elizabeth Shaughnessy was trying to smooth things over. Some day she hoped, and from the depth of her being, that this woman would be her mother-in-law, and yet she was a little afraid of her. Yes, the truth was, she was a little afraid of her. She thought she wasn't quite good enough for

Michael. All mothers felt like that about daughters-in-law, so she understood, and so she felt sure that Elizabeth Shaughnessy would finally accept her into the family, whereas she would never reconcile herself to accept Corny Boyle. This thought brought her eyes flicking towards Mary Ann. It was hard at this moment to think that Mary Ann and herself had been bitter enemies from the day they first met until just a short while ago. She did not delude herself that the first day she came to this house, when she led the dapple, Mary Ann's thirteenth birthday present from Mr. Lord, up the road, and was asked to stay to tea, that it was from that day that she and Mary Ann had become friends. No, on that day Mary Ann had tolerated her because her mind was taken up with other important things. Corny Boyle, for instance, and her pony, and her posh friends from Newcastle, to mention a few. Even in the days that followed Mary Ann's acceptance was touched with condescension, although she gave her back with good measure everything she dealt out. . . . In a way, they had still been at war. It was only in the last few months Mary Ann had been different. But then she herself had been different. They both seemed to have grown up over night, and recognizing this they had come together and talked. They had talked about Michael and they had talked about Corny. So now at this moment she could understand what Mary Ann was going through. She also knew that because his daughter was unhappy Mr. Shaughnessy was in a tearing rage. She had never seen him look so thundery. She could remember back to the times when he used to come home roaring drunk to Mulhattan's Hall. She could remember the day he had danced and sang in the road; and Mary Ann had come and taken him home and she had gibed at her: 'Your da is a no-good drunk,' she had shouted. And mimicked Mary Ann's oft-repeated phrase, 'Me da's a grand man.' And yet now there was nothing more she wanted in life than to be a member of this family, and to call Mike Shaughnessy 'Da'. In a way, although she loved her own father, there was something greatly attractive, greatly endearing about Mike Shaughnessy, and it would be an added happiness the day he became her father-in-law.

'What are you dreaming about?' The gentle dig in the ribs from Michael turned her face towards him, and she laughed and said, 'Horses.'

Michael let his eyes rest on her. He loved to look at her. He knew she hadn't been thinking of horses; he had come to know all the flowing movement and expression of her vivacious dark face. Sarah was beautiful, she was more than beautiful. To him she was everything a fellow could dream of. She had a lot of sense in her, which was strange when he thought of her father and mother, though he must say he liked Mr. Flannagan; he liked him much better than he liked her mother. But Sarah was like neither of them. She had a sort of deep wisdom about her. If he was going off the deep end about this, that, or the other, she would come out with something that astounded him with its profundity. He who had attended the Grammar School up to a year ago could not think to the depth that Sarah's mind took her. He wondered how his mother would take it if he wanted to get married before he started college. Likely she would go mad.

'Michael, you're not eating anything.' Lizzie brought his eyes from Sarah, and he said, 'Well, what do you expect after all that dinner?'

'I've never known your dinner stop you eating your Saturday tea.' Lizzie now turned to Mary Ann and said, quietly, 'Shall I fill your cup again?'

'No, Mother, no, thanks. I've had enough.' As she turned her glance from her mother, she met the full penetrating force of Mike's eyes on her. They were looking into her, probing the hurt, and feeling it almost as much as herself. In his eyes was a reflection of her own anger, and she thought in the idiom that no convent-school training, no English mistress who had selected her for personal torture while dealing with clauses had been able to erase: 'Eee! there'll be ructions if I don't stop him. But he's not to go for Mr. Lord. I'll tell him what I think, meself.' She knew she could tell Mr. Lord what she thought, she knew that she could show her temper to him, answer his own arrogant manner with what her mother would term 'cheek' and get away with it, but, not so, her da. Mr. Lord liked her da. She felt that although she in the first place had to point out to Mr. Lord, and emphatically, the qualities that made up her father, he had come to respect and like him from his own judgment. But that wasn't saying that he would stand her father accusing him of sending Corny off to America, and that is what Mike would do if she didn't stop him. She was thankful that Mr. Lord wouldn't be back on the farm until Tuesday. In the meantime she must get at her da. But she knew she wouldn't have much weight with him unless she could prove to him that she wasn't all that much affected. This would be nigh impossible if she continued to go around looking as if the end of the world had come. But it had for her. Her world seemed to have been sliced in two, so that she was faced with a gulf over which she must either jump or remain in a state of pain for ever. She made an attempt at the jump by looking at Sarah and asking in a voice which she strove with great effort to make ordinary, 'What are you wearing for the wedding?'

Sarah, looking back at her with the threaded intuition of youth, immediately played up by raising a laugh. 'If this weather keeps up, black stockings, woollen undies, and a wind-cheater.'

Lizzie laughed, louder than she would have done on another occasion. Michael laughed, his head back in the same attitude that his father used when his laughter was running free. Mike only allowed a quirk to appear at the corner of his mouth, but he nodded towards Sarah as he said, 'Sensible idea.'

'Fancy having a white wedding at this time of the year. And those two, with a nuptial mass!' Michael bowed his head and shook it from side to side as he chuckled to himself, and then added, 'I shouldn't have been surprised if Len had said he was going up to the altar in tails.'

Mary Ann too wanted to laugh at the thought of Len, the cowman, going up to the altar in tails. Len was dim – they all knew that Len was dim – and Cissie, his girl, was even lower down in the mental grade. She was round and placid, and ever smiling; and she had a stock phrase, with which she punctuated every question and answer. She could hear her now, 'Well now, Mrs. Shaughnessy, I've always wanted a white weddin'.' 'And well now, with Mr. Lord showing his appreciation of Len so, standing the spread for us, and givin' Len a rise and all that, well now, I thought we should do things fittin' like.' Part of Mary Ann felt sorry for Cissie but she didn't really know why. Sometimes she thought it was because, as she said to herself, Cissie had never had a chance, there had never been a Mr. Lord in Cissie's life. Yet at the same time she recognized that all the Mr. Lords in the world couldn't have made much difference to Cissie. Cissie, like Len, was dim. But that didn't say they shouldn't have a nuptial mass. . . .

This point was as good as any other on which to start an argument with Michael. She knew she had to do something, and quickly, to switch her thoughts from weddings in general to a wedding in particular, which of late had been finding a prominent place in her thinking. So, as she had done from as far back as she could remember, she attacked Michael in her usual way. 'What's funny about a nuptial mass, about their having a nuptial mass? They've as much right to have a nuptial mass as you or anybody else!'

'Oh! here we go again!' Michael rolled his eyes towards the ceiling before bringing his head down and bouncing it towards Mary Ann, emphasizing each word as he said, 'I didn't say they hadn't the right to have a nuptial mass. But those two won't have a clue what it's all about. They'll sit through the service without a clue. Do you think they will be affected by the spirituality of the whole thing? Can you imagine Len thinking?'

'How do you know if they'll be affected spiritually or not? Because Len has never been to a grammar school it doesn't say that his spiritual awareness isn't as alive as yours!'

'Aw. . . . Bulls, heifers, cows and calves!' Michael always managed to impregnate this saying with the same quality that another would give to strident blasphemy and it affected Lizzie in this way; she often thought she would rather hear Michael swear than say that. It wasn't the words themselves but the stringing of them together, and the inflexion of his voice as he said them. 'Now, that's enough, Michael. And you too, Mary Ann! The pair of you stop it.'

'Well, Mother, I ask you.' Michael knew he was being pulled up, and why. But he smiled at Lizzie and said pityingly, 'Well, I ask you. Len and Cissie in a nuptial mass! If one of them had been a little different, a bit bright, it mightn't have appeared so bad, but they are a pair . . .'

'Yes, you've said it there, they're a pair.' Mike was speaking now and they all looked towards him. But he was looking at Michael only. 'And they're paired properly. What do you think Len's life would be like if he was marrying a more intelligent girl? . . . Hell, that's what it would be. There's something in nature, if let alone, that helps us with our picking. We're not always aware of it at the time, sometimes not for years. Len's marriage won't break up, because he's picked according to the level of his mind. He doesn't know it, he never will, and he'll be all the more content. It sometimes comes about that you don't get the one to fit both your mind and your body, then things happen. . . . Take it on a lower plane, so to speak. Take it in the breeding of stock. . . .'

'Mike!' Lizzie's back was very straight; and Mike turned his face full to her and lifted his hands in a flapping motion, as if wiping away his name, before saying, 'Look, Liz. There's neither of them at school any more. They're no longer bairns! And all right, Sarah's here, but Sarah deals with animals.'

'Well, it's no conversation for the tea-table, and I'm not having it. I know where it will lead. We'll have the stockyard on our plates before many more minutes are over. Likening people to animals!'

'There's not a lot of difference that I can see.' Mike's voice was suddenly quiet; and there was a tinge of sadness in his tone as he went on, 'I've a sick cow in the barn now. Nobody will have it, nobody will believe that it's because Brewster's gone. But from the day she watched him mounting the ramp into that van, she's gone back. . . . Cows are women. . . .'

'Mike!' Lizzie had risen to her feet.

'All right, you won't have it.' Mike had scraped his chair back on the floor and was looking up at her. 'You won't have it, but nevertheless it's true. . . . You know, your mother did everything under God's sun to prevent you and me coming together, didn't she? Well, if she had succeeded it would have been a bad thing, a loss to both of us, and you know it. The same thing is happening now and you're glad. You're glad, Liz. That's what hurts me, you're glad.'

Mike was on his feet now glaring at Lizzie, and she put her fingers to her lips as she stared back at him, muttering, 'It isn't true, it isn't true. You know it isn't true.'

'Aw, I know you, Liz. I can read you like a book. Only remember this, you can't push big houses and money into a heart. A heart's only made for feeling.'

Mike's voice had come from deep in his chest on the last words, and they all watched him walking down the long farm kitchen towards the door. And when it closed on him Lizzie turned towards Mary Ann, her voice breaking as she said, 'He's blaming me. He's blaming me for it all! What had I to do with Corny going to America? I had nothing to do with it.' She was appealing to Mary Ann, seeming to have forgotten Michael and Sarah. 'You believe that, don't you?'

Mary Ann got to her feet. She too seemed to have forgotten the couple sitting opposite, their heads bent in embarrassment; and she put her arms about Lizzie as she said, 'Don't cry, Mother. Don't cry. Yes, I believe you. There, there, don't cry.' She pressed her mother into her chair again, and going to the teapot, poured her out a fresh cup of tea; and as she handed it to her she said again, 'There, now, don't worry. I know you had nothing to do with it.'

But even as she said this, she was thinking along the lines of Mike. She knew her mother was glad and relieved, even happy, at the way things had turned out. She also knew that she must talk to her da before he met Mr. Lord, or the place would blow up.

CHAPTER TWO

'How d'you think it's gone, Mary Ann?'

'Wonderfully, wonderfully, Len. It was a wonderful wedding.'

'Aye. Aa feel it was.'

Mary Ann smiled at Len, and her smile was as sincere as her words had been. For to her mind it had been a wonderful wedding, surprisingly wonderful. The nuptial mass had not been ludicrous, as Michael had foretold. In fact, as she had looked at the white-robed Cissie and the unusually spruce Len, she had felt that they were deeply threaded with the spirituality of the moment, as very likely they were. Cissie had even looked pretty. She was detached from all dimness in this moment. Cissie was a bride, and Mary Ann had wanted to cry.

She said to Len, 'You'll like Harrogate.' At the same time she wondered why on earth they had chosen Harrogate. Harrogate was stuffy – snobbish and stuffy. Cissie had said it was because there were things to do; it had a winter season. That was funny, if you came to think about it. The Spanish City in Whitley Bay would be more in their line.

'You know, Aa wish we weren't goin' away.... Well, you know what Aa mean.' Len laughed. 'Aa mean not so soon like. Aa would uv liked to stay for the dance later on. Aa bet it's the first time there's ever been a dance in this old barn. Anyway, for many a long year.' Len looked along the length of the barn to where Lizzie was supervising the clearing of the tables and added, 'By, your mother made a splendid turn-out, didn't she? With Cissie's folk not being up to anything like this, it's made her feel ... well, you know what I mean.'

Mary Ann nodded. Yes, she knew what he meant. As well

23

as all the bought cakes, her mother had cooked nearly all the week for the wedding spread. Hams, tongues . . . the lot.

'An' the old man's all right at bottom; curses you up hill and down dale one minute, then stands your weddin' expenses. He's all right, he is, if you understand him like. Look, there he is now. He's laughin'. Look, he's laughin' with that Mrs. Schofield. By, she's a nice woman, that. She's got no side, has she?' He looked at Mary Ann. And she, looking to where Mr. Lord was being entertained by Mrs. Schofield, nodded before saying, 'Yes, she's nice.'

Lettice Schofield was the mother of Mary Ann's school friend. She had first come to the farm on Mary Ann's thirteenth birthday, and had since then not infrequently looked them up. Everybody liked Mrs. Schofield, but everybody thought her a bit dizzy. Perhaps they liked her for that reason. At least everybody but Mike. Mike didn't think Mrs. Schofield was dizzy, he never had. From that birthday party he had said, 'There's depth in that one. All this Mrs. Feathering is just a barricade against something.' And over the past three years there had been times when Mary Ann thought her father was right, and others, when she listened to Mrs. Schofield's light brittle chatter and her high tinkling laugh, when she had been inclined to think with Janice that her mother acted silly, like a girl . . . and she nearly thirty-four years old. Another thing that made Mary Ann wonder at times about Mrs. Schofield was the fact that Mr. Lord was always entertained by her, and she knew only too well that Mr. Lord could not suffer fools gladly. So, on the whole she was inclined to think that her da's opinion of Mrs. Schofield was correct. But whether she was thinking along the lines of her da, or her friend Janice, there always remained in her a liking for Mrs. Schofield, a funny kind of liking, a sort of protective liking. It was a bit crazy when she came to analyse it, for it made her feel as if she were older than the mother of her friend. But the main trend of her thinking at this moment was not on Mrs. Schofield, but on Mr. Lord, and she thought bitterly as she looked at him, 'Yes, he can laugh and be amused. He's got his own way again.'

'Come on, me lad.' Mary Ann turned her head to where Mike was pushing his way through the crowd of guests towards Len. Her da stood head and shoulders above everybody in the barn. Dressed in his best, he brought a thrill of pride to Mary Ann, that for a moment obliterated thoughts of Mr. Lord.

'Come on, lad. Do you want to miss that train?' He beckoned with his one arm above the heads of the gathering, and Len, laughingly jostled from all sides, pushed towards him.

Mary Ann, left alone for a moment in a little island of space, watched Mrs. Schofield leave Mr. Lord to go and say goodbye to the bride. Then to her consternation she saw Mr. Lord rise slowly and come towards her.

It was the first time they had met face to face since his return, which had not been on Tuesday as expected, but yesterday morning, which was Friday, and since then he had, she felt sure, kept out of her way. In fact, out of everybody's way, until two hours ago when the wedding party had returned from the church. From which time he had allowed himself to be entertained by Mrs. Schofield.

Mr. Lord was standing close to her now and he looked at her for a long moment before speaking, and then he took the wind completely out of her sails by saying, 'You're wrong, you know, Mary Ann.'

As always when stumped, she blinked, but she continued to stare up at him.

'You have been blaming me for Cornelius's decision regarding America.' He always gave Corny his full name when speaking of him. 'Well, I want you to know I had nothing whatever to do with making up his mind. Oh, yes.' He raised his hand. 'I'm not going to deny that I have pointed out the advantages that would attend his taking up a position in America, and I have gone as far as to tell him I could secure him a post. Oh yes, I have done all that. But that was some time ago. More recently, I gave up the idea of trying to persuade him because I realized he was a very determined young man and would not be influenced by me, or anyone else, but would go his way. So I was surprised, as no doubt you were, when his decision was made known to me. He was the last person I expected to see in my office, and our meeting was brief, for in accordance with his character he came straight to the point. He told me what he wanted, and asked some questions. . . . Usually I am the one who asks the questions, and I don't take kindly to cross examinations.' He smiled his tight smile down on her. Then finished abruptly. 'Cornelius Boyle knows exactly what he wants. I should say he will go far. . . .

'Now, now, now, Mary Ann, don't be silly. You're not going to cry. This is a wedding, remember.' He took her arm in a firm grip and she allowed him to walk her towards the barn door.

She hated him, she did. Well, he could make all the excuses he liked, but she would never marry Tony just to please him. That was what he was after. . . . Oh, she knew, she knew what his subtle game was. And played so smoothly, you couldn't get at him.

'If you start crying everyone will blame me.'

'I'm not crying.'

'Very well, you're not crying, not yet. But if you do start I will get the blame. Especially from your father, because he, too, thinks like you, doesn't he?'

They had reached the left side corner of the barn when he pulled her to a stop. And looking at her with gentleness that always managed to break her down, he said softly, 'Whether you believe it or not, Mary Ann, anything I do, I do for your own good. Out of the essence of knowledge garnered through a long and trying life, I can see what is right for you . . . I know what is right for you, and I want you to have what is right for you. . . . You believe me?'

She was not crying, but her large brown eyes were so misted she couldn't see his face as she gazed up at him. He had done it again. She hated him no longer. What he said was right. Whatever he did was for her good. If only he would do something for Corny to stop him from going away. Her love gave her courage to say, 'I like Corny, Mr. Lord.'

'Yes.' He nodded at her. 'Yes, of course, you like Cornelius. I know you like Cornelius. Anyone would be blind, or stupid, if he didn't realize you like him. And go on liking him, there's no reason why you shouldn't. And you should be proud that he wants to go to America and make a position for himself, so that when ... when the time comes, he will have something to offer you. He would have nothing to offer you if he stayed in England.'

'He was getting on well at the garage. He's had a rise.'

Mr. Lord turned his head with a quick jerk to the side as if he was straining to look up into the sky, and it was into the sky that he sent his words: 'Had a rise!' The scorn in them made Mary Ann stiffen, and she made to pull her hand from his grasp when he brought his gaze once more to bear on her and again softened his scathing comment by saying, 'What is a rise in that work? A few shillings a week! You give Cornelius a year in America and he will be making twice as much as the manager of that garage. Believe me.... Well. Well, now.' He had turned his head quickly towards the gate of the farmhouse, where a car was backing in, and he ended abruptly, 'No more of this now. Here's Tony.'

Mr. Lord did not go towards his grandson but waited for him to come up to them. And although he kept his gaze fixed on the approaching figure, the expression in his eyes, which could have been taken for pride, was veiled with a mask of impatient arrogance.

Tony was tall and thin. A faint replica of Mr. Lord himself. Perhaps he was better looking than Mr. Lord had been at his age. His skin, even in the winter, kept a bronzed tinge as if he had just returned from a southern beach. In some measure, too, he had about him a touch of his grandfather's aloofness, which at the age of twenty-seven added to his attractiveness.

From a child Mary Ann had been conscious of this attractiveness, and in a childish way had looked upon Tony as hers. She had begun by liking him, then she had loved him. . . . That was until she met Corny. But she still liked Tony very, very much, and was aware of his attraction, as were most of the girls who came into contact with him. His charm and natural ease of manner were part and parcel of his character. But he also had a vile temper, which could rip the charm off him like a skin, to disclose stubbornness and cold arrogance for which one hadn't to look far to find the source. And it was mainly when he was fighting with that source that these two facets came into evidence.

As Mary Ann watched him approach them now, she said to herself, 'He's wild about something.' She knew Tony as well as she did her da, or ma, or Mr. Lord.

'Hello, there, you're late. The wedding's nearly over.' Mr. Lord's tone was clipped.

'Yes, I'm sorry. I couldn't make it. I told you I might be late.' Tony nodded to his grandfather while looking him straight in the face. He did not look at Mary Ann, although he asked, 'Where's Mike?'

Was he mad at her? Why was he pointedly ignoring her? She had done nothing. She said to him, 'My father's gone to the house with Len.' She always gave Mike the title of father when speaking of him in front of Mr. Lord.

'Thanks.' Still Tony did not turn his gaze on her, not even in a sweeping glance.

As she watched him stride away, she looked up sharply at Mr. Lord, saying, 'He's wild about something.'

The old man dusted his hands as if they had been soiled, and then he said, 'Young men are always wild about something. That's why they are young men. Once they stop being wild they are no longer young men.'

Mary Ann, looking at him for a moment longer, saw that he was not worried about Tony being wild. He was not coldly questioning why his grandson's manner was so abrupt, and this was unusual. And why he was not questioning was because he already knew.

She looked hard at the old man, who was looking to where Tony was now hurrying across the yard, not towards the farmhouse, but towards the gate that led up to the house on the hill. And she realized, as she had done so many times in the past, that this old man was clever, clever and cunning. He was like the devil himself. He could make you believe in him, in the goodness of his intentions, even while he plotted against you. And, as she had done in the past, she knew that she would hate him at intervals, but during the longer periods, and in spite of everything, she would always love him. And then she asked herself: What could he have done to upset Tony?

Corny arrived at six o'clock in Bert Stanhope's old car.

Bert Stanhope was the chief mechanic in the garage. He was also the leader of the 'Light Fantastics', a suitably fantastic name for the four members of his band. For Bert himself was short and stubby, while Joe Ridley was as thin as a rake, and possessed a club-foot. Arthur Hunt, on the other hand, was of middle height with muscles straining from his coat sleeves. He had come by these, he proclaimed, through playing the mandoline. Topping them all by a clear head and shoulders was Corny.

Corny now eased his long legs out of the front seat of the car, and after raising his hand quickly in a salute to Mike, who was coming out of the barn, he turned his head in the direction of Bert, to ask, 'What did you say?'

'Aa said, "Is that the place we're doin' it?"'

'Yes, that's the barn.'

'Coo, lor! It'll be like the Albert Hall, only barer.'

Joe Ridley, surrounded by what looked like an entire band of wind instruments, remarked caustically, 'We'll have to blow wor brains oot to put anything ower in there. The sound'll all come oot through them slats up top.'

'You'll get them blown oot if we don't put it over, me lad.'

They were all laughing at their leader's reply when Mike reached them.

'Hello, there. You all set.' He looked around the four young men, but addressed himself to Corny.

'Aye. Yes, Mr. Shaughnessy.' Corny had always given Mike his full title, and perhaps this was another reason why Mike was wholeheartedly for him. 'This is Bert Stanhope. It's his band, and this is Joe Ridley; and Arthur Hunt.'

Mike nodded with each introduction, then looking at the paraphernalia spread round their feet, he asked seriously, 'Where are the others?'

'The others?' Bert flicked an inquiring and puzzled glance towards Corny before finishing, 'What others?'

'Well, with all this lot, I thought it must be the Hallé Orchestra that had come!'

There was more laughter, louder now, as the young fellows picked up the instruments and made for the barn. Corny, about to follow them, was stopped by a light touch on his arm, and Mike, his face serious now, said, 'I want a word with you.'

'Now?' Corny was looking straight at Mike. Their eyes were on a level.

'No, it needn't be now. Perhaps when you have an interval.'

'All right.' As Corny turned away, Mike said quietly, 'Mary Ann's just gone over to the house, if you want to see her.'

Corny did not turn to meet Mike's gaze now, but answered evenly, 'They want to start right away. We're a bit late. I'll see her later.'

Mike said nothing to this but watched Corny stride towards the barn, before turning and making his way to the house.

And there he banged the back door after him as he went into the scullery. But when he entered the kitchen he stopped just inside the door and looked across to the fireplace where Tony was standing, one foot on the fender, his elbow resting on the mantelpiece and his face set in a stiffness that spoke of inner turmoil.

'Oh, you all alone?' Mike attempted to be casual.

Tony moved from the fireplace and stood on the edge of the mat, rubbing his left shoulder with his right hand, a characteristic action of his when worked up about anything.

'Where's Mary Ann?'

'I think she's upstairs. I've heard someone moving about, and Lizzie's still in the barn. Look, Mike, I didn't intend to say anything to her. I was going to ignore the whole affair, but I've just got to tell her that I'm not in on this business of Corny's deportation.'

'Deportation is right!' Mike nodded at him. 'That's the most suitable word I've heard for it yet. But don't worry, I don't think she would believe for a moment you had a hand in it.'

'Oh, I don't know so much, Mike. She said the other day, over some little thing that I did, she said I was as wily as my grandfather. She might be thinking that, although I'm opposing the old man on the surface, I'm glad that Corny is going.'

30

'And are you?' The question was flat sounding.

'Aw, Mike, no. No.'

'But you like her?'

'Yes, of course I do. You know that, Mike.'

'Do you more than like her? I've got the right to ask this, Tony. Do you more than like her? Do you love her?'

Tony turned his head quickly and looked towards the fire, then bringing his eyes back to Mike he said slowly, 'Yes. Yes, Mike, in a way, I suppose I do. I always have done. But it's an odd kind of love. I don't understand it quite myself. I'm always fighting against her inside myself. I suppose this is the result of the Old Man's plans. If he hadn't pushed it but let it take a natural course, things might have been different; at least on my side. But no matter what I had felt it wouldn't have made very much difference as long as Corny was in the picture. And you know, Mike—'

'And when he's out of the picture?' Mike cut in. 'What then? On your side, I mean.'

'I don't know, Mike. I've got to wait and see. The odd thing is I've never met anyone I like better. I was brought up, so to speak, on her personality.' He smiled now, before adding, 'And as you know, it'll take some beating.'

Mike turned from Tony and, pulling a chair from under the table, straddled it. And with his one hand he thumped the top with his closed fist as he said, 'I'm mad over this business, Tony, flaming mad. I know the old boy, he's worked on that lad for years.' He looked up at Tony. 'You know this is the kind of situation that always makes me want to get drunk.' He gave a little jerk to his head. 'I'd better not let Lizzie hear me say that. But at this moment I'd like to get blind drunk. You see, all my early married life, and occasionally even now, I've had to fight against Lizzie's mother. You know the old girl. Well, I see in the old man a male replica of Madam McMullen. He's aiming to direct and ruin Mary Ann's life as surely as Lizzie's mother tried to ruin ours. And I tell you, Tony it boils me up inside. . . . Ssh!' Mike got to his feet quickly. 'Here she's coming. Look, Tony. I wouldn't say anything now. Let it pass off, for the night at any rate. Talk to her later. Let her dance the night and have a bit of carry on, and forget it if she can. Although she'll be hard put to it with Corny up there blowing his heart out through that cornet, and nothing will convince me but he'll go on doing that where she's concerned, America or no. . . . Ssh!'

Although it was Mike who had been doing the talking he admonished Tony to silence with his last Ssh! and when the door opened and Mary Ann came into the kitchen he flung his arm up over his eyes and cried, 'Oh, Lord, what a dazzle!'

'Don't be silly, Da.' Although Mary Ann's voice was chiding, she smiled at Mike but did not look towards Tony, until he said, 'A new dress, is it?'

'Yes.' She nodded her head once.

'It's nice. Red suits you.'

'It's not red, it's cyclamen.'

'Oh . . . oh. Cyclamen, is it? Well, anyway, it's very charming. Although, mind, I think it makes you look older.'

The last was a covered compliment and would have at any other time pleased Mary Ann, for next to wishing to be taller she longed to appear older. Although she would soon be seventeen, she sometimes, because of her height, looked no more than fifteen years old.

'The band's come,' said Mike, his back half towards her now. 'Listen, they've started. Come on, wrap yourself well up. Wait, I'll get my big coat and put around you; your top looks half-naked, you'll catch your death.'

When Mike went out into the hall, Tony, moving towards Mary Ann, said, 'May I have the first dance, Miss Shaughnessy?' His smile was kind, and she returned it. But she did not enter into his playful mood.

Mike, coming into the room again, put his coat about her and they all laughed at the picture she presented; then, one on each side of her, they went out of the house down the road to the farm gate, and across the yard to the barn. And when they were inside the doorway, Mike took his coat from her, and she turned to Tony, and they danced. . . .

Lizzie was standing in the far corner of the barn behind the refreshment table, which also served as the bar. And it was the bar at this moment that was worrying Lizzie. Mr.

Coot was attending to the bar and also to himself. In her estimation he'd already had too much, and the night was young yet. The bride's father had not been satisfied with the amount of wine and beer Mr. Lord had provided, but had had to bring his own quota. Instead of spending so much on drink, Lizzie thought to herself, they could have bought something different for the young couple instead of that clarty cheap tea-set. Or provided some of the eatables. Thriftless lot. She had better see Mike and tell him to keep an eye on Mr. Coot and his personal friends.

She was looking here and there in between the dancers for Mike when she saw Mary Ann and Tony dancing together. At the sight of her daughter's dress, all thought of Mr. Coot left her mind for the moment. Oh, that dress! Why on earth had she picked a red dress? It wasn't her colour and the style was all wrong. It was the first dress she had let her buy on her own, and she had to pick red! It looked cheap, and it didn't suit her; it made her look older. She could be eighteen . . . nineteen. She kept her eye on her daughter as she waltzed nearer. And as the couple passed the table, Lizzie smiled at them. Anyway, Mary Ann was dancing nicely. It was the first time she had seen her dance except in the kitchen at the Christmas do's. Her steps and Tony's seemed to match. somehow, she didn't look out of place with Tony, not like she did with . . . Lizzie's eyes flicked towards the temporary platform where the band was arrayed. Corny, his legs apart, his elbows level with his shoulders, his head back, was blowing his heart into his cornet. She could see the full meaning of Mike's phrase now. He was cornet mad, that boy. And, yes, yes, from the bottom of her heart she was glad he was going to America. And she prayed God that he would go soon and Mary Ann would have a chance to settle down with . . . She turned her eyes to Tony and Mary Ann again. Then she brought her gaze to the right of her, where Mr. Lord was sitting, once again being entertained by Mrs. Schofield. Let him scheme, let him plan, she was with him every inch of the way. Although she would not be able to open her mouth to him about the matter, she knew that the day her daughter married his grandson would be one of the happiest in both their lives.

She saw Mike now and she came round from behind the table and threaded her way towards him, and when she reached him she turned and stood by his side, letting her gaze follow his as he looked at the merry-making. But under her breath she said, 'You'd better keep your eye on that Mr. Coot. He's going it some with the bottle.'

When Mike did not answer or turn his eyes towards her she was forced to look at him, and she said, still in a whisper, but with an edge to it, 'I'm saying something, did you hear me?'

'Yes, I heard you, Liz, but it happens to be a weddin'.'

'But you don't want it broken up, do you, with a drunken brawl?'

'Who says there's going to be a drunken brawl?'

'The night's young, and I'm telling you he's pretty well loaded now.'

'And he mightn't be the only one afore the night's out.'

Something jumped within Lizzie's chest. It was a frightening feeling. But one that was familiar – at least had been familiar up to these last few years. And now the feeling attacked the muscles of her stomach, bringing with it a slight nausea and she was back in the past, when each week-end had been a dread, and she didn't know from one day to another how they were going to get by. She was staring through glazed sight at the dancers while she cried out wildly inside herself, 'It's not fair, it's not fair, he's taking it out on me.' Then her vision clearing, she turned her eyes without moving her head towards the seat of state, in which Mr. Lord still sat; and she ended her thinking with, 'Well, far better he take it out on me than on the old man. But if he gets one too many himself it will be on both of us.' On this she was swamped with apprehensive fear, and the fear made her bold. With her eyes still directed towards the swirling couples, and her voice almost drowned by the noise and laughter, she said, 'If you do anything to spoil this night, Mike, I'll walk out . . . I'm telling you, I'll walk out.'

'Will you, Liz?' Mike too had his eyes fixed on the dancers, and his tone was deceptively even as he went on, 'I should have thought you knew better than that, Liz. Threats have always been as effective on me as water on a duck's back.'

34

The band stopped. The dancers clapped and called for more. The band started again and Mike, without any further words, walked from Lizzie's side and along to where Mr. Lord was seated. As Lizzie watched him go her hand went instinctively to her lips. Then slowly it dropped away and her shoulders went back, and her chin moved up just a little as she watched her husband bending over Mrs. Schofield. She watched him put his arm around Mrs. Schofield's slender waist while she rested both her hands on his shoulders. she watched for a moment longer as he laughed down into Mrs. Schofield's pretty face, and she watched Mrs. Schofield laugh up at him; and then she turned abruptly away.

She had, up to this minute, liked Mrs. Schofield, even though she thought her a bit dizzy. He had always maintained there was another side to her.... Oh, she wished it was tomorrow and the wedding well behind them. She wished it was next week or the week after, or whenever it was Corny Boyle was leaving. Once he was gone Mary Ann would settle down. She would do everything in her power to see that she did settle down. But, oh, she did wish this night was over, and she wished that Mrs. Schofield hadn't come.

When the band stopped for a break, Mary Ann was standing waiting to the side of the platform for Corny. She had no pride left. During the hour and a half the band had been playing, Corny hadn't looked at her; at least, when she was looking at him. It was as if she didn't exist for him; or, once having existed, he had decided to forget her. She knew that her father would try to get at him during the interval. And if not, her mother would insist that he had something to eat. Or Mr. Lord would raise an authoritative finger to beckon him to his side. And then the interval would be over, and when the dance finished he would pack up and go back with the other lads, and she didn't know whether he was coming tomorrow or not. She just had to talk to him.

As he stepped down off the wobbling planks, she looked up into his big face, which was redeemed from ugliness only by the mould of the mouth. This feature, taken separately, could be described as beautiful, yet it almost went unnoticed in the ruggedness of the whole. 'Hello,' she said. It was as if they had just encountered each other.

'Hello.' After looking down at her for a moment he thrust his head upwards, and gazing towards the refreshment table he exclaimed, 'Lord, but I'm starvin'.'

'I'll get you some sandwiches ... stay here, and I'll get them. Look, there's a seat.' Her voice was rushed, eager, and he looked down on her again. Then jerking his head, he said abruptly, 'I can get it.'

'Corny, I've got to talk to you.'

'Aw, Mary Ann. . . .'

'You'll go with the others as soon as the dance is finished, won't you.'

'Aye, it's the only way of gettin' back. I can't do anything else.'

'Well, I've got to talk to you now.'

'Leave it till the morrer.'

'Are you coming tomorrow?' Her eyes were wide and fixed hard on him now.

He looked anywhere but at her as he said, 'No. No, I wasn't. I promised to take our Stan's motor-bike to bits.'

As she stood gazing up at him she made a great effort to use the pride that was in her and turn from this gangling individual and march away, her head in the air and her step firm. But, as with her da, she could bring no pride to her aid when dealing with Corny, at least not as yet. In the past she had sold her soul to the devil over and over again in her own small way to defend her father. And she would do the same for this boy. She did not question why she should love Corny, she only knew that she did. And it was a love that could not be killed by ridicule or parting. Or even a statement from his own lips to the fact that he did not love her. That was a strange thing. And she had dwelt upon it quite a bit these past few hours. Corny had never said in words that he loved her; but in every possible way his actions had spoken for him. He had never even paid her a compliment that she could remember, and he had certainly never said, 'Oh, Mary Ann, I love you.' And his desertion now was not to be verbal either. He spoke, as usual, in actions, and his actions, like the proverb, spoke louder than his words.

'Comin' for some grub?' Bert was calling to him from the far side of the stage. And Corny, looking over his shoulder, answered in an over-loud voice, 'Be with you in a tick,' and then, walking towards the seat that Mary Ann had proffered, he said quietly now, 'Sit down, I'll get you something.'

She remained standing looking at him. 'I don't want anything. . . When are you going away?'

'Aw, Mary Ann, man.' He tossed his big head from side to side. 'Let's forget it.'

'When are you going away?'

'All right, all right, if that's how you want it.' Again his head was tossing. But it had ceased its moving before he said, 'The fourteenth.' His voice had dropped and his head with it. His eyes were not looking at her, but were shaded by the wide lids, and they flickered once when her voice, cracking with surprise, cried, 'The fourteenth! That's just over a week. . . . Oh, Corny!'

'Look, Mary Ann, don't go on. I'll come over the morrer. . . . Yes, I will, and talk about it. . . . Look, I'll go and get something to eat. Sit there, I'll be back.'

He did not wait for more protestations but hurried from her and threaded his way towards the far corner and the refreshment table.

Mary Ann sat down. She felt lost, sick, and she wanted above all things to lay her head on her arms and cry.

Up to a moment ago this corner of the barn had been comparatively empty, but now people were making their way back to the forms that lined the walls, carrying plates balanced on the tops of cups of coffee or glasses of beer. And as she was forced to answer, and even smile when she was spoken to, she was thinking, 'There's no place for him to sit now. And it's too cold outside, and he won't come over to the house.' She looked around now, not for Corny, but for Mike. Just to stand near her da would be a comfort. Moreover, she realized that she should be sitting close to her father from now on; because when she last saw him there had been a glint in his eye that told her he was well past his restricted number of whiskies.

Corny had pushed his way to her with a dinner-sized plate

full of food, but his attention was not on her, for he kept looking towards the stage. And then he brought out under his breath, 'Lordy, I hope they don't play about with the instruments. Bert will go crackers if anything's busted up.'

Mary Ann, following his perturbed gaze, saw Mrs. Schofield, her head back, her mouth wide with laughter, holding a trombone, and Tony, who was sitting at the piano – which incidentally had been brought down from the house but had not so far been played – calling to her: 'One . . . Two . . . Three.'

The sound that issued from the stage now caught the whole attention of the barn. And everybody was laughing as they looked towards Mrs. Schofield. It was evident that she had some knowledge of the trombone but was laughing so much herself that she could not keep in time with Tony, but the guests, catching the theme of 'The Old Bull and Bush', began to sing.

Mary Ann didn't join in, nor did Corny, but he whispered to her in reluctant admiration, 'She could play that, you know. With a little practice she could be good.'

Mary Ann looked at Mrs. Schofield, who was consumed with laughter and only intermittently keeping in time, and thought, 'This is what Janice means when she says her mother is dizzy.' And she felt a little ashamed of Mrs. Schofield. Ashamed of her, and ashamed for her. She was too old to act the goat like that. Mary Ann at this moment gave thanks that her mother would never do anything like that.

But it would appear that Mary Ann was alone with her feeling concerning Mrs. Schofield, for the rest of the company were enjoying her with high delight. And when one song was finished there was a call for another, and another.

Then Mike was on the stage, standing by Tony, and he let his deep rich voice soar through the barn as he led the singing. That was all right; Mary Ann liked to hear her da sing. And as long as he was singing he wouldn't be drinking. Yes, it was all right until Mrs. Schofield put down the trombone and went and joined him. And then Mary Ann watched her da put his arm around Mrs. Schofield's shoulder and lead her to the front of the stage, and with their heads together they sang duets to the great amusement of the company, with the exception of herself and her mother. For Mary Ann caught sight of her mother's face, and she knew that she was upset. She also knew that her da was letting rip like this on purpose because he was vexed, not only with Mr. Lord but with her ma. And it was all on account of her and Corny. As Lizzie had said a short while ago, now Mary Ann also said to herself, 'Oh, I wish this night was well over.'

There was just one other person who was not pleased with the spectacle. And that was Mr. Lord. He had found Mrs. Schofield a very entertaining companion; when you got past the frivolity of her veneer there was a serious side to the woman. He had found her intelligent and observant, and possessed of a quality that, in his opinion, was rare in most women – wit. Many of them had a sense of humour, but humour and wit were on two different planes. Yes, indeed, he had liked Mrs. Schofield and he did not relish seeing her making a spectacle of herself with Shaughnessy, and his grandson. Shaughnessy, too, he noted, had taken on more than was good for him, and in a very short while his good humour would turn to surliness, and from that . . . Well, he wasn't going to be present when Shaughnessy brought up the subject of why young Cornelius Boyle had decided to go to America. He was well aware of Shaughnessy's championship of the boy. And it was not only because of Mary Ann's affection for the fellow, but because Shaughnessy saw in the big, bony unlovely Cornelius a replica of himself as he was at that age. And in championing his daughter's choice, he was also pandering to the vanity in himself. Oh, he knew Shaughnessy, he could read Shaughnessy.

'Well, I must be making my way up the hill, Mrs. Shaughnessy.' Mr. Lord was facing Lizzie now, bending towards her to make himself heard. And she only just managed to keep the relief out of her voice as she answered, 'You must be tired, it's been a long day. . . . Thank you very much, indeed, for all you have done.'

The old man raised his bushy brows into his white hair, and brought his chin into his neck as he said with a rare twinkle in his eye, 'We're never thanked for the right things by the right people, Mrs. Shaughnessy. The ones who should be thanking me are past thinking of anything at this moment but the next drink. I have done nothing to deserve your thanks, but there it is. That is life.' He nodded his head slowly. 'And I am grateful for your thanks, Mrs. Shaughnessy.'

They looked at each other for a long moment.

'Good night, Mr. Lord.'

'Good night, Mrs. Shaughnessy. And don't worry. Everything will turn out all right.' He did not explain to what he was referring, there was no need. Lizzie looked back into his pale eyes as she said, 'I'm sure it will, Mr. Lord. I sincerely hope so from the bottom of my heart.' The last words were merely a whisper.

Again he nodded. 'We understand each other, Mrs. Shaughnessy. It's a very good thing when two people understand each other. Good night, Mrs. Shaughnessy.'

'Good night, Mr. Lord. Good night, Mr. Lord. You'll be able to manage?' She pulled the barn door open for him.

'Yes, quite well, Mrs. Shaughnessy, quite well; there's a moon.'

He paused for a moment and looked up into the sky, then turning his head towards Lizzie he said, 'Don't ler her stay up too late. Young girls should get their rest.'

Lissie did not answer but inclined her head towards him, and stood for a moment watching him walk across the moonlit farmyard. He was telling her to protect Mary Ann from the moonlight, the moonlight and Corny. For a moment, just for a fleeting moment, Lizzie experienced a feeling that she thought could be akin to that which was eating up Mike. Why should Mary Ann be kept from the moonlight and Corny? The moon was made for the young. But as she closed the barn door again, the feeling passed. He was right; moonlight was dangerous. A dose of it created a madness that some people had to pay for all their lives. She was not going to stand by and see Mary Ann paying such a price. . . .

The dance ended at eleven o'clock, but long before this time Tony and Mrs. Schofield were running a shuttle service taking people home. Tony's first car-load had contained the prostrate form of Mr. Coot, who, true to Lizzie's prophecy, had become blind drunk very early in the evening. But not aggressively so as she had feared. Whereas Mike, who was not as drunk as he could have been, was tinder dry for a row. Mr. Lord's disappearance had brought forth his caustic comments, and Mr. Coot's recumbency had aroused his scorn. Tony he frowned on more and more as the evening advanced, and it would appear the only person who pleased him was Mrs. Schofield. But it seemed that as Mike's boisterousness increased, Mrs. Schofield's merriment went the other way, until, towards the end of the evening, although still smiling, her gaiety had diminished. Perhaps this was because Mrs. Schofield did not drink. Even a natural gaiety is hard to sustain hour after hour on lemonade. Or perhaps it was because Mrs. Schofield was really a nice woman, an understanding woman.

Yet Lizzie's liking for Mrs. Schofield did not return, not even when she witnessed her persuading Mike from getting into the car and accompanying her in her taxi-ing. You can't like a woman who is trying to prevent your husband from making a fool of himself even when you know that she is in sympathy with you. . . .

The barn was almost deserted when the band finally packed up. And Mike, swaying just the slightest, stood with his arm around Corny's shoulder, and he grinned widely at him as he muttered thickly, 'Cum on, me young buck, cum on. You and me 'ave got some talkin' ta do.'

'I've got to go, Mr. Shaughnessy. They're waitin'.'

'Waitin'? What for? Let them get themselves away, you're comin' in with me. Why, the night's young, lad.'

'I'll come in the morrer.'

'You'll cum in the night!'

'Da!'

Mike turned to look at his daughter, saying, 'Ah, there you are. I was just tellin' Corny here the night's young.'

'Da. Come on indoors, please.'

'We're all goin' indoors, me dear.'

'Listen, Da.' Mary Ann gave a rough tug at Mike's arm, pulling him to attention. 'Listen. Corny wants to go home; they're waiting for him.' She inclined her head backwards. 'Let him go! Do you hear me, Da? Let him go!'

Not only did the tone of her voice catch Mike's attention, but it brought Corny's eyes hard on her. His neck jerked up out of his collar as if he had been suddenly prodded with a sharp instrument, and he looked down on her with a wide, startled expression as she went on, 'You go now, Corny.' Her words were spaced, her voice level. 'Go on. And don't come back tomorrow, or any other time. Go to America, and I wish you luck. . . . Come on, Da.'

As she had done so often in her young life, she tugged at Mike's arm and guided him away, and this time unprotestingly away, leaving Corny in a wilderness of words he could not voice. And as she went, she clung on desperately to the fringe of her old courage, which she had dragged from its retreat to save her from utter desolation after an evening of torment, an evening of being rejected, overlooked by the only one that mattered. Just a short while ago she had rehearsed a plea she would make to Corny when she had him to herself. For somehow she would get him to herself, at least that is what she had thought.

Mary Ann had never yet in her life recognized total defeat. Her agile mind had always supplied her with a plan. But in this telling moment if it had presented her with a plan that would keep Corny at her feet for life, she would have rejected it.

As they entered the garden Mike's docility vanished and he pulled them to a stop, exclaiming, 'Why the hell! I'm not havin' this. Where is he?' He flung round, only to be dragged back again by Mary Ann, and, her voice as stern as Lizzie's ever could be, she said to him, 'Look, Da, listen to me. I'm telling you, I don't want to see him.'

'Aa . . . ah! So you're playing the old fellow's game, eh?' He swayed slightly towards her.

'I'm playing nobody's game. Come on in.' Suddenly her tone changed and she was the little girl again, pleading with him. 'Aw, Da. Come on. Come on to bed . . . I've had enough for one night.'

He peered at her through the moonlight, and then without further words he put his arm about her, and together they went up into the house.

CHAPTER THREE

'WHAT are you goin' to be when you leave your typin' school . . . a secretary?'

'Yes, I suppose so, Mrs. McBride.'

'Do you want to be a secretary?'

'No, not really.'

'Then what did you go in for it for?'

'Oh, well.' Mary Ann gave a faint smile and, looking down, said, 'I fancy I'll be able to write.'

'Write?'

'Yes, stories and things, you know. I've always been able to make up poetry.'

'Well! well!' Fanny stopped basting the joint and gazed down on Mary Ann where she sat at the corner of the kitchen table. 'Now, that's an idea, a good idea, for you were always the one for tellin' a tale. Oh, you were that. . . . Remember the things you used to spin around, about all the cars, and the horses your da had, and the big house you lived in?'

Mary Ann nodded, and she kept smiling up at this old friend of hers as she listened to her recalling the escapades she got up to in the days when they lived in the attics at the top of this grim house. But she knew, as Mrs. McBride kept prattling on in her loud, strident voice, that they were both just marking time, waiting for the moment when Corny's name would be mentioned. She was bitter in her heart against Corny. Although she had dismissed him with a cold finality the night of the wedding, she hadn't imagined for a single moment that that would be the last she would see of him. When he hadn't come on the Sunday, she had known he would turn up one night during the week. But as the days ticked off towards the fourteenth of November, her pride sank into oblivion once more, and she paid earnest, even frantic, attention to her praying, beseeching Our Lady to bring him before he sailed. But her prayers weren't answered. And the day of his departure came without a word or a note from him.

Her da was still mad, and part of his temper now was directed towards Corny himself. Even her mother was annoyed at Corny's cavalier treatment. And she had overheard her saying to Michael in the kitchen, 'After the way he's been welcomed in this house. Every weekend for years he's been here. And never once was she invited back!'

Michael had answered, 'Well, you can understand that. The fellow wouldn't want to take her to the set-up in Howdon.'

'Well,' her mother said, 'I hope it shows her she's well rid of him.'

When their Michael had answered, 'I wouldn't count on it doing that, Ma,' she had wanted to fly into the kitchen and cry, 'Well, it has! Me ma's right. Me ma's right. I never want to set eyes on him again.'

That was a week ago. And now here she was, drawn to Mrs. McBride's, waiting, as each minute passed – glossed over with topics that didn't matter – for her to speak about her grandson.

Fanny pushed the dripping-tin back into the oven, and threw the coarse sacking oven-towel on to a chair. Then going back to the table, she sat down opposite Mary Ann. Heaving a sigh that hardly disturbed the huge sagging mountain of her breasts, she put her head on one side and looked at Mary Ann with compassion in her glance. 'Well!' she said abruptly.

Mary Ann, staring at her old friend, bit on her lip, looked downwards, then back into the wrinkled face, and muttered, 'Oh, Mrs. McBride, I feel awful.'

'You do, hinny?'

Mary Ann nodded and blinked, but the blinking could not check her crying, and the tears welled from her eyes.

'Aw! there now, there now, don't cry. It had to be like this, lass. It had to be like this.'

'He . . . he went off and never even said good-bye to me.

He needn't have gone off like that and ... and after him coming to us every week. He ... he never missed, and then to go off ...'

'Now wait a minute.' Fanny held up her hand. 'There was a reason for him goin' off like that. And you know it.'

'I don't, Mrs. McBride. I don't.' She was shaking her head desperately.

'Aw, come on, come on. Face up to facts. If he had come to say good-bye to you, he would have never seen America.'

Mary Ann's mouth was open and she moved her head in a slow painful motion, her tears still running down her face.

'It's a fact,' said Fanny. 'He stood in this kitchen ... Stood? No, I'm tellin' you a damned lie. Stand, he didn't do, he raged about the room until I threatened to hit him with the frying-pan if he didn't let up. And talk. I never heard that lad talk so much in all me born days. All mixed up, seemingly without sense or reason, until I shouted at him. "If you don't want to go, don't go," I said. "Blast Mr Lord. You'll get other chances." "Where?" he said. "If I was even managing that garage I wouldn't be able to make much more than fifteen quid a week, and what can you do on that?" "What can you do on that?" I said to him. "I wish to God I had the half of it, that's all." '

Fanny paused now, and after nodding towards Mary Ann she went on more slowly. 'It was after I said that, that he held his head in his hands and said, quiet like, in a way that made him sound like a settled man, "Gran, you don't know what you're talkin' about. I'm not askin' her until I have enough to start off decent, and if I don't get goin' now, it'll be too late. Unless I start doing things on the side with the cars to make a bit like the rest of them. And I don't want to get mixed up in anything, I've seen where that can lead. ..." '

'Oh! Mrs. McBride. If he had only told me ...'

'Wait a minute, wait a minute. I haven't finished yet,' said Fanny. 'You know how I like your mother, don't you? I think of Liz with more affection than any of me own. But apparently she doesn't see me grandson in the same light. She's got ideas for you, Mary Ann, and—' Fanny spread her arms wide. 'It's natural, isn't it? She's your mother. But my

45

Corny is no fool. Perhaps I say it as shouldn't, but he's a big chip, a great big chip of meself, and he read through Liz right from the beginnin'. The same as he knew what old Lord was up to all the time. Old Lord wants you for Mr. Tony, lass, and you know, I can see his point an' all. And I'm not blaming your mother for wantin' to fall in with his little scheme. For it would be a wonderful thing if her daughter, her Mary Ann, could marry the old man's grandson. . . . Now, now, don't take on so, I'm just statin' facts, and there's no hard feelin's atween Liz and me, and never atween you and me. We know each other too well, don't we now?' She reached forward and patted Mary Ann's hand.

It was all too much for Mary Ann. Turning on a loud sob, she buried her face in her arms on the table, and Mrs. McBride, pulling herself to her feet, stood over her, tapping her shoulder and saying, 'Come on, now. Come on.' Then after a moment she said, 'Stop now, an' I'll give you somethin'. He left it to me for to do with what I thought best. "If you think she needs it, Gran, let her have it," he said. "If you don't, put it in the fire." '

Mary Ann raised her tear-stained face and watched Fanny take her wobbling body to the fireplace, where she reached up and extracted a letter from behind the clock. When she placed it in her hand, Mary Ann looked down on it. There was no name on the envelope, no writing of any kind; and when automatically she turned it over, she knew from the condition of the flap that it had been steamed open. This did not affect her, it did not bring any feeling of resentment against her friend. Fanny had likely wanted to know what her grandson had said, and whether she should pass it on or not.

Slowly Mary Ann slit open the envelope and read the very short letter it contained.

If you read this it'll be because you have been upset at me going and you didn't really mean what you said the other night. I'm going to stay in America for a year. If I know I can make a go of it I'll come back then and tell you. If I feel I can't – that is make a go of it – then don't wait but do what they want you to. Perhaps in a year's time you'll want to do that anyway because you always liked him.

Corny.

Would you come and see me Gran now and again? She gets lonely for a bit of a crack.

'Oh! why couldn't he tell me this?' Mary Ann shook the letter in her hand as she looked up into Mrs. McBride's face. 'Why couldn't he say it?'

'Well, he was never very ready with his tongue, especially when it was about anything that really mattered.'

'I'll wait. Oh, I'll wait, Mrs. McBride.'

'Well, now, hinny.' Fanny put her hand heavily on Mary Ann's shoulder. 'Make no rash promises. You're only sixteen, you know. You're very young yet.'

'I'm getting on seventeen, Mrs. McBride.'

'Well, aye, you might be, but you know you still look such a bairn. And a lot of things can happen in a year, God knows that.'

'Nothing will ever happen to change me, Mrs. McBride.'

'Aw, well, we'll wait and see. But now you feel a bit better, don't you?'

Mary Ann nodded.

'Would you like a bite of dinner?'

'No thanks, Mrs. McBride.'

'A bit of bread dipped in the gravy?'

Mary Ann gave an involuntary shudder when she thought of the black fat surrounding the meat. But she smiled and said, 'Thanks, all the same, but I'll have to be off. You know what me ma is if I'm not there on time. . . . Good-bye, Mrs. McBride, and thanks.' Impulsively she reached up and kissed the wrinkled cheek. And Fanny held her tightly for a moment, and as she did so she whispered, 'You're not the only one who'll miss him, you know, lass.'

'I know that, Mrs. McBride . . . and, and I'll come and see you more often.'

'Do that. Do that, hinny. You're always more than welcome.'

'Good-bye, Mrs. McBride.'

47

'Good-bye, lass. Give me love to Lizzie, and don't forget Mike. Tell them I'll drop in one of these days.'

'Oh, do, do, they'd love to see you.'

After more repeated good-byes, Mary Ann went down the steps of Mulhattan's Hall with a lighter tread than she had ascended them, and as she hurried through the quiet Sunday-stripped streets towards the bus stop, she gripped the letter in her hand inside her coat pockets. She had no experience of love letters with which to judge this, her first one; but even so she knew it was lacking in the niceties that went to make up such a letter. Yet every line had brought Corny closer to her. The terse, taciturn, blunt individual was near her once again. There had been no sign in the letter of his lessons in English. Corny could, she knew, speak all right when there was nothing to deflect his attention from the rocks and pitfalls of grammar. But when he was angry, or disturbed in any way, he fell immediately back into the natural idiom. But what did she care how he talked? He could talk broad Geordie for the remainder of his life if only he was here with her now. But she had his letter, and his promise, and to this she would hang on for the coming year. And longer, yes, longer, if necessary. As long as ever he wanted.

CHAPTER FOUR

THE farm had fallen under a spell of peace. It was like an enchanted place because everybody was happy. Mike sang and joked once more. Lizzie bustled about her house. She cooked more than ever. She took an interest in books that went in for pictures of big houses, and she laughed quite a bit. And Mr. Lord seemed to be very pleased with himself these days. He appeared to be floating on a firm cloud of achievement. As for Tony, Tony smiled and laughed and teased Mary Ann; and on occasions took her out for a run in the car. This was a new departure and might account for Mr. Lord's cloud of achievement. ... Then Michael and Sarah; they were living in a world of their own and enjoying a separate happiness – they were not involved with Corny Boyle.

This change in the atmosphere as far as Mary Ann and Mike were concerned had been brought about simply by Corny's letter. Mary Ann had, on the quiet, shown the letter to her da, and Mike had grinned widely and said, 'Stick to your guns. Don't let on. Let them go on thinking and planning what they like.' He had not intimated who 'they' were, but she knew he was referring to her mother and Mr. Lord. He had added, with a warning lift of his finger, 'Don't show that to your mother, mind.' And looking back at him she had said, 'As if I would.' And they had laughed together. But some time later Mike had said to her, 'I would show that letter to Tony if I was you.'

'To Tony?'

'Yes. It would put things straight in his mind, and he won't start walking up any garden path.'

So she had shown the letter to Tony, with the result that after a long moment of looking down at her, with perhaps just a trace of sadness in his expression, he had suddenly punched her playfully, saying, 'What do you say to playing them at their own game?' And she knew that here, too, Tony was referring not only to his grandfather but also to her mother, Lizzie, with whom he was on very good terms. But she had asked, 'What do you mean?' He didn't explain fully what he did mean, but said, 'Well, we needn't fight, need we, and give them cause for worry? I'll have to take you out for a run now and again, and to a show. It'll make the year pass quicker. What about it?' She had laughed freely for the first time in weeks. Her da was happy again, so was her mother. What did it matter if it was for different reasons. And Tony was nice. She had always liked Tony. As Corny had said, she had always liked Tony. But that wasn't loving. There was all the difference in the world.

So everyone, with the exception of Michael and Sarah, began putting on an act.

It was on the Thursday morning that Mary Ann received a letter from Janice Schofield, asking if she could come up and see her on the Friday evening. During working hours Mary Ann, escaping the keen eyes of Miss Thompson and wishing to show off her typing prowess, wrote Janice a sketchy reply, the gist of which was: Of course, she could come up on the Friday evening.

Mary Ann had been rather surprised to receive a letter from Janice. At one time during her school days, they had been good friends; but Janice had never been close to her like Beatrice Willoughby. Beatrice, to use schoolgirl jargon, was her best friend, and Janice her second best. Janice was nine months older than Mary Ann and had been left school for more than a year, while Mary Ann had just finished in the summer term. Beatrice, on the other hand, was still at school making her way to college. ... Years ago Mary Ann had thought she, too, would like to go to college, but Corny had changed her mind about this matter, and strangely, when she had put forward her idea of taking up shorthand and typing, there had been little or no objection from any quarter. This, she had reasoned, was because her da had Corny in mind and further education was going to serve no purpose. In fact, it might do Corny a disservice. Her mother's reaction, she knew, was patterned on Mr. Lord's, and this is where the word 'strangely' applied most. For Mr. Lord had not gone off the deep end about her proposal to become a secretary.

Two more years at school and three at college would not have helped Mr. Lord's scheme at all. Five years is a long time when a man is over seventy.

Mary Ann wondered what Janice wanted to see her about, and she hurried home on the Friday night and changed into her new loose sweater and pleated skirt so as to look her best when Janice arrived. For Mary Ann knew that she would come all dressed up – 'killingly smart', as their Michael termed it, 'and smellin' like a poke of devils'. Janice worked on the cosmetic counter in a large store, in Newcastle and undoubtedly this had a lot to do with her choice of perfume.

Lizzie had lit the fire in the sitting-room, and at ten minutes to seven, Mary Ann and Michael went down the road to the bus stop. Michael to meet Sarah, and Mary Ann to meet Janice. But only Sarah alighted from the bus.

At eight o'clock Mary Ann, accompanied this time by Mike, met the bus again, but still there was no sign of Janice.

'You'd better phone her up,' said Mike, 'and find out why she hasn't put in an appearance.'

They now had an extension of the phone in the house, and the operator, after trying several times to get Janice's number, informed Mary Ann that there was no reply. So there was nothing for it but to wait until the next morning and see if there was a letter from her.

But on the Saturday morning there was no letter from Janice. As always, Mary Ann was in a tear to get to the bus, and she did not phone the Schofields' until she returned at lunch time, when once again she was told there was no reply.

Lizzie said now, 'Likely their phone's out of order; you should take a trip over there this afternoon and see her. It's a lovely day, it will do you good.'

'But it's such a long way. It's right outside the town, Mother.'

'Well, it's just as long for her to come here. . . . Why don't you ask Tony to run you over? He's nearly sure to be going into Newcastle this afternoon.'

Lizzie had her face turned from Mary Ann when she made this proposal, and Mary Ann allowed herself the re-action of raising her eyebrows slightly, but that was all.

Not for a long time had she asked Tony to take her any-where, even from the night he had proposed that they, too, should put on an act she had left the invitations to him. But today, when she did ask him, he expressed delight at the opportunity of running her into Newcastle. He would do more than that, he said. He would take her to the Schofields. He would very much like to see his theatrical partner again. Oh, yes, Mrs. S. and he should team up.

He repeated much of this when he called for her, and Mike and Lizzie and he all laughed together, but Mary Ann thought he was overdoing it a bit.

Lizzie smiled warmly down on Mary Ann as she watched Tony reach over and tuck the car rug around her; she even waved them off as if it was a special occasion.

They were out on the road going past the cottages when Tony gave Mary Ann a sidelong quizzical glance as he re-marked, 'Everybody's happy . . . everybody. For the Lord himself gave his blessing on our excursion before I came out.'

Tony was referring to his grandfather. And now her laugh-ter joined his. Oh, Tony was nice, he was. He was good fun. She liked him ever so much. For a fleeting second she even wished that she didn't know Corny. But it was just for a second.

Mary Ann had not been to the Schofields more than three times during her acquaintance with Janice. But Mrs. Schofield had been to the farm many times; in fact, Mary Ann had lost count of Mrs. Schofield's visits during the past few years. The Schofields' residence, one would be right in calling it that, was an imposing house standing on a piece of land unusually large even for such houses in that select dis-trict. You entered the grounds through a long drive, which was bordered by larches. Although the trees were bare they were entwined with the dark, shining green of canes. These, in turn, were laced with dead bramble. The effect was the same as entering a tunnel, although not quite so dark. The gravel of the drive was covered with matted grass and, except for two deep car ruts, appeared like a field track. The front of the house, too, when they came upon it, had the appearance of being buried under masses of undergrowth. It looked as if it was fighting the clematis, climbing roses, and virginia creeper hanging in dead profusion, even from its tiles.

Perhaps it was the unexpected condition of the house that made Tony bring the car to a stop before he reached the front door. He sat with his head bent forward, staring upwards through the windscreen for a moment, before saying, 'Great Scott! There hasn't been much work done here for some time, I should say.'

'It wasn't as bad as this the last time I was here.' Mary Ann was speaking in a whisper. 'But that's nearly two years ago. It was rather nice then. It was summer. Mrs. Schofield used to do the garden herself. There's a beautiful rose garden at the back. . . . Will you wait until I see if they're in?'

'Of course, of course.' Tony brought his gaze round to her. 'I'll come in with you for a moment. I meant what I said, I'd like to see her . . . not Janice.' He nipped her nose, and they both laughed. Then he added, 'She's not a patch on her mother.'

'She's all right.' Mary Ann felt bound to defend her friend. 'You've just got to know her.'

'I don't want to, thank you very much.'

They were out of the car now and walking towards the front door, which was covered by a glass porch, quite a large porch. They stood for a moment, as people do, hesitating just that second before ringing the bell, and it was as Tony's hand was uplifted that the yell came to them. Bawl would be more appropriate in describing the sound of the man's voice. It came from the right, from inside the room to the right of the front door. This room had a large high window, which protruded into the drive with squared sides. Looking through the glass of the porch they were right opposite one side of the window, which was a pane wide but half-covered by a twist of dead stems. The bawl had been in the form of a

53

curse. It was a word that Mary Ann hadn't heard before, although Mike at times swore freely. And its effect on Tony was to make him bring his startled glance down on her, and then to take her arm and move her quickly back towards the drive. But before they reached the entrance to the porch they had stopped again, and were once more looking towards the window. And there to be seen quite plainly was Mrs. Schofield. She was walking backwards into the far corner of the recess, and advancing on her was a man. When Mrs. Schofield could go no further the man, too, stopped, and his voice came clear and penetrating to them. 'You would bloody well put up with it and like it, and if you make any more of your highfalutin' shows I'll bring her here. . . . You're always on about needing help, aren't you?'

'You can't do this to me, I'll . . . I'll leave you.'

The man threw his head back and laughed. 'That's what I've been wanting you to do for years, but you won't will you? You're afraid of what your dear, dear friends would say. That wonderful, charming Lettice couldn't hold her man! You wouldn't like that, would you? Oh, no!'

'I'll go when I'm ready.' Mrs. Schofield's voice came to them in trembling tones like those of an old woman; and immediately there followed the man's voice, saying, 'You'll go when . . . I'm . . . ready. You'll stay here until Jan is married. And then I'll have the great pleasure of escorting you to the door with my foot in your backside. . . . You stuck-up bitch, you!'

Mary Ann was standing with her hand pressed tightly to her mouth, and as she saw the man's arm come up she closed her eyes and turned her face towards Tony's chest. Automatically Tony's arms went round her shoulders, but he did not look at her, and when the sound of the second blow came to Mary Ann she felt his body jerking as if the man's fist was hitting him.

There were footsteps sounding inside the house now, and Tony, loosing his hold on Mary Ann, turned and faced the front door.

Her fingers still tightly pressed to her mouth, Mary Ann stood looking apprehensively at Tony. She had often seen him in tempers, but she had never seen him look like this.

There was not a vestige of colour in his face, it had a bleached look. Even his eyes appeared to be drained of all pigment. She was as frightened at this moment for Tony as ever she had been for Mike. There was going to be a fight. She knew there was going to be a fight; and it would be a terrible fight. Mr. Schofield was a big man, as big as her da. She had only met him once and she hadn't liked him. Tony was tall, but he had no bulk with which to match Mr. Schofield. Yet he had something else that perhaps might kill Mr. Schofield; it stemmed from the livid passion showing on his face.

The footsteps had gone, and the door hadn't opened. A full minute passed before Tony turned his neck stiffly and looked towards her. Then his gaze lifted almost reluctantly towards the window again.

Mary Ann, too, looked through the window. Mrs. Schofield was now sitting in a chair, her face turned into the corner, and she was crying, but no sound reached them. What they did hear was the whirr of a car engine starting up. The next second there shot from the side of the house a Humber Snipe with Mr. Schofield at the wheel.

If Tony's car had been opposite the front door the man must surely have seen it, but from where it was standing on the far side of the drive underneath the overhanging trees, it must have escaped his notice, for he did not stop. Within seconds, the loud grinding of changing gears told them that he was on the main road.

Mary Ann was feeling sick. She always felt sick when there was fighting. But this was a different kind of sickness. She was puzzled, bewildered, and absolutely out of her depth. Mrs. Schofield was bright and gay, and had a lovely life. That's what people thought about Mrs. Schofield. She was light as thistledown, she was amusing ... she amused Mr. Lord. This couldn't be Mrs. Schofield; this woman who had backed away across the room and almost whimpered when she talked. Mary Ann had lived in the slums of Jarrow and yet she had never seen a man actually strike a woman. She had heard of Mr. and Mrs. So-and-So having rows and going for each other, but she had never actually seen them fight; and never once in her life had she seen her da raise his hand to her ma, not even when he was paralytic drunk.

'What are we going to do?' She was whispering up to Tony. 'Oh, poor Mrs. Schofield.' She shook her head and swallowed against the threatening tears.

When Tony did not answer but kept staring through the window, she asked softly, 'Shall I ring?'

'No.' His voice was sharp. 'She won't answer.' He moved from her, out of the porch, on to the drive; and she followed him. And when he stood on the overgrown flower-bed before the window and tapped gently on the pane, she herself was startled, so quick was the jump Mrs. Schofield gave from the chair. She watched her stand for some minutes staring in painful amazement through the window at Tony, before screwing her face up, and then burying it in her hands.

'Open the door.' Tony's voice was quiet. And when Mrs. Schofield only shook her head slowly from side to side, he called louder, 'Open the door.'

A few seconds later the front door opened, and Mary Ann, following Tony, saw Mrs. Schofield's back disappearing down the dim hall.

They were in the room now, and Mrs. Schofield was standing looking through the window, and Tony was standing behind her talking to her back. Quietly he said, 'We saw what happened, so it doesn't matter. Let me look at your face.'

'No, no, please . . . and please go away.'

'I'm not going away.'

Mary Ann noticed he did not say we. And then he went on, 'How long have you put up with this?'

'Oh, please.' It was a low, beseeching cry. And when Mrs. Schofield's head drooped, Tony took her gently by the shoulders and turned her around.

Mary Ann gave a sharp gasp before going to the side of this woman who to her had been the personification of frivolity and lightness. 'Oh! Mrs. Schofield. . . . Oh! I'm sorry. Your poor mouth. Will . . . shall I get some water?'

Mrs. Schofield's head was held level now, and although the tears were running down her swelling cheekbone and over her bruised lip, she managed a faint smile as she said, 'Don't worry, Mary Ann. It's all right, it's all right. Come and sit down.'

Tony, with his fingers just touching her elbow, led Mrs. Schofield to the couch, and when he had seated himself on the edge beside her, with his body turned fully to her, he asked pointedly, 'Why do you stand it?'

As Mary Ann watched Mrs. Schofield's mouth quiver she wanted to say to Tony, 'Don't ask any questions. Can't you see she's upset enough,' but she continued to look at this surprising woman as she moved her eyes slowly about her drawing-room. It was as if she were looking at the articles about her with surprise, as if seeing them after a long time. And then she answered him absently with, 'Why? Yes, why?' Her head continued to make small pathetic jerks until her eyes came to rest on Tony, and then she said, in that voice that held a peculiar charm for all who heard it, 'I suppose it's because I was born here. I was brought up in this house. My whole life has been spent here.'

'Is it worth it?'

'No! No! Oh, no.'

There was vehemence in the tone now, and as Mrs. Schofield went to cover her face once again with her hands, she stopped, and seeming to be becoming fully aware of Mary Ann's presence, she swallowed and drew in a deep breath, before turning and looking at her and saying, 'You've come to see Janice, I suppose, Mary Ann?'

'Yes, Mrs. Schofield. She was going to come last night, and she didn't, and I couldn't get through. I tried several times.'

'No, you wouldn't. The line's broken.' She didn't go on to explain how the line was broken, but added, 'Janice is upstairs.'

Before Mary Ann could make any reply to this, Tony brought out in an amazed tone, 'Upstairs! and all this going on?'

Mrs. Schofield did not answer Tony, but, turning to Mary Ann, asked, 'Would you like to go up to her, Mary Ann? It's the second door at the top of the landing, on the right-hand side.'

'Yes. Yes, Mrs. Schofield.' Mary Ann glanced towards Tony, but Tony was looking at Mrs. Schofield.

Out in the hall she stood for a moment gazing about her.

The house inside was clean, tidy and clean, not bright like their house was bright, but not dirty. She did not go immediately up the stairs, for she was overwhelmed with pity not untouched with shock. She had just experienced the first great surprise of her life. She had been shown in one swift swoop the meaning of . . . putting a face on it. Mrs. Schofield must have spent all her married life putting a face on it. She could see her now on the night of Len's wedding, standing on the platform playing the trombone when she could stop herself laughing. And later that night she would have gone home to perhaps a similar scene to that which had just taken place. . . . Ee! it was awful. Poor Mrs. Schofield. She went slowly up the stairs and knocked on the second door to the right. And when it was opened, Janice said, 'Oh, you.' Then looking past her and towards the stairs, she asked, 'How long have you been here?'

'Not very long. I tried to phone you, but couldn't get through. I thought something was wrong when you didn't come last night, after saying you would.'

Janice turned her back completely on Mary Ann and walked back into the bedroom; then after she had sat down on the side of the bed, she said, 'Well, come in, don't stand there.'

Mary Ann went into the room, closing the door behind her. She felt rather gauche in Janice's presence, and very, very young. Janice was sitting with her hands nipped between her knees, and she looked at her hands as she asked, 'Did you hear anything going on?'

'Yes, we did.'

'We?' Janice's head came up.

'Tony's with me.'

'Oh, my God!' Although Janice said this in a very swanky tone, it sounded much more of a blasphemy than if, say, Mrs. McBride had said it.

'Well, he would get an earful.'

'I think you should come down. Your mother's lip's all swollen.'

Janice looked down at her hands once more and began to rock herself, before she said, 'Oh, it won't be the first time. And anyway, she asks for it.'

'Asks for it?' Mary Ann's voice was high and sharp. 'She's nice. I've always said that.'

'If that's the kind of niceness you want, yes. But she's always got on his nerves. She should never have married him. She should have taken someone polished, and re-feened. Someone who liked to go to concerts, yet someone who would laugh at her jokes when she was being funny ha-ha. But most of all somebody who would keep up this damn mausoleum.' She released her hands from between her knees and flung them sidewards. 'Oh, she gets on my goat too.'

'But he hit her, Janice . . . twice!'

'He was drunk and worried about me.'

'About you?'

'Yes. It all came out last night. That is what I wanted to see you about. I was in a blue funk yesterday, but now all the beans are spilt it doesn't matter. . . . I'm going to have a baby.'

Mary Ann's mouth dropped into a large 'O', before she brought her lips together again, saying, 'Janice!'

'Oh! For God's sake, don't look like that, Mary Ann. You look like the Virgin Mary, only more damned good.'

Although Janice had attended the Convent she wasn't a Catholic, and Mary Ann had always resented her digs at the Virgin Mary. But now all she could say was, 'Are you . . . are you married?'

'Oh, be your age. . . Why I thought of coming to see you I don't know. Of course I'm not married. What do you think all this hoo-ha is about? And I'm telling you, I don't care much if I do or I don't. But Father's going to play the gigantic square and make him do . . . the right thing. Oh, my God!' Janice jerked herself from the bed. 'The right thing! And live a life like theirs! I wouldn't have believed it, but Daddy's taken it worse than she has. You get surprises if you've got anything left to feel surprise with. She didn't blink an eyelid, yet Daddy, he nearly went through the roof. And him running one in Newcastle and another in Pelaw.'

It must have been Mary Ann's puckered expression that made Janice close her eyes and fling her head back as she cried defiantly, by way of exclamation, 'A woman . . . he's always had a woman, but now he's got two.'

Mary Ann knew that she should sit down. She had a

frightened feeling. It was like the time she had thought that Mr. Quinton wanted her mother. She wasn't as green as Janice thought she was. It wasn't Janice's knowledge that was shocking her, but the open flaunting of it. She herself would rather have died than talk like this about her parents. Then Janice surprised her still further by turning on the bed and flinging herself face downwards.

'Oh, don't, Janice, don't.' Mary Ann grasped Janice's hand which was pounding into the pillow, and when she began to cry with a hard, tearing sound, Mary Ann knelt on the floor and put her arms around her and her face on the pillow as she murmured over and over, 'Oh, don't, Janice, don't. Don't cry, don't cry so.'

When Janice finally stopped crying she seemed to have washed away the hard covering of her personality, for, sitting once again on the side of the bed, one hand only now nipped between her knees, she looked at Mary Ann and said quietly, 'I won't have a life like theirs, I'd rather take something and finish it.'

'Oh, Janice! Don't say such things, don't. And you needn't have a life like theirs. . . . Is . . . is this boy nice?

'No. No, he's not. He's as far removed from me as Daddy is from . . . from her.' Janice now turned her head to the side and said, 'I've got a lot of my father in me so that's why I know that if I marry Freddie I won't be able to stick it. I think that's why I grew to dislike her . . . my mother. Because she had the power to stick it. To put a face on it. She should have left him years ago. And she might have, too, if it hadn't been for Grandpa. He died only three years ago. They were both barmy about this house and garden. There's something to be said on both sides, because it was Daddy's money that was keeping it going. That is until he turned nasty . . . and he can be nasty, hellish. He cut out the gardener, and the maids . . . and, oh . . . oh, lots of things. And the more things he did the more face she put on, and that drove him almost round the bend. . . . But I won't marry Freddie, I won't.'

'He can't make you if you don't want to.' Mary Ann was holding Janice's hands tightly between hers now. 'Look, come and stay with us for a while.'

Janice turned and stared into Mary Ann's face. 'Would your mother let me?'

'Yes. Yes, of course she would.' Mary Ann hadn't stopped to consider whether Lizzie would fall in with this arrangement or not. She only knew she wanted to help Janice.

'I'd be glad to get away from here. If only for a few days. But I'm beginning to show ... and there's, there's your Michael!'

Yes, there was Michael, and Sarah. But Mary Ann, overriding this as well, said casually, 'What does it matter? They're not to know.'

'Oh, they'll know. Everybody will know shortly. It would be better in the long run, I suppose, to do what I'm told.'

'Does he ... Freddie, want ... want to get married?'

'Oh, yes. He would jump in feet first at the idea. He's only in the dock office and he'll know when he's on a good thing; Daddy would set him up. Oh, I know exactly what'll happen. He'll set him up, and he'll buy us a house and a car. He's rotten with money, and he'll spend it on anything or anybody outside this house.'

The bitterness was creeping back into Janice's tone, and Mary Ann shook her hand and said, 'Well, wait and see. And think about coming to us. You needn't worry about phoning or anything, just come. My mother will love to have you.'

Janice, now looking down into Mary Ann's upturned face, smiled and said, 'You're sweet, you know, Mary Ann. I used to be jealous of you and Beatrice being close pals. I always wanted you for a friend, a complete friend. Because you were different somehow. I suppose it was because you had nothing in your family life to hide.'

'O ... oh!' Mary Ann's head went back on a little laugh now. 'Oh, Janice, you don't know the half of it. I'm beginning to think we all have something to hide. I've been fighting for me da since ... oh, I can't remember the time when I wasn't putting him over as somebody wonderful; when I wasn't covering up his drinking bouts. It isn't like that now, but things still happen and I always seem to be covering up for him. You do things like that when you love someone. . . . Nothing to hide! Do you know, I've always envied you.'

'Envied me? God! Envied me? The times I've been going to run away, or commit suicide; or throw myself over the banisters to stop them havin' a row. . . . Envy me!'

The two girls sat looking at each other on the side of the bed. And their hands held tightly for a moment, before Mary Ann said through a break in her voice, 'I'd better be going down now, Janice; Tony will want to be getting away. But remember what I said. Come any time . . . any time. Good-bye, now.'

'Good-bye, Mary Ann, and thanks. But I'll let you know if I'm coming. I'll drop you a line, or phone. Good-bye. I feel better now. Good-bye.'

In the drawing-room Tony was no longer sitting on the couch but on a chair some distance from Mrs. Schofield, and as Mary Ann entered the room it did not seem as if she had interrupted their talking, it was as if they had been sitting quiet for some time. She stood in front of Mrs. Schofield when she said, 'I've asked Janice to come and stay with us for a while, Mrs. Schofield.'

'That's nice of you, Mary Ann. But hadn't you better ask your mother first?'

'Oh, my mother won't mind . . . she won't.'

Mrs. Schofield did not speak, she only moved her head slightly. And then Mary Ann added, 'I'll have to be going now.' She turned sharply and looked towards Tony, and he rose from the chair but made no comment.

Mrs. Schofield, too, rose to her feet, but she did not accompany them from the room, and Mary Ann was slightly puzzled when Tony took leave of her with just a single good-bye; a rather curt-sounding good-bye.

As the car went through the tunnel of the drive, Mary Ann said softly, 'It's awful, awful.'

Tony made no response to this. He slowed the car up as he neared the end of the drive, then, when he had swung into the main road, he quickly changed gears and they went roaring towards the city.

Mary Ann realized that Tony was quiet because, like her, he was upset. He, too, must have seen Mrs. Schofield as a gay creature. And she supposed that men could be shocked as much about such things as women could. She said now, as if they were continuing a conversation, 'I hope she doesn't marry that Freddie.'

'Who? Who are you talking about?'

'Janice.'

'Is she going to be married?'

'Well.' She glanced at him. Did he, or didn't he know? She said softly, 'Well, you know she's going to have a baby.'

'Good God!' The car almost jerked to a stop, then went on again. 'So that's it.' He was not speaking to her but answering some question of his own. She did not take it up for he did not look in the mood to talk. He looked like her da did at times, but more so like Mr. Lord when he was very angry inside. So they didn't speak again until they reached the farmyard. And there he turned the car before stopping. Then reaching over to open the door for her, he said, 'Are you going to tell your mother?'

'Yes.' Mary Ann hesitated. 'I'll have to if Janice is coming.'

'Yes.' He nodded his head without looking at her, and said again, 'Yes.'

She closed the car door, then watched him speeding back along the road down which they had just come.

Mike had been going in the direction of the byres, and he turned on the sound of the car leaving the yard again and, coming to her, said, 'My! you're soon back. Where's he gone?'

Mary Ann, looking up at Mike, meant to say 'I don't know,' but instead she bowed her head and burst out crying.

'What's the matter? What's happened?' Mike's voice was deep.

'Nothing. Nothing.'

'Tony said somethin' to you?'

'Oh, no, no. Come in a minute, will you? I've ... I've got to tell me ma.'

In the kitchen, with Mike sitting at her side and Lizzie sitting in front of her, she held their silence with her story. And when it was finished she looked from one to the other, and they returned her gaze, still without speaking. Then Mike, getting up and walking to the pipe rack, lifted a wire cleaner from the top of it and rammed it down the stem of his pipe before shaking his head and saying, 'I think this is one of the biggest surprises of me life.'

'Yes, that's how I felt, Da. I couldn't take it in.'

'Poor soul! Look at her the night of the wedding. Who could have been more full of fun?' Lizzie had forgotten her irritation towards Mrs. Schofield on that particular night, and her sympathy at this moment was very genuine. 'Did you actually see him hit her?'

'Yes, Ma.' Mary Ann reverted to the old form of address. At moments such as this Ma seemed more fitting, for the three of them were joined in their pity. 'I didn't see him do it the second time; I hid my face.'

'You never know, do you?' They both looked towards Mike as he went on pushing the cleaner down the stem of the pipe. 'I would have staked me last shilling that she was the happiest woman alive. Mind you' – he wagged the pipe towards Lizzie – 'I've said, haven't I, that she wasn't as dizzy as she made out. I knew from the minute I first clapped eyes on her there was a depth there. But it never struck me that all this light fantastic was just a cover . . . did it you? Did you ever have an inkling?'

'No. No. Like you, I would have sworn she was happy.' Again Lizzie added, 'Poor soul.'

'You don't mind me asking Janice here?' Mary Ann now asked of Lizzie.

'No, no. It will be better if she's away from that set-up for a time. But with a man like that, it looks as if he'll get his own way, and make her marry the fellow. Which, I suppose, will be all for the best. At least best for the child. . . . Oh, dear God, it's awful, when you think of it. I've never liked Janice very much, but now I'm sorry to the heart for her. And it's not a bit of wonder she's gone wrong, not a bit.'

'Oh, I'm not as sorry for her as I am for the mother.' Mike put the pipe into his mouth. 'That young un's got a tough core, she'll get by. . . . But you see, don't you, Liz, money isn't everything.' Mike now thrust out his arm and wagged his finger at Lizzie. It was as if money, and its value, had been under discussion. 'Schofield's rotten with money. I understand he's got his fingers in all sorts of pies. Real estate, shipping, the lot. He's as bad as the old man. And where's his money got him? What has it done for him? Except help him to run three homes!'

'Mike!'

'Oh, don't get on your high horse, Liz. She's told us all about it, hasn't she? It's herself that's told us.' He flapped his hand towards Mary Ann. 'Her education's been advanced this afternoon. But as I was sayin' about money . . . see what it does?' Mike bounced his head once, then turning on his heel, went out, and Lizzie, sitting straight in her chair, remarked in hurt tones, 'Why has he to go off the deep end like that? Who was talking about money?' She looked at Mary Ann and shook her head. Mary Ann said nothing. She knew that her da had been pointing out to her ma that people who married for money were not always happy. And she knew that her mother was being purposely blind to the parable.

The sound of Michael coming in the back way at this moment brought Mary Ann to her feet, and she said hastily, 'I'll go upstairs and do my face. Don't tell him about Janice, will you not? He doesn't like her very much and if she's comin' here it will make things awkward.'

'Go along. All right. Don't worry.'

Mary Ann had not reached the hall door when Michael entered from the scullery, and as he watched her disappearing back he remarked, in a brotherly fashion, 'What's up with her? Has she been crying? Why did they come back so quickly?'

'Oh . . . Janice wasn't very well.'

'What's she been crying for?'

'She's upset. Just a little upset about something.'

'What?'

'Oh, Michael, don't ask so many questions.'

'Oh, all right, if it's private. Only if I started to howl my eyes out, there'd be a reason for it.'

Lizzie turned and looked at her son and smiled fondly at him as she said, 'There would, if you howled your eyes out; that would be the day when you howled your eyes out.'

Lizzie was to remember these words and to think, 'Isn't it strange the things we say? It's as if we have a premonition of what's going to happen.' But at this moment she had no feeling of premonition. She just said to her son, 'It's time you were getting yourself changed as Sarah will be here and you not ready.'

'Mother.'

'Yes, what is it?' Lizzie had gone to the sideboard and taken out the teacloth.

'I want to ask you something.'

She turned and glanced at him. 'Well, I'm listening, go on.'

'It's about my holiday.'

'Your holiday? It's late in the year to start talking of holidays.'

'Father owes me a week. He said I could have it at any time. You remember?'

'Yes. But we'll soon be on Christmas. And you don't want your holiday with snow on the ground, surely?'

'Yes, that's just it, I do.'

'Where are you going?'

Michael turned from her penetrating gaze and walked towards the fire. 'I want to go to Switzerland.

'Switzerland?'

He swung round sharply to her. 'Yes, Mother, Switzerland.'

'But that'll cost a penny, won't it?'

'Well, I've never had a real holiday in my life. South Shields, Whitley Bay, Sea Houses. But now I want to go abroad. It will only be for a week.'

'Well, well. If you want to go, I suppose you'll go. What does Sarah say to this?'

Michael now looked down towards the mat. Then without raising his head, he cast his eyes up towards Lissie as he said, 'That's it. We want to go together.'

Lizzie's lips closed with a light pressure; the line in between her brows deepened, and then she said quietly, 'Together? You and Sarah away in Switzerland?'

'I'm nearly twenty, Mother.'

'Yes, I know that. And don't tell me now that Sarah's eighteen. I know that too, and I'm going to tell you right away I don't hold with young people going away on holiday

66

together. And there's your father. Just think what he'll say to this.'

'I've asked him.'

'You've asked him . . . well! . . . What did he say then?'

'Do you want to know word for word?'

Lizzie made no reply. But her shoulders went back a little, and she drew her chin in.

'He said it's my own life; nobody can answer my conscience but myself. He said, "If you ever intend to marry a girl never take her down first if you can help it. . . ." '

'Michael!' Lizzie's voice seemed to hit the back of her throat and check her breathing. Twice in the matter of minutes life in the raw had been let loose in her kitchen.

'Well, I'm only telling you what he said, and I know he's right. And I'm just repeating it to put your mind at rest. . . . You understand?'

Lizzie understood all right; but it didn't alter the fact that she didn't want her son to go on a holiday alone with Sarah Flannagan or any other girl. She knew men, even the best of them were what she called human. Well, he'd certainly had his say. Lizzie wiped her lips. 'Is there anything more you have to tell me?'

'What father said? Well, he said there were worse things than a man getting drunk; and I'm beginning to believe him. . . .'

'No, I didn't mean I wanted to hear anything more your father said. He'd said enough, I should imagine. As for worse things than getting drunk, there's two opinions on that point. And I should have thought you knew that.'

'Yes, I do, Mother.' Michael's tone was soft now and he came towards her, and putting his arm about her shoulders he said, 'Don't worry, we'll do nothing we shouldn't do, let me tell you.' He smiled at her now. 'Sarah will see to that.'

Lizzie pulled herself away from Michael's hold. She didn't like this kind of talk; not from her son, her Michael. She knew that one day, and not in the far distant future, she would have to give up this boy of hers, but until that day came he would remain her boy. Not someone who discussed the possibilities of intimacy on holiday. What were young people coming to! She knew that young people went away on holidays together even when they weren't engaged, and she was also well aware of what happened; but she didn't want that kind of thing in her family. And Michael having a good deal of his father in him was bound to be ... human. Oh dear, oh dear, one thing on top of another. She had thought she would have no more worries when she left Mulhattan's Hall. It just showed you. The word Mulhattan's Hall conjured up first Mrs. McBride, and then Mrs. Flannagan, and she turned swiftly towards Michael and said, 'What about her mother? What does she say to this?'

'I don't know.' Michael held out his hand with a sort of hopeless gesture. 'I won't know until Sarah comes. She's asking her this afternoon.'

They continued to look at each other for a moment longer, then Lizzie, with a deep flick, spread the cloth over the table, and Michael, with an equally deep sigh, went upstairs to change.

It was after dinner on the Sunday and the family were relaxing in the front room. Mike was asleep in the deep chair, his long legs stretched out towards the fire. Lizzie sat opposite to him at the other side of the hearth. She was pursuing her favourite hobby of looking at antique furniture and big houses. Michael was sitting at one end of the couch reading *The Farmers' Weekly*; and Mary Ann, with her legs tucked under her, was sitting at the other end. She had two books on her lap. One was *The Art of the Short Story* and the other was Fowler's *Modern English Usage*. But she was reading neither at present. She was staring across the hearth rug into the fire. Her thoughts darting from Corny to Mrs. Schofield then back to Corny again, then on to Janice and back to Corny again. Then to Tony, and strangely not to Corny now but to Mrs. Schofield. For she was seeing them wrapped in that strange silence when she entered the drawing-room of that unhappy house yesterday. Then once again she was thinking of Corny; hearing Mrs. McBride talk of him; seeing Mrs. McBride give her his letter. Her mind dwelt on the letter. She had read it countless times in the past few weeks. She could, without any exaggeration, have quoted it word for word backwards. But the thought of it at this moment brought her legs from under her, and in order not to disturb her da nor yet her mother nor Michael, she went quietly out of the room and upstairs to her bedroom.

After the heat of the sitting-room the chill of the bedroom made her shiver, and she swiftly went to the top drawer of the dressing chest, and there, from the box in which she kept her handkerchiefs and the flute which Corny had given her for her thirteenth birthday, and which, in spite of her promise, she had never learnt to play, she took out the letter. To read it she had to stand by the window, for the sky was dark with coming snow, and her heart quickened as it always did when she came to ... 'If I know I can make a go of it, I'll come back then and tell you.' There was a statue of Our Lady on a little shelf above the head of her bed and she turned her eyes up to it as she did night and morning, and now she prayed: 'Make the time go quickly, dear Mother ... please.'

When she folded the letter again she held it to her cheek for a moment as she looked out of the window. One minute her eyes were dreamy, lost in the promise of a year ahead. The next minute she was bending forward towards the window pane, her mouth open and her eyes screwed up. It couldn't be! But it was; yes, it was. She stared one moment longer at the figure walking primly towards the house gate, and then she thrust the letter into her handkerchief box, banged the drawer closed, and went belting down the stairs. as she thrust the sitting-room door open, all concern for her father's afternoon nap was gone as she cried, 'Mrs. Flannagan! ... It's Mrs. ... It's Mrs. Flannagan ... Mrs. Flannagan's coming.'

'What! Who?' Lizzie and Michael had turned towards her, and Mike, shaking his head and blinking rapidly, pulled himself into a sitting position. 'Good God! Flannagan? The old 'un? You said her ... Mrs.?'

Before Mary Ann could make any further retort, Michael cried, 'Oh Lord!' And Lizzie, turning on him, hissed under her breath, 'This is you and this Switzerland business. Good gracious, on a Sunday afternoon, and me looking like this!'

'Let me get out.'

As the knock came on the front door, Mike, buttoning up his shirt neck, pushed past Mary Ann and made for the stairs. And Michael, about to follow, was checked when Lizzie hissed, 'Now, Michael, you're not going to leave this to me, you've got to face it.'

'Oh, Mother! ... Well, let her get in, I'll come back in a minute ... it mightn't be about that at all.'

'Michael!' Lizzie was whispering hoarsely to Michael's disappearing back as Mary Ann, on the second knock, went towards the door.

'Oh, hello, Mrs. Flannagan.' The feigned surprise, and even pleasure, in Mary Ann's voice, said a lot for her advancement from the days when, next to the justifiable hate she had for Sarah, she considered Mrs. Flannagan not only an enemy of her ... ma and da, but someone in close association with the devil himself.

Mrs. Flannagan was dressed very nicely. She had always attended to her person with the same meticulous care she gave to her house. These qualities of cleanliness were considered by Mrs. Flannagan offsprings of virtue and as such had been enough to arouse Fanny McBride's hate, and Mary Ann, always a staunch ally of Mrs. McBride, would have hated Mrs. Flannagan if for no other reason but that Mrs. McBride couldn't stand ... the upstart.

'I hope you don't mind me comin' like this, Mary Ann?' Mrs. Flannagan's tone held none of the old condescension.

'No, no. Come in, Mrs. Flannagan. You must be frozen. Isn't it cold?' Mary Ann closed the door behind the visitor. 'Will I take your hat and coat?' She was playing for time to allow her mother to compose herself, and perhaps tidy her hair; but at this moment Lizzie came to the sitting-room door.

Lizzie couldn't be blamed for the slight tilt to her chin as she looked at this woman who for many years had been the bane of her existence. Life was strange. But she had no time to delve into this deep problem now, she would keep that for when she lay in bed awake tonight. She was glad, oh she was, that she had insisted on having the new square carpet for the hall. In spite of Mike's saying 'It's madness, lass. It's madness, with all the feet tramping in and out.' But she had always wanted a proper carpet in the hall, with a matching colour going up the stairs. Mike had said, 'Why pick on a mustard colour?' And she had informed him that dark mustard would go with the old furniture, the pieces that her flair had guided her to bid for at the auction sales. And now on one of these pieces, a small hall table, stood a wrought-iron basket showing off a beautiful plant of pink cyclamen. Oh, she was glad her hall looked nice. If only she'd had a chance to change into something decent. But her skirt and blouse were really all right, and what was more, oh, of much more significance, she was mistress of this fine home. . . . Yes, life was funny.

Lizzie fell into the part of hostess. With only a slight touch of reserve to her manner she held out her hand to Mrs. Flannagan, saying, 'If I'd known you were coming, I would have had Michael meet the bus.' The censure wasn't too tactfully covered, it wasn't meant to be. But Mrs. Flannagan was, today, out to placate, and she answered, 'Well, I know I should have phoned, Mrs. Shaughnessy. But it was the way Sarah sprung it on me. And it made me rather vexed.' She smiled. 'So I said, "Well, I'll go myself and see what Mr. and Mrs. Shaughnessy have to say about it." . . . But very likely you don't know what I'm talking about?'

'Yes. Yes, I think I do.' Lizzie inclined her head. 'But come in and sit down; it is cold today, isn't it?'

Mary Ann followed Mrs. Flannagan into the sitting-room. She had a great desire to laugh. Laugh loudly. . . . Go and see Mr. and Mrs. Shaughnessy. Oh! Mr. Shaughnessy would have a laugh about this for weeks ahead. The times Mrs. Flannagan had called her da a drunken no-good. . . . All of a sudden she was glad Mrs. Flannagan had made this unexpected visit. After yesterday, she needed light relief, she felt they were all in need of a little light relief. She sat down opposite Mrs. Flannagan and watched her look around the sitting-room with open amazement. And she found herself even liking her when she said generously, 'What a beautiful room, Mrs. Shaughnessy, what a beautiful room. Did you do it yourself?'

'We all helped, Mrs. Flannagan. Mike's very good at papering and painting.' Lizzie's chin, still high, moved a little to the side.

'But my mother chose the furniture,' Mary Ann put in. 'She's always picking up nice pieces.' She looked with pride towards Lizzie, and Lizzie smiled back at her. And then inclining her head towards her guest, she said, 'Would you like a cup of tea?'

'That's very kind of you, Mrs. Shaughnessy. . . . Yes, I would. I'd be obliged.'

'I'll make it, Mother.'

Mary Ann jumped up and left the room. And as she went laughing into the kitchen, Michael, standing to the side of the door, pulled at her arm.

'What has she said?'

'Nothing, nothing. We've only reached the polite exchange stage so far. You've got all that to come, me lad.' She dug her brother in the chest.

'Oh! They get you down.' Michael put his hand to his head. 'Who?'

'Oh, mothers. The lot of them.'

'Me ma's right about this.' Mary Ann's face took on a straight pattern as she nodded solemnly at Michael. She had only heard that morning about the proposed holiday in Switzerland, and her first reaction had been one of shock. And then she had thought . . . well, it would be all right, they were Catholics. But this statement had been countered by a cynical voice that was making itself heard in her mind quite a lot of late, and it said, with a little smear of a laugh, 'What difference will that make when it comes to . . .' She had shut the door of her mind on the voice before it had dared to go into forbidden topics. But she found now that she was vexed with Michael's attitude towards her ma, because her ma, she knew, put Michael first, and always had done, the same as her da had put her first and would always do so. And Michael knew this, and up to now he and her ma had been very close. If she hadn't had her da's unstinted love she would have at times been jealous of Michael. She said again, 'Me ma's right.' And he turned on her, whispering fiercely, 'What do you know about it? Your ideas are so infantile, you should still be in white socks.'

'Well!' She drew herself up. Then with sisterly affection she finished, 'I hope you get it in the neck.'

At this moment the kitchen door opened quietly and Mike entered, and at the sight of him both Mary Ann and Michael were forced to laugh.

'Oh, Da! She must have you frightened at last.' Mary Ann was spluttering through her fingers.

Mike, unloosening the button on the coat of his best suit, and hunching his shoulders upwards, said, 'All right, laugh. I'm on me own ground; but I still feel I need some armour against that one.' Then looking at Michael he said kindly, 'I've always had the idea that Sarah was adopted.'

'I don't think I'll hang anything on to that hope.' Michael returned his father's grin. 'She takes after her mother in some ways . . . she's finicky about her clothes.'

'Well, I wouldn't stand there, both of you,' Mary Ann thrust at them. 'I'd go on in and get it over.'

'After you.' Michael held out his hand with an exaggerated gesture to his father. And Mike, following suit, replied, 'No, after you. This visit, don't forget, is for the benefit of your soul.'

'Ha!' On this telling exclamation Michael led the way out of the kitchen, and Mary Ann, in case she missed much, flung the things on to the tea-tray and only a few minutes later carried it into the sitting-room, there to see her da ensconced in the big armchair with his legs crossed, his pipe in his mouth and his whole attitude proclaiming the master of the house, and to hear Mrs. Flannagan repeat an earlier statement, 'It's a beautiful room. Mr. Shaughnessy.'

'My wife has taste, Mrs. Flannagan.'

Mrs. Flannagan lifted her watery smile up to Lizzie's face, and Lizzie, slightly embarrassed, and praying inwardly that Mike was not all set to have his own back on this she-cat-turned-dove, said, in a smooth tone that tempered the abrupt plunge into essentials, 'It's about Sarah and the holiday you've come, Mrs. Flannagan?'

'Yes, yes, Mrs. Shaughnessy, you're right. You see, I would never have dreamed of coming without an invitation.' She flickered her eyes around the company asking them all to bear witness to her knowledge of propriety. 'But this, I felt, was an emergency. You know what I mean.' She eased herself to the edge of the chair. And as she did so Michael coughed, and Mike made a funny sound down the stem of his pipe that brought Lizzie's sharp warning glance on him. 'Now as I said to Sarah, this thing has got to be talked over; not that I don't trust you, Michael.' Mrs. Flannagan's head now went into a deep abeyance. She had lost her nervousness; she had forgotten for the moment that she was in the enemy's camp, so to speak. For Mrs. Flannagan, at rock bottom, was no fool; she knew that Mike Shaughnessy's memory was long. And although she didn't want to do anything to put a spanner in the works of the match, she wasn't going to let her daughter appear as a ... light piece, her own phraseology for any female who gave to a man her company in the first hours of the day. 'I do trust you, I do, Michael, but ...' Mrs. Flannagan seemed to be stumped for words with which to make her meaning plain, but this obstacle was overcome for her by Mike.

'But taking into account human nature, Mrs. Flannagan?'

Was Mike Shaughnessy laughing at her? Mrs. Flannagan stared back into the straight countenance of the big red-headed man. There was no sign of laughter on his face, but that was nothing to go by when dealing with him. She knew this from experience, but now she clutched at his explanation, which was really what she had wanted to say but had found a little indelicate. Now however she affirmed, 'Yes. Yes, you're right, Mr. Shaughnessy. Human nature has got to be taken into account. And ... and the look of the thing, it's the look of the thing, and what people will say. And once give a dog a bad name, you know. . . .'

'Yer ... ss, I know. I know, Mrs. Flannagan.' Mike was nodding at their guest. 'Don't I know, Mrs. Flannagan.'

Oh my. Mary Ann had a little uneasy fluttering inside her chest. This could lead to anything. Her da was going to rib Mrs. Flannagan. He was going to lead her on, and on, and then knock her flat. She knew the tactics. In the hope that it might divert the topic, she put in quickly, 'You haven't drunk your tea, Mrs. Flannagan.'

'No. Oh, no.' Mrs. Flannagan smiled at Mary Ann and took two very ladylike sips from her cup. It was as she took the second sip that she gulped slightly, for Michael was speaking, and with no prelude.

'I hope some day to marry Sarah, Mrs. Flannagan.' His voice was quiet, his tone very level, and his air not that of a boy not yet twenty, but of a man who knew his own mind.

Mrs. Flannagan's head made a half-moon turn as she took them, one by one, into her glance again. Then after a gulp that had nothing ladylike about it whatever, she addressed Michael pointedly. 'There, that's what I said to her. I said, "It would be different altogether if you were engaged or something." That's what I pointed out to her. I said, "If there was an understanding or something."'

Oh, Lord. Mary Ann's head dropped. This was enough to break up any romance. Poor Michael. Poor Sarah.

'Michael will do what he thinks is right in his own time, Mrs. Flannagan.'

'Yes, yes, I'm sure he will, Mrs. Shaughnessy.'

'You might as well know I don't hold with this business of holidaying together any more than you do.'

'Oh, it isn't that, Mrs. Shaughnessy.'

'No, no, it isn't that.' Mike's voice was a deep bass as he repeated Mrs. Flannagan's words. And it was evident he meant to go on, when Michael cut in sharply on them all, and he was on his feet when he spoke. 'Leave this to me, Father . . . and you, Mother.' And now he looked straight at Mrs. Flannagan while he said, 'Sarah and I have the same ideas about an engagement. We've talked it over. In the meantime we want to go away together. . . We don't intend to sleep together. . . .'

'Michael!' Lizzie, too, was on her feet, and Mike, sitting up straight in his chair, said quietly, 'It's all right, it's all right. It happens, don't be so shocked. Nor you, Mrs. Flannagan. Go on, son.'

Michael swallowed before saying, 'What we do want is to go away for a time and enjoy ourselves, and be together all day. And see different places . . . together. On our own. And you know' – he was now not looking at Mrs. Flannagan but casting his glance sideways at Lizzie as he went on – 'It's not held as a sin any longer when a fellow and a girl go off holidaying together. It might be frowned on but—'

At this point Michael stopped and jerked his head round towards the sitting-room door. Mary Ann, too, was looking towards the door. Her attention had been drawn to it before Michael had stopped talking, and now Lizzie said, 'What is it?' and following Mary Ann's gaze she asked abruptly, 'See if anyone's there. It might be Tony.'

Mary Ann was at the door before her mother had finished speaking, and when, pulling it open with a quick tug, she almost fell on to the high breast of her granny, she let out a scream.

Her granny. Of all days her granny had to come today. Of all times her granny had to come precisely at this time, when Mrs. Flannagan was here. She had always considered her granny a form of witch who went round smelling out mischief for the sole purpose of enlarging it. As far back as she could remember she had hated her granny. There was no alteration in her feelings at this moment. In the presence of her granny she lost all her girlish charm. Mrs. McMullen had the power to bring out the very worst in Mary Ann, and she always put this power into motion as soon as her eyes alighted on her grand-daughter.

'Well, knock me over. That's it, knock me over.'

'Oh, no!' Mary Ann heard her mother's stifled murmur, and above it came Michael's audible groan. Mike alone made no sound. But Mary Ann knew that of all of them her father would be the most affected by her granny's visit. Whereas he would only have chipped Mrs. Flannagan, and revelled, no doubt, in the superiority of his family's position now that the tables were almost completely turned, the afternoon, nevertheless, would have gone off with a veneer of smoothness, but when her da came up against her granny veneers were useless. For her granny hated her da, and would do until the last breath was dragged from her.

'What are you gaping at? Standing there looking like a mental defective.'

'I'm not then. . . .' Whether Mary Ann was denying that she was standing gaping, or that she was a mental defective was not plain. The only thing that was plain was the aggressive note in her voice.

'Well, there's one thing I can always be sure of when I visit my daughter, and that's an all-round welcome.'

Mrs. McMullen was now in the room, and her chin went

up and her abundantly covered head, both of hair and hat, were slightly to the side as she feigned surprise at the sight of Mrs. Flannagan.

'Well! well! And who would have expected to see you here! . . . Good afternoon, Mrs. Flannagan.'

'Good afternoon, Mrs. McMullen.' Mrs. Flannagan was smiling her thin smile but it was evident that she was more uneasy now than she had been before Mrs. McMullen's entry.

'Well, Lizzie.' Mrs. McMullen looked at her daughter.

'Hello, Mother. . . . I wasn't expecting you.'

'Are you ever?'

'Well, you rarely come on a Sunday. I've never known—'

'All right! All right! I rarely come on a Sunday. But I live alone, don't forget, and people do forget that old people are living alone and without company. So I felt that I would visit my daughter, and have a look at my grandchildren.' She made no mention of her son-in-law who was now sitting, legs uncrossed, his spine tightly pressed against the back of the chair.

'Sit down. Give me your hat. . . . Will you have a cup of tea?'

'Well, I won't say no. I'm practically frozen to the bone.'

'Pour your granny out a cup of tea, Mary Ann.'

'Why does she have to look so gormless?' Mrs. McMullen had turned her gimlet eyes on her grand-daughter, and Mary Ann, rearing up now well above the side table and Mrs. McMullen's seated figure, spat out, 'Do you make a list of all the sweet things you're going to say before you—'

'That's enough!' Lizzie was not only speaking to Mary Ann as she extended her one hand towards her, but was already addressing Mike with a warning look, for Mike had pulled himself to the edge of the chair – his face dark with temper.

It was at this point that Mrs. Flannagan, seeing herself in the light of peacemaker, turned to Mrs. McMullen and remarked, 'I was just saying to Mr. Shaughnessy, what a delightful room this is.'

Mrs. McMullen's head moved in a series of short waves as she calmly and aggravatingly surveyed the room; then her verdict came. 'It's too light.' There followed a pause when no one spoke, and she went on, 'Never put good pieces of dark furniture against light wallpaper. I've told her.' She looked towards Lizzie. 'I was picking up things in antique shops long before she was born and I've always said dark paper, dark furniture . . . haven't I?'

Lizzie did not answer her mother. And Mrs. McMullen took a sip from her tea, only to comment, 'No sugar.'

'I did sugar it.'

'Well, I should say that in this case the sugar is about as sweet as the donor.'

It was evident to all that Mrs. McMullen was in a temper. She was usually in a temper. It seemed to be her natural state. But she generally waited until she could diplomatically fire her darts. Unfortunately, whatever had upset her today had robbed her of her finesse. And then she gave evidence of the source of her annoyance by turning to Michael for the first time.

'What you want is a visit from the priest.'

'WHAT!'

'You heard what I said.'

There was a wrinkled query spreading over the faces of them all as they looked towards the old woman, ageless in her vitality. 'You heard what I said. A priest . . . going away with a young lass for a week!'

The comments to this remark seemed to come simultaneously from all directions of the room.

'Mother!' This was Lizzie.

'Look here, Gran.' This was Michael.

'Really, Mrs. McMullen!' This was Mrs. Flannagan.

'Well, I'll be damned! Your cuddy's lugs got working quick, didn't they? Did you find it draughty standing in the hall?' This from her beloved son-in-law.

Only Mary Ann made no comment, for she was thinking rapidly. She would have to get her da away out of here else there would be a row. This would have to happen when Mrs. Flannagan was here, wouldn't it?

Mrs. McMullen, it would appear, had not heard her son-in-law's remarks, for she turned now to Mrs. Flannagan, and her tone was sympathetic as she said, 'I can well understand how you feel, I would be the same in your shoes. And you're right to put your foot down and forbid such a carry on. . . .'

'But . . . Mrs. McMullen, it . . . it isn't like that.' Mrs. Flannagan was definitely floundering. She held out a wavering hand towards Mike, who looked livid enough to explode, and he cut in on her in deep, deep tones.

'If my son wants to take Sarah away, then he has my permission and my blessing on the trip. . . . Are you listening?'

'Mike. . . . Look, wait a moment.'

'I'm not waitin' any moment, Liz. I'm making this clear once and for all. My son is not a boy, he's a man.' This was the second time Mike had spoken of Michael as my son, not our son, and he had stressed the 'my' this time.

'You know my opinion, Mrs. Flannagan.' Mrs. McMullen was entirely ignoring Mike, and doing it in such a way that a saint would have been forgiven for springing on her and putting a finish to her mischief-making existence. 'You must be very worried, and you're quite right to put a stop to it. . .'

'But, Mrs. McMullen, wait. . . .' Mrs. Flannagan was leaning towards the old woman now with her hands raised in an agitated flutter. 'You've got me slightly wrong. I trust Michael with Sarah.' She glanced with her thin smile towards Michael's stiff countenance. 'Mr. Flannagan and myself think very highly of Michael, and now that, well . . . they're going to be engaged, I can't, as I was saying to Mr. Shaughnessy a moment ago, see any harm in them having a holiday together, now they're going to be engaged . . . You see, Mrs. McMullen?'

Mary Ann had never liked Mrs. Flannagan, and she had imagined that she never could, but at this minute she had a strong desire to fling her arms around her neck and hug her. True, she had precipitated an engagement, but that's what she had come for. Still, no matter how she had accomplished it she had got one over on her granny. But, what was much more significant, she had sided with her da against her granny. This was indeed a change of front and a blow to her granny, because Mrs. Flannagan and her granny had been on very polite speaking terms simply because they both had a joint enemy in her da. And now Mrs. Flannagan had blatantly left her granny's ranks and come over to their side. Oh, if only her da would use this turn in the situation and play up. And her da, being her da, did just that.

Undoubtedly Mrs. Flannagan's statement came as a surprise to Mike, and that is putting it mildly. Perhaps before the end of her visit she might have indicated that if the couple were engaged, they would have her blessing to take a trip together. Whether she had cunningly grasped at the situation to use a little motherly blackmail didn't matter. She, Mrs. Flannagan, the thorn that had been in Mike's other side for years, had openly flouted his mother-in-law, and had openly agreed with him. Whatever he had thought of her in the past, this afternoon he would be for her. He reached for his pipe and once more lay back in his chair and crossed his legs, before saying with a smile, which he directed entirely upon Mrs. Flannagan, 'Yes, you're right. An engagement makes all the difference. You can trust your daughter as I can trust my son. And I don't think there'll be any need for a priest. Do you, Mrs. Flannagan?'

Mrs. Flannagan blinked, she preened, she returned Mike's smile in the face of Mrs. McMullen's thunderous countenance as she replied banteringly, 'Well, not just yet awhile, Mr. Shaughnessy.' And she continued to smile across the hearth-rug towards this big rugged, red-headed man, who had more than once threatened to throw her down the stairs if she didn't mind her own so-and-so business. But those things were in the past. For now she was delighted that her Sarah would marry into such a family. Into a family that would soon be connected with Mr. Lord, and him owning a shipyard. She knew why Corny Boyle had been sent packing. She couldn't get much out of Sarah these days, but some time ago she had let slip that old Lord had his grandson all lined up for Mary Ann.

'What do you say to this?' Mrs. McMullen had turned her whole body towards Lizzie, and her attitude would have intimidated anyone less strong. From anyone less used to the subtleties of this woman it would have brought forth the truth. And if Lizzie had spoken the truth at this moment she would have said, 'I'm as against it as you are.' But she could never desert Mike openly in the face of her mother. Nor could she stand on one side while Mike was taking sides with Mrs. Flannagan. Where Mike stood in this she must be also. She looked down into her mother's face and said, with just a little side dig of censure at Mrs. Flannagan, 'I think we are all concerning ourselves far too much about something which isn't entirely our business. Michael and Sarah will do what they want in the long run, with or without our consent.'

'You've gone soft, me girl.'

A silence followed this remark, and Mrs. McMullen moved her body slowly round again and surveyed the company. And when her eyes came to rest on Michael, his dropped away, and he tried his best at this juncture not to laugh. . . . Talk about manoeuvring and counter-manoeuvring. They had settled his life between them. He was already engaged; if they only but knew it, he had been engaged to Sarah from the first moment he set eyes on her, and she to him. But let them have their say, let them think they were fixing everything. There would be no harm done.

He looked towards his father, and Mike, catching his eye, gave the faintest of winks. As Michael grew older he found he liked his father more and more. It hadn't always been like that. He knew now that Mike was enjoying the situation, he had got one up on the old girl, even if it meant joining forces with Mrs. F. It was as good as a play, the whole set-up.

Lizzie broke the awkward silence now by saying, 'I think I'd better set the tea.'

'I'll help you, Mother.' Mary Ann, glad of the chance to escape, was about to move from behind the table when Mrs. McMullen, turning her cold fish eyes on her, remarked, 'Nice goings on among your friends, eh?'

'What?'

'Is that all you two can say?' Mrs. McMullen flicked her eyes between Michael and Mary Ann: 'WHAT!'

'No, it isn't all I can say.' Mary Ann defended herself, standing squarely in front of her grandmother now. 'And what do you mean about my friends?'

'That Schofield piece, no better than should be expected.'

At the name of Schofield, a swift glance passed between Lizzie, Mike and Mary Ann. Then Mary Ann's eye came to rest on her granny again. It was true what she had always maintained, her granny was in league with the devil. Father Owen had told her years ago that the devil walked the earth in different guises, and for a certainty, she would maintain, he had taken on the guise of a bitter, envious, hateful, cantankerous old woman. How else would her granny know of Janice's trouble? But now Mrs. McMullen gave her the answer.

'A come-down for the Schofields, I'd say, wouldn't you, them having their daughter tied up compulsorily with the Smyths?'

'Which Smyths are you talking about?' Lizzie, now, not Mary Ann, snapped the inquiry at her mother.

'The Smyths above me, you know them well enough. Two doors up. It's their Freddie she's got mixed up with. And there was her dear papa yesterday afternoon in his car as big as a house, and May Smyth in tears after. But they weren't too salt, for there's money there.'

'What do you know about it?' Mike's voice was harsh. 'You're just surmising, as always. Putting two and two together, a putrid two and two.'

Mrs. McMullen did not turn her superior expression on her son-in-law, but looked up at her daughter as she said, 'Mrs. Smyth told me the whole story after Mass this morning.'

'She's a blasted fool then.'

Mrs. McCullen continued to ignore Mike as she went on, still looking at Lizzie. 'Of course it didn't surprise me, with a mother like she's got gallivanting here, there, and everywhere. Never in, I should say. Every bazaar and flower opening, there she is, with that Mrs. Willoughby and Bob Quinton's wife. They have nothing better to do, the three of them, but going around showing themselves off on platforms and not attending to their families. It will be the Willoughby one next . . . and you, me gel.' Now Mrs. McMullen brought her face sharply round to Mary Ann's dark countenance.

'You should go on your bended knees every night and thank God you haven't got a mother who gallivants—'

'When I go on my bended knees every night, it isn't to thank God but to ask Him—'

'Mary Ann!' Lizzie had to shake Mary Ann by the arm to bring her riveted attention from her granny.

'Oh, leave her alone, leave her alone.' Mrs. McMullen flapped her hand at her daughter. 'I suppose it shows some good quality when she tries to defend her friends. And they need some defending is all I can say. . . . With the girl in a packet of trouble, and the mother joy-riding up the country lanes with that young fellow.'

Mrs. McMullen did not go on to give the name of the young fellow, but she looked around her silent audience, waiting for one of them to prompt her disclosure. But when no one spoke, she wagged her head before ending, 'I wonder what the almighty Mr. Lord will say to his grandson running round with a married woman?'

'Oh, you! you wicked old . . .! You always were a wicked creature, you . . .!'

'Stop that.' It was Mike speaking now, his voice low and steely. 'Let your granny go on, she came to give us this news. She won't rest until she tells us.'

But Mary Ann didn't allow her grandmother to go on. She was quivering with rage as she blurted out, 'You're lying. Tony never saw Mrs. Schofield until yesterday.'

Mrs. McMullen's eyebrows went up just the slightest at this new piece of information and she replied coolly, 'Yesterday? I'm not talking about yesterday. I'm talking about today, not an hour gone. The police were holding the traffic up, there'd been an accident, and as I sat in the bus I happened, like any ordinary person, to look at the passing cars. He was letting them pass one by one as the lorries were half over the road, and there, sitting side by side, was your Mr. Tony and the Schofield woman. And something else I'll tell you, she had her head down, but that didn't prevent me from seeing one of the best black eyes I've spied for a long time.'

'It's a pity someone hadn't the guts to give you—'

'Please, Mike, please!' As Lizzie appealed to Mike she had

her eyes closed, and looking up into her white face he obeyed her plea. But, pulling himself to his feet, he remarked, 'Let me out of this. I'm in need of fresh air.'

As Mike reached the sitting-room door, Mary Ann was behind him, and as they went into the hall Michael came on their heels.

All three stood in the kitchen and looked at each other, and then Michael asked quietly 'Is it true, do you think, about . . . about Janice Schofield?'

'Yes, it's true enough, more's the pity.' Mike took in a deep breath.

'And about . . . Tony?'

'No, it isn't. That part isn't true. Mr. Schofield hit Mrs. Schofield yesterday, and Tony and I saw him. Tony was taking me to see Janice. That's all there was to it.' Mary Ann stopped gabbling and again they looked from one to the other, but not one of them said, 'Why is he with her today though?' Yet Mary Ann knew that both Michael and her father were asking themselves this same question. She sensed Michael's bewilderment at the situation, but she more than sensed her father's real reaction to this latest piece of news. He would welcome the idea of Tony having an affair. . . . And she herself, how did she feel about it? If Corny had been here, perhaps she would have just shown a friendly interest, mixed with a little wonder that Tony should take out a woman so much older than himself, for Mrs. Schofield must be nearly thirty-five. . . . But Corny wasn't here. And she was amazed at the feeling of resentment that had whirled up in her quite suddenly against Mrs. Schofield. She liked Mrs. Schofield. Yesterday, she had loved her. If pity is akin to love, then she had loved her. But this afternoon she was out with Tony!

She turned her eyes from her father's penetrating gaze and said aloud, with the fervour of the younger Mary Ann who had cared nothing about self-discipline, decorum, and putting a face on things, 'I could kill me granny! And you know, one of these days I feel sure I will, I won't be able to help it.'

CHAPTER FIVE

JANICE neither wrote nor phoned during the following week to say that she was coming, and Lizzie, her sympathy now ebbing, said testily, 'She might have at least let us know. I suppose she doesn't think there's a room to be got ready, and other things.' She had gone to some pains to make the spare room attractive, and she had added, 'Only three weeks to Christmas and everything to do. People don't seem to have any consideration at all these days.'

Mary Ann did not in her usual way make any defensive retort. She understood how her mother felt. She was feeling slightly annoyed herself. Janice might have phoned. Moreover, she was curious to know what was happening. She had been tempted twice already this week to bring up the subject with Tony, but strangely enough she had found herself shy of broaching it! For Tony, from the time he had said, 'Are you going to tell your mother?' had, it would seem, dismissed the Schofields from his mind, for he had made no reference whatever to them. This would have seemed strange enough if Mary Ann had not known he had met Mrs. Schofield since the incident at the house, but now that she knew he had taken Mrs. Schofield out on the Sunday it was more than odd. His silence, she felt, put upon the situation a cloak of secrecy that wasn't ... nice. And it was this cloak that prevented her from inquiring about Janice.

Yet when he called into the house he laughed and talked with her ma and da, and seemed in very good spirits. And she asked herself on these occasions, didn't he himself think it was odd, knowing that she had told them about Mrs. Schofield, that he shouldn't mention the matter?

Then there was her mother's attitude towards this

business. The fact that Lizzie hadn't referred to her granny's denouncement added another cloak of secrecy to the affair, and strengthened this feeling of the situation being beyond the pale of . . . nice.

Her mother had said last night that everything happened around Christmas time and that she wished it was over. She knew that her mother was worried about Michael going to Switzerland with Sarah, for it was now settled that they would have their holiday together. And in bed last night she herself had felt a keen jealousy against the two of them. It did not last long and she went to sleep on the thought: 'When Corny comes back I shall have my holiday with him. Me ma won't be able to say anything, she can't after this. . . .'

When yet another week had passed and still no word had come from Janice, Lizzie dismissed the subject with the emphatic statement, 'That's the last bottle I'm putting up in that bed.'

It was a week before Christmas and on a Friday night that Mary Ann brought home news of Janice. Lizzie was in the kitchen and anxiously looking towards the clock – Mary Ann was half an hour late, which was unusual. Lizzie got worried when she was five minutes late – you heard of such dreadful things happening to girls these days.

The sound of Mike scraping his boots on the scraper outside the scullery door brought her hurrying through the kitchen, and as he opened the door she said, 'She's not in yet.'

'No! What's keeping her, I wonder? She phoned or anything?'

'No.' Lizzie shook her head. 'Would I be like this if she had? Hadn't you better go down and meet the next bus?'

'Aye. Yes, I'll do that.' He rebuttoned the top of his great-coat, saying as he did so, 'The buses will likely be late, the roads are icy.' Then as he was about to turn from her he laughed as he cocked his head upwards. 'Listen, that's her running. All your worry for nothing again.' He pushed past her and, taking off his coat, sat down on the cracket in the scullery. He was unlacing his boots when Mary Ann came in.

'What's kept you?' Lizzie's tone was sharp and indicative of her anxiety.

'I lost my bus. I came on the one on the top road.'

'What's the matter?' Mike lifted his head from its bent position, and his fingers came to a halt where they were entwined in his laces. Mary Ann stood looking down at him for a moment, and her voice shook just the slightest as she said, 'Janice phoned just after I'd finished.'

'Oh? Well ... go into the kitchen, you look froze. Get something to eat before you go any further.'

Mary Ann went into the kitchen, and she turned her white, peaked face towards her mother as she said, 'I don't want anything to eat, not yet, just a drink.'

'What's the matter?' Lizzie's voice was now quiet.

'It's Janice. She's married.'

'Married? Oh.' Mike, coming into the room, picked up her words. 'Well, she could have let you know sooner, couldn't she?' He sat down in his chair, and Mary Ann looking from him to her mother, said, 'No.'

'You're upset about something.' Lizzie put her hand around her daughter's shoulders. 'Sit down and I'll get you a cup of tea.'

Mary Ann sat down, but immediately turned her face into her mother's waist. It was an action that she had not indulged in for a long time. But at this moment she had a frightened feeling. Life could be terrible. Life, she knew, was hard and painful. She had been educated in that kind of life all during her early childhood, but there were other things in life, terrifying things. She drew her head from the shelter of her mother's flesh and looked up at her as she whispered, 'She tried to kill herself!'

'Oh, my God!'

'Did she tell you this?' Mike was leaning towards her now, his hand outstretched holding hers.

'Yes, Da. I had just finished work and Miss Thompson told me I was wanted on the phone. It was Janice. She sounded just as if ... well, as if she was drunk. She was laughing most of the time, except at the end. She kept talking and talking. She said she was married last Friday and her father was going to set Freddie up in business. He had bought them a car and a bungalow on the Fells Road. And then she stopped laughing and carrying on and said she was sorry about not letting me know she wasn't coming, but she hadn't expected to go anywhere for she had taken some stuff and locked herself in her room.' Mary Ann's lips began to tremble. 'From what she said I think she would have died but her mother climbed up the trellis and got in through the window – the house is covered with creeper – and after her doing that she ... she said, Ma, Janice said that she hated her mother, that she should have left her alone. . . . Poor Janice. She must have been in an awful state.'

'Poor mother, I should say.' Mike now hitched himself up to Mary Ann and, patting her hand, said, 'Don't be upset, lass. Madam Janice will come through all right, you'll see. I wish I could say the same for her mother.'

'Where was she married?' asked Lizzie. 'Newcastle or Shields?'

'Newcastle, Ma. At the Registry Office.'

'But she couldn't . . . he's a Catholic.'

'Oh my God! Liz.' Mike shook his head.

'All right, all right. There's no need to use that tone.'

Mary Ann rose from her chair, saying now, 'I'll get washed, Ma.'

'Will I set your tea on a tray and have it in the front room? Michael and Sarah are there.'

'No, Ma. I'll have it here.'

Almost before she had closed the door behind her, she heard her da speak. It was the bitterness of his tone that made her pause for a second to listen, as he said, 'If the old man gets his way, what about it then? Tony's no Catholic and I'm damned sure you'll not get him to turn. He's as stubborn as they come, and no blame to him.'

'I'll meet that obstacle when it arises. And what's the matter with you going for me like this?'

'Because it makes me flaming mad, Liz, when you put a second-class label on people who aren't Catholics.'

'Oh! How can you say such a thing? What about us, eh?'

'I'd be a better man in your eyes if I changed me coat.'

'Oh, that's unfair, Mike. That's unfair. Oh, it is.'

88

As her mother's voice trailed away in sadness, Mary Ann went slowly up the stairs. Why was it that nothing was going right inside or outside of the house lately?

Some minutes later when Mary Ann descended the stairs into the hall again, she approached the sitting-room door with a discreet cough. She would say Hello before she had her tea. But when she opened the door – without knocking, of course – such action would have slapped diplomacy in the face – she did not find Michael and Sarah sitting on the couch, but Michael sitting on his hunkers in front of Sarah, and he looked up quickly at Mary Ann, saying, 'She's off colour.'

'Are you feeling bad?' Mary Ann bent over the back of the couch.

'No, not really bad. I just can't explain it.' Sarah dropped her head backwards and looked up into Mary Ann's face. 'A bit head-achey, a bit sick ... achey. Just like when you're going to get the flu; but I don't feel as if I've got a cold. Oh!' She smiled up at Mary Ann. 'I think the real truth is I'm after a few days in bed. As much as I love those horses, it's been pretty stiff going in more ways than one these last few mornings. I had to break the ice on the trough with a hammer this morning.'

'I know,' said Mary Ann. 'Prince's water was the same. Me da's kept him inside for days, he doesn't like the cold. And I haven't ridden him for nearly three weeks.'

'But look here,' Michael drew Sarah's attention to him again with a tug at her hand, 'you don't want to take this lightly. And don't try to be brave and laugh it off. I think it's as you said, you want a few days in bed, you're under the weather.'

'Yes, sir.' Sarah's voice was demure, and she laughed now, and Michael, getting to his feet, his face straight, passed off his concern by saying, 'Now look, don't you go and get any-thing serious. After all the schemozzle there's been about our holiday, you're going to go on it if I have to take you in a box!'

Twenty-four hours later, Michael, remembering these words, was to droop his head and press his chin into his neck with the horror of them. But he now looked at Mary Ann and said, 'She hasn't had a bite of anything to eat all day.'

'Does me ma know?'

'No, but I'm going to tell her. You stay there.' He dug his fingers down towards Sarah, and added, 'You'll eat what I fetch in.'

When the door had closed behind him, Sarah, looking at Mary Ann, who was sitting beside her on the couch now, said, 'I won't, you know, I just couldn't.'

'Perhaps your stomach is upset.' Mary Ann nodded knowingly. 'Whenever there is trouble of any kind it always goes to my stomach.' She laughed. 'Even if I get into a temper, I'm sick. Oh! Last Sunday night I felt like death after dear grandmam's visit. . . . Oh, Sarah, I do hate that woman.'

Sarah, nodding sympathetically, said, 'I'm not very fond of her myself. Never was.'

'That needn't worry you, for she's no relation of yours, but she's my granny, and the only one I've got. And oh, I hate the thought of her being my granny. Do you know, I felt so hateful on Sunday that I could have killed her. I could, I'm not just kidding, I could. I've always prayed, as far back as I can remember, that she would die. But on Sunday I actually felt that I could have killed her. It was a dreadful feeling, Sarah. I felt awful after and, as I said, I was sick.'

'Talking of killing' – Sarah's head fell back on to the couch again – 'it doesn't seem so very long ago since I felt that way about you, and you about me, remember?'

Mary Ann, her face straight now, nodded her head, and bit on her lip before she said, 'Seems daft now, doesn't it?'

Sarah did not answer this, but staring up towards the ceiling, she said slowly and quietly, 'I'll die if anything separates me from Michael . . . I'll die.'

'Oh, Sarah, don't talk like that. Why are you talking like that? Don't be silly, what can separate you from Michael?' As Mary Ann looked at Sarah's face, her eyes staring upwards, she was amazed to see two large tears roll down in the direction of her nose. Leaning swiftly forwards she touched Sarah's cheek, saying under her breath, 'What is it? What is it, Sarah?'

'Nothing.' Sarah lifted her head with a heavy movement from the back of the couch, and groping for her handkerchief, she remarked, 'I feel altogether odd, I can't remember ever feeling like this before, sort of depressed.' Then after blowing her nose, she lifted her eyes to Mary Ann, saying, 'I know how you feel about Corny, and I think you've been marvellous. I should have gone round looking like ... well, as your da would say, a sick cow. Do you still miss him?'

The conversation wasn't keeping to pattern, but Mary Ann said, 'Yes, awfully. I just seem to be passing the time towards the end of the year ... not this year but what I think of as this year. I get terrified when I think he won't come back.'

'You could never like Tony?'

'Not that way.'

'He'd be a catch.'

'Could you give up Michael for someone similar to Tony ... a catch?'

Sarah shook her head, and then clapped her hands swiftly over her mouth and muttered through her fingers, 'I'm – I'm going to be sick.'

Mary Ann, leading Sarah into the kitchen, exclaimed to her mother and Michael, 'Sarah's sick ... she wants to be sick.'

'Oh! my dear.' Lizzie, taking up a position on the other side of Sarah, hurried her towards the scullery. And that was the first of a number of trips between the front room and the scullery during the next hour. At half-past eight, Lizzie, standing in the kitchen looking at Mike, said, 'She's in no fit state to go home. We'll have to get word to her mother in some way.'

'I'll phone the house and see if Tony's in.'

Tony was in, but on the point of going out, and when, a few minutes later, he came into the farm kitchen after a brief word with Sarah, who was now lying on the sitting-room couch, he looked from Lizzie to Mike and said, 'I would get a doctor.'

'What are you thinking it is?' Mike narrowed his eyes towards Tony. And when Tony said what he thought might be the matter with Sarah, Lizzie cried out, 'Oh no! no! Not that.'

'I hope it isn't. I may be wrong. But those symptoms look

pretty familiar, I've seen someone with them before. I'd phone the doctor if I were you, and I'll slip into Jarrow and take a message to her mother.'

The kitchen became very quiet, the house became very quiet, and the quietness was heavy with fear.

Mike phoned the doctor. He came within half an hour, and within a few minutes of his arrival the life of the house changed.

It was suspected that Sarah had polio.

The waiting-room was quiet. It had coloured pictures on the wall, and modern low tables and comfortable chairs. Michael, sitting on the edge of a chair, had his elbows on his knees, his hands clasped between them, and he kept his gaze fixed on his hands, except when the waiting-room door opened. It hadn't opened for some time now. Mary Ann sat next to him. She kept going round the edge of her handkerchief with the finger and thumb of her right hand, while she smoothed the small piece of cambric material with the other. Opposite to them, across the low table, sat her mother and Mrs. Flannagan. They had all ceased to talk. From time to time her da would push the waiting-room door open. Or Mr. Flannagan, or Tony. And then they would go out again and sit in the car.

At a quarter to twelve a grey-uniformed sister entered the waiting-room, followed by a doctor. The sister remained silent as the doctor talked. He was very, very sorry, yes, the young girl had polio. How serious it was, was yet to be seen. He advised them to go home. They'd be kept informed. No, it wasn't advisable for any of them to see her. Perhaps tomorrow. Everything that possibly could be done would be done, they could be sure of that.

'I'm staying,' said Michael.

'I wouldn't,' said the doctor. 'You can do no good. Come in first thing in the morning and see how things are going then.'

'I'm staying,' said Michael again.

The doctor nodded.

The doctor now looked at Mrs. Flannagan and said, 'You are the mother?'

'Yes.' Mrs. Flannagan had lost her spruceness. For the first time that she could remember, Mary Ann saw her other than neat. Her face was tear-stained; her hair, like thin wire, stuck out from each side of her hat. She seemed to have shrunk and was now no bigger than Mr. Flannagan. It seemed odd, too, to see her sitting there with one hand clasped in the tight grip of her mother's hand.

Mike and Mr. Flannagan came into the room, and the doctor said again, 'It would be better if you all went home, for you can do nothing, nothing at all.'

He was passing Mary Ann now, and he put his hand on her head as if she was a child, as indeed she looked at this moment. And he seemed to be addressing her solely when he said, 'The only thing now is to pray and leave the rest to God. . . .' And it was with a sort of gentle inquiry that he added 'Eh?' to his words.

Michael, not to be deterred, stayed in the waiting-room and Mr. Flannagan stayed with him. Mrs. Flannagan went back to the farm with Lizzie and the rest. . . .

Three days later Sarah was fighting for her life, kept alive only by the miracle of the iron lung. On the seventh day it was known that she would live, but without the use of her legs, and Michael sat at the kitchen table, his head buried in his arms and cried. And Lizzie cried, and Mary Ann cried and Mike went out to the cowshed.

Lizzie stood by Michael's side, her hand on his head, but she could say nothing. She could not find words adequate for comfort, until some minutes elapsed, and Michael, lifting his head slowly from his arms and shaking it from side to side in a despairing movement, muttered, 'And I said I would take her on that holiday if I had to take her in a box . . . Oh! God.' And Lizzie, remembering the time not long ago when she herself had said, 'That'll be the day when you howl your eyes out,' whispered brokenly, 'We say things in joke, take no notice of that. She's alive, and they can do wonderful things these days.'

Mary Ann's throat was swollen with the pressure of tears as she stood at the other side of the table and looked towards Michael. Poor Michael. But more so, poor Sarah. She was feeling for Sarah, at this moment, anguish equal to that which she would have felt if they had been sisters. It was impossible to remember that they had ever been enemies. She thought, 'Her poor legs, and she loved to ride. Oh, what will she do?'

It was as if Michael had heard her thinking, for he stood up and, brushing the back of his hand across his eyes and around his face, he said, 'As soon as she comes out we'll get married.'

'Michael.'

Lizzie had just spoken his name, there was no indication of shock or censure, but he turned on her sharply, saying, 'You can do what you like, Mother, say what you like, put all the obstacles on earth up, but as soon as she's out of that place we're getting married.'

'Yes, yes. All right, Michael, all right.'

'Don't say it like that, Mother.' He was yelling at her. 'As if I'd get over it and change my mind, and by the time she's out I'll be seeing things differently. I won't, I won't ever.'

'Don't shout, Michael.' Lizzie's voice was very low. 'I understand all you feel at this minute, believe me. . . .'

'But you wouldn't want me to marry Sarah, crippled like that, would you? She would handicap me, wouldn't she? What would happen to my career?'

'Now, now, now.' This was neither Lizzie nor Mary Ann, and they all turned to see Mike standing in the kitchen doorway. His face looked pale-ish, his eyes were bright, and his voice and manner were quiet. How much he had heard of the conversation Mary Ann didn't know. But little or much she knew he had got the gist of it, for looking at Michael, he said, 'Don't worry at this stage. Just go on praying that she'll get better quickly, and then do what your heart tells you you've got to do.'

Mary Ann watched Michael looking towards her da. She watched their eyes holding for a long while before Michael turned away and went out of the kitchen and up the stairs. It was strange, she thought, Michael was her ma's, her ma and Michael were like that – metaphorically, she crossed her fingers – yet lately it had been her da who had seen eye to eye with him, while her mother seemed to cross him at every point. Perhaps, like all mothers, she was afraid of losing him, and he knew it, and this was bringing a slight rift between them.

Lizzie had the palms of her hands pressed tightly together. If her fingers had been lifted upwards, they would have indicated her praying, but they were pointing towards the floor, and she rasped her palms together as she said under her breath, 'He says they're going to be married as soon as she comes out.'

'I heard.' Mike nodded his head. 'Well, you'll have to face that, Liz.'

'But how will he manage? He's just starting out, Mike.' Lizzie's voice was soft. There was no tone of opposition in it, just helpless inquiry.

'People have managed like that afore, they're shown a way.'

'But if she can't walk. If she's in a chair. . . .'

'Liz!' Mike walked over to her and put his arm around her shoulder. 'Listen to me. Things'll pan out. Just remember that. Whatever you think or do, things'll pan out one way or the other. But this much I think you'd better get into your head and accept it. Whatever condition Sarah comes out in, she'll be the only one for him. . . . Now it's no use saying he'd get over it. Don't start to think along those lines, because I know this . . . he'd rather have his life a hell of a grind with Sarah than be on velvet with anybody else. . . . Now don't cry.'

But Lizzie did cry. She turned her head into Mike's shoulder, and as he held her and spoke softly to her, he looked across the room towards Mary Ann, but she herself could hardly see him, her vision was so blurred. She felt a weight of sadness on her that she had never before experienced. It sprung, she supposed, from Sarah's condition. Yet she knew that not all her feelings were due to Sarah. Vaguely she realized that life was opening her eyes wide, stretching them with knowledge, painful knowledge, such as the fact that her mother was crying, not so much because Sarah was crippled for life, but because her son was determined to take on a burden that to her mind would cripple him too.

It was the worst Christmas Mary Ann had ever known.

No one felt like jollification. Presents were given and received without much enthusiasm. Mr. Lord bought Mary Ann a portable typewriter for her Christmas box, and although she was pleased with the gift, she simulated delight that she didn't altogether feel. But Mr. Lord was very thoughtful and kind during this period. And she wanted to please him.

The old man had shown great concern over Sarah. Twice a week he sent her gifts of flowers, he had looked at Lizzie and said, 'There's no need to inquire if the boy will stand by Sarah. I feel that Michael knows his own mind, and it's a very good thing. Perhaps it will be very good for both of them. And he can rely on all the help he needs when the time comes.'

Lizzie had said nothing, but Mary Ann had wanted to fling her arms about the old man's neck, as she had done years ago, by way of thanks.

Corny did not send Mary Ann a Christmas box, but he sent her a letter which was of much more value in her eyes. Although the letter was brief, she read volumes between the lines. He liked it in America. He liked the people he was staying with, they were very good to him. He liked his job. The boss was very good to him. He had been put into another department which meant more money. He could get a car if he liked, but he wasn't going to. He was saving. It was funny not being at home for Christmas but everybody was nice to him. Mary Ann felt a stir of jealousy against this oft-repeated niceness. But she told herself he hadn't known what to say, he was no hand at letter-writing. His writing was as terse as his speech. Her Corny was a doer, not a sayer. She liked that idea, and she told herself a number of times: Corny was a doer not a sayer. The letter ended with the same request as had his first one: Would she go and see his granny?

The only other thing of note that happened over the Christmas was an announcement in the paper to the effect that Mrs. Lettice Schofield of The Burrows, Woodlea End, Newcastle, was seeking a divorce from her husband.

PART TWO

The Year Passes

CHAPTER SIX

'Look,' said Mike, as he leant towards Michael across the little table in his office, 'I know the old fellow means well, at least I want to keep on thinking that. But I'd rather you didn't start your life, your real life along with Sarah, beholden to him.'

Michael with one elbow raised high resting on the top of the small window, rapped his ear with his fingers as he stared out across the farmyard towards the chimneys of the house, where they reared up above the roof of the byres. 'I know, I know what you mean.' His voice was deep and very similar to Mike's now, except for the inflexion garnered from the Grammar School. 'I don't want to take the place, for the very reason you've just stated, but another reason is that Sarah's cut off enough where she is now. Although she's with her mother, she's cut off. She feels lost, they don't speak the same language. She's closer to her father, but he's out all day. And then there's not a blade of grass to be seen, looking out from that window on to the street. It drives me mad when I'm sitting with her. I can't imagine that we ever lived opposite. The only good thing in taking the bungalow is that she would see a tree or two, and the fields. But then it's a good two miles away, and although there's houses round about, Sarah doesn't want other people.' He brought his eyes from the window towards his father. 'She's already one of us. She's always seemed to have been one of us. She hasn't said this, but I know that she looks upon us as ... her people. As I said, she likes her da, but I can tell you this, she likes you ten times more.'

Mike dropped his eyes away from his son as he said, 'That's good to hear, anyway.'

There was silence in the little office until Mike said,

'There's a way out of this.' He cast his eyes on the open ledger as he spoke, and Michael kept his eyes on the view across the farmyard as he replied, 'Yes, I know. But who's going to put it to her?'

He did not say put it to Mother ... but to 'her', and this phrase hurt Mike. Although it meant that he and his boy were closer than ever before in their lives, it also meant that Michael had moved farther away from Lizzie during the last few months. Somehow, he would rather that the situation were the same as it had been years ago ... yet not quite. He did not want his son to hate him and he had, at one time, done just that. No, he didn't want that again, and please God he would never deserve it, but he didn't want Lizzie to be hurt. Michael was Lizzie's, at least she had always considered him so. It was as if years ago she had said to him, 'You have got Mary Ann, Michael is mine.'

At this moment the door was pushed open and Mary Ann, coming round it, said, 'Oh, there you are.' She looked at Michael. 'I'm going in to Sarah's, Tony's running me down. Is there anything you want to go?'

'No.' He shook his head. 'Tell her I'll be there round about six.'

'What's the matter?' Mary Ann looked from one to the other. 'Anything wrong?'

'No, no.' Mike got to his feet. 'We're just talking about the bungalow.'

'Oh, the bungalow.' Mary Ann nodded her head, and looking again at Michael she said, 'Are you going to take it?'

'I don't want to.'

Again she nodded her head. 'Then why don't you ask her?'

Again, the 'her' was referring to Lizzie, and Michael, moving out into the yard, said, 'I couldn't stand a row. And if she did consent, having Sarah on sufferance would be worse than anything so far.'

Mike and Mary Ann, left together, looked at each other, and when Mike's eyes dropped from hers she said to him under her breath, 'Something should be done, Da. What's going to happen to Sarah up there by herself all day? It won't work. He just couldn't take that place.' She looked at Michael's broadening back as he went across the yard, then her gaze lifted up the hill towards Mr. Lord's house, and her tone indignant now, she commented, 'If he's going to advance him the money for a bungalow why couldn't he have one built here? He's got piles of land.'

'There's such a thing as laws about building on agricultural ground.'

'Poloney!'

'Not so much poloney as you think.' Mike nodded solemnly at her. 'Once you start that, it's like a bush fire, one house goes up and then the place is covered.'

Mary Ann looked her disbelief, then after sighing she remarked, 'Well, I'm off, Da. See you later. . . . Good-bye.'

His good-bye followed her as she went across the yard towards the road that led up to Mr. Lord's house. She knew that he was standing watching her.

In the far distance she could see the hood of Tony's car. She glanced at her watch. He had said half-past two on the dot, and now it was twenty-five to three. She walked slowly up the hill, through the gate, over the back courtyard to where the car was standing. There was no sign of Tony and, going to the back door, she knocked as she opened it, a courtesy she still afforded Ben.

'Hello, there.' The old man's tone was gruff, and he hardly raised his eyes from the occupation of silver cleaning to look at her. But Mary Ann, over the years, had come to know Ben, and a 'Hello there' she had come to consider a very affectionate term.

'Lovely day, isn't it, Ben? How's your hip?'

'Same as afore.'

'Well, it's your own fault.' She stubbed her finger at him. 'You should have taken it easy these last few weeks while Mr. Lord was away. It's your own fault.'

'And have him come back finding fault in every corner, like an old fish woman.'

'You should let Mrs. Rouse do it.'

'Ugh! Ugh! I have to go behind her all the time now.'

Mary Ann smiled, then said, 'Is Tony upstairs?'

'No. In the study . . . on the phone.'

'Oh.' Mary Ann went out of the kitchen and across the large hall towards the study. There was no sound of anyone speaking on the phone, and she stood outside the door for a second before saying, 'Are you there, Tony?'

'Yes. Come in.'

When she entered the room she saw him sitting at the desk, and he turned his head towards her, saying quickly, 'I won't be a minute, I want to get this off.'

She sat down in the hide chair to the side of the fireplace, and her small frame seemed lost in its vastness. She liked this room: the brown of the suite, the soft blue of the deep carpet; the low, ranging bookcases set against the panelled walls. She looked towards Tony, his head bent over the letter. He looked nice ... he always looked nice, but today she seemed to be seeing him in a different light. She realized with a kind of pleasant shock that he was very handsome, in a thin, chiselled kind of way. She supposed Mr. Lord had once looked like this. Her gaze was intent on him when he turned his head quickly and looked at her. 'I'm glad you came up,' he said. 'I hoped you would, I want to talk to you.'

As she watched him turn to the desk again and quickly push the letter into an envelope, she experienced a quiver of apprehension. It went through her body like a slight electric shock, and felt as unpleasant. Tony and she had exchanged nothing but polite pleasantries for months. He had continued to take her into town on a Saturday, and sometimes he picked her up later, but where he went in the meantime he did not say. Nor did he ask where she spent her time. He no longer seemed interested in anything she did, but she knew that Mr. Lord was under the impression that they were together during these Saturday afternoon jaunts. She had an idea now, in fact she knew, what he was going to talk about. And when he came towards her, and pulled a small chair close to the big one before sitting down and leaning forward, she could not meet his eyes.

'Mary Ann.'

'Yes.' She still did not raise her eyes.

'If Corny had not come on the scene, would you have liked me enough to have married me?'

She lifted her head with a jerk, and her eyes flicked over

his face for a moment before she looked away towards the window beyond the desk. and she seemed to consider for quite a while before she answered.

'I don't know . . . I suppose I might, and yet I don't know.' She paused again. 'There might have been someone else. You just don't know, do you?' Now she was looking at him full in the face.

'No, you just don't know. But as things stand you want Corny, don't you? Tell me . . . please.'

'Yes . . . yes, I want Corny.' She felt she was blushing right into the depths of her stomach.

'Yes, I knew you did. But I wanted to hear you say it. I don't want you on my conscience. I have enough to face up to without that. . . . I'm going to marry Mrs. Schofield, Mary Ann.'

Although Mary Ann had known that he had wanted to talk about Mrs. Schofield, that he might say to her, 'I'm friendly with Mrs. Schofield . . . I like Mrs. Schofield,' she had not expected him to say, slap bang, that he was going to marry her. This statement suggested an intimacy between him and Mrs. Schofield that deepened the blush. She could have said she was going to marry Corny, and Michael could say he was going to marry Sarah, but in either case it would not have been the same as Tony marrying Mrs. Schofield. Mrs. Schofield was a married woman. And then there was Mr. Lord. Mr. Lord would go mad, she knew he would go mad. She said as much.

'What will he say? He'll go for you, he won't stand for it. He'll go mad.'

'I know that. But whether he will or no, I'm marrying Lettice as soon as the decree nisi is through.'

Mary Ann put her fingers over her lips and swayed a little. She felt some part of her was in pain, and it was for Mr. Lord. At this moment she would gladly have fallen in with his wishes and married Tony if that had been possible, just to save him the pain that she knew the failure of his cherished plans would bring him. And the pain would not be alone. There would be with it anger and bitterness. Once before she had seen what extreme anger and bitterness did to him. That was the time when he had discovered that Tony was his grandson. And what had been the result? He had a heart attack and nearly died. She clasped her hands tightly now between her knees and asked, 'How are you going to tell him?'

'I don't know. Lettice wanted to come and tell him herself. But I wouldn't have that.'

It was funny hearing him speak of Mrs. Schofield as Lettice. She hated Mrs. Schofield at this moment, yet remembering back to the time when she liked her, she also remembered that Mr. Lord liked her too. Here was a ray of hope. She said to Tony, 'You should have let her come. He liked her. She could get it over better than you, I'm sure of that. There'll only be a row if you tell him, and that's putting it mildly. Don't forget what happens when he gets worked up.' She leant further forward. 'Do you realize this might ... it might kill him.'

'I've thought of all that. It's been hellish this last few months. In fact since that day ... you remember, that Saturday when I saw him hit her, I knew then what was going to happen to me. I think I knew before. You see, Mary Ann' – his voice dropped almost to a whisper – 'I was attracted to her long before that day. When she used to come up here, to your house, I always made a point of being there. Perhaps no one noticed. They wouldn't, would they?' He smiled a sad smile at her. 'But that day when I saw that pig of a man – and he is a pig of a man, Mary Ann, and that's putting it mildly – when I saw him hit her, I knew it was all up with me. It was as if the blow that struck her had sprung my mind wide open, and I saw the fix I was in. And I'm not going to say at this juncture that I tried to fight it and make a brave stand against it. Oh, no. Although I knew what it would mean to the old man in the end I went ahead, and I still count myself lucky that I did. She is a grand person, Mary Ann. A very, very sweet person.'

Mary Ann dismissed the unique qualities of Mrs. Schofield, and said, 'He'll cut you off.'

'Yes, I expect that. But I've got quarter shares in Turnbulls. He signed those over to me two years ago. They'll give me a start somewhere, and Lettice doesn't want much. ... It seems odd though to think that those very shares were the first thing he allowed me to put my name to, although I was supposed to be his heir. And he only gave them to me as an inducement to fall in with his plans concerning his ... protégée.' Tony's hand came out and grasped Mary Ann's. 'I could wish at this moment for him that his plan had worked out, because, you know, I like his protégée very much.' He squeezed her fingers.

Mary Ann swallowed and blinked her eyes, the tears were welling in her throat, and as she pulled her hands from his she said with a touch of the cheeky asperity he knew so well, 'I'm not crying because of you, don't think that.'

'I wouldn't for a moment, Mary Ann.'

'I just don't know what's going to happen to him when he finds this out.' She sniffed twice, blew her nose, then asked, 'When is he coming back? It was next Tuesday, wasn't it?'

'As always he's changed his plans. You know his old trick of dropping in when he thinks nobody is expecting him, that's likely what will happen this time. I had a wire this morning to say he was staying on another week. But I shouldn't be surprised if he came in tonight, or tomorrow night, or then, on the other hand, not for another month. We should know by now, shouldn't we?'

'But he'll come.' She bounced her head at him. 'And you'll have to tell him. . . . When are you—' she paused and her voice sunk again as she ended, 'getting married?'

'It could be in three weeks' time.'

'But if he shouldn't be back by then you won't leave, will you? You won't leave and get married before he gets back?'

'No, Mary Ann, I won't do that.'

She turned her eyes from him, and feeling again that she was going to give way to tears, she jumped up from the chair, saying, 'It's awful. He'll die.'

'No, he won't.' Tony had his arm around her shoulders now. 'He's tougher than you think.'

'If he gets into a paddy, he'll have a heart attack, you'll see.'

'Oh, Mary Ann, don't make it worse for me, please.'

'I don't want to.' Her voice was soft now. 'But I'm frightened for him, Tony.' She looked up. 'And you won't make matters any better because you'll lose your temper and there'll be a pair of you. You know you can't keep your temper with him. I don't think you should tell him. I think you should leave a letter for him, something like that.... Oh, I don't know what to suggest.'

'I won't leave a letter for him, Mary Ann. What I've got to say, I'll say to him.'

'And kill him!'

'Don't!' He swung away from her. 'Don't keep suggesting that. It's got to be done.' His voice had risen now. 'And I'll have to stand the consequences, but don't keep saying that.' They stared at each other in hostility, and then Tony, taking his breath in on a deep sigh, said, 'Come on. We had better be going. Sufficient unto the day.' He opened the door for her and she went past him, through the hall and into the kitchen. And she did not say good-bye to Ben, where he sat still rubbing away with his rheumaticky hands at the silver, and this caused him to stop his work, and even rise to his feet and go towards the door from where he watched her getting into the car.

When a few minutes later Ben returned to the table, he looked at his work for a moment before touching it, and remarked, 'What now, eh?'

Mrs. Flannagan's front room was fourteen feet by twelve feet. In it was a three-piece suite, a small sideboard, a corner cabinet, besides two small tables and an ornamental coal scuttle. The floor was covered by a small carpet and a surround of highly polished check-patterned linoleum.

Sarah was sitting on the couch, her legs painfully immobile beneath the rug. Her back appeared bent as if she was leaning towards them, and her complexion, which had been a thick cream tan, had now a bleached look. The only thing about her appearance that remained untouched by her illness was her hair. It was still black and shiny. She held out a half-finished nylon petticoat towards Mary Ann, saying rather hopelessly, 'Look at those stiches, I'll never be able to sew.'

Mary Ann looked at the stitches. 'You're doing fine; they're only half an inch long now, they were an inch on Wednesday.'

They both laughed, and Sarah moved her shoulders into the cushion. Then the smile disappeared from her face when, looking at Mary Ann, she said below her breath, 'Oh, I wish I had that chair. I want to get out. I want to get out. I'll go mad with much more of this.'

'They said next week, didn't they?' Mary Ann's voice was low also. 'But Tony would come and take you out tomorrow. He's offered time and time again. Why won't you go?'

'Oh.' Sarah moved her head wearily on the pillow. 'To be carried into a car and all the street out. It's bad enough in the ambulance going to the hospital. I don't want to be carried and lifted for the rest of my life. And I'm not going to.' She pulled her body forward now until her face was close to Mary Ann's, and then she whispered fiercely, 'I've been praying and praying and praying. I'm going to use my legs again, I am. I don't care how long it takes – ten years, twenty years.' Her voice was becoming louder now, and Mary Ann, getting up and putting her arms around her, said, 'That's the spirit. You feel like that and you will. Oh, I'm glad to hear you say that. It's like an answer to my prayers. In fact, I'm sure it is. Every night after I've left work I slip into church and say a decade of the rosary for you, just for that, that you'd get the urge to use your legs. . . . Isn't it funny?' Her voice was high with excitement.

'Oh, Mary Ann.' Sarah leant her head wearily between Mary Ann's small firm breasts. 'You've been so good, always coming in. People stop after a while, you know. They used to come in a lot at first, but not now. And I'm seeing too much of me mother. Oh, I know I shouldn't say this because she's been so good, but she keeps on, she keeps on, finicking about, polishing, dusting, tidying up, all the time, all the time. . . . Mary Ann?' It was a question.

And Mary Ann said, 'Yes, Sarah?'

'Do you think that Michael really wants to marry me?'

Mary Ann drew away from Sarah and actually gaped at her as she repeated, 'Really wants to marry you. He'll go round the bend if he doesn't. What's put that into your head?'

'Oh, I think people are saying things. I know they are. I hear that Mrs. Foster in the kitchen with me mother. It's not what she says, it's what she leaves unsaid ... the pauses. They don't think it right that I should marry Michael, not like this, I know they don't. But if I don't, Mary Ann' – she looked into Mary Ann's eyes now and repeated – 'if I don't, I'll do meself in, I will.'

Another one talking about doing herself in. Janice, and now Sarah. Was this what sorrow did to you, took away all desire for life. She couldn't see anything bad enough happening to her to take away the desire for living. She loved life, she loved breathing. She used to stop sometimes, on the road from the bus to the farm, and say to herself, 'I'm breathing.' It wasn't silly for she knew within herself, deep within herself, that it meant a great deal, something she couldn't as yet explain. She was breathing, she was alive. She felt at times that no matter what happened she wanted to live. ... To know all about living and then write about it. She dreamed of writing about living. Yet two girls that she had known intimately talked about dying, about killing themselves, and one had already tried. She shuddered and grasped hold of Sarah's hands as she said, 'Don't say such things, Sarah. And now get this into your head, there's only one person in the world for Michael and that's you. And if you don't know it by now, you never will. He's driving us all crazy about you.'

Sarah's smile spread across her face. It was a sweet smile, and it made her beautiful, more beautiful than when she had been the outdoor, hard-riding, youth-filled girl. But the smile faded, and on its going she said, 'Your mother's not pleased, and I can't blame her. I can understand how she feels.'

'What's got into you all of a sudden? Don't be silly. Of course mother's pleased, she'd rather have you for Michael than anybody else.'

'Has she said so?'

'No, there's no need. I know.'

'You're just being kind as usual, Mary Ann. You're always trying to fix people's lives. I used to laugh about it one time, but I give you leave to fix mine right now.' She shook her head. 'But if your mother wanted me for Michael she would have asked me to go there, to live with you. I wouldn't have been a burden, I wouldn't. I feel that if I could go and live with you all I would get better. When I was in hospital, Michael sort of said that we'd have ... the front room. It was like a dream that I hung on to. I thought your mother must have suggested that we could, and I thought it was wonderful of her, because it's a beautiful front room, and you can see the farm from the window. I dreamed of that front room. Then when I came home Michael said Mr. Lord was going to put up the money for the bungalow. There was no more mention of the front room, and I knew somehow that your mother had never said anything about it.... I don't want that bungalow, Mary Ann. I don't want to go and live all that way off. I want to live close to Michael, where his work is. And with your da near abouts. Your da infuses strength into people, Mary Ann. It's funny that, isn't it? For me to say that, I mean. But he does. I always feel that I could get up and walk when he's talking to me. Not that I don't like your mother, I do. I think she's a fine woman ... sort of a lady. I've always thought of her as a lady. ...'

'Oh, Sarah, Sarah! Look, don't worry. Everything'll come out all right. And you will live with us, I promise you will.'

Sarah smiled through very bright eyes now at Mary Ann, and it was doubtful if she was seeing her as she said, 'You've always made rash promises, you're the Holy Family rolled into one, not that they make rash promises. ... You know what I mean. You were always going to the side altar praying to them, weren't you?' She laughed now, a sharp loud laugh to stop herself from crying as she said, 'I remember I stopped going to their altar because I didn't want to do the same thing as you.'

'Oh, Sarah.' Mary Ann could not cap this with any amusing reply. She felt she couldn't bear much more today. There had been Tony just an hour ago, and now Sarah in this state. It was awful, awful. Everything was awful.

She stood up and looked towards the window merely to turn her face from Sarah's for a moment, and as she did so she saw coming down the steps of Mulhattan's Hall, right opposite, the great wobbling figure of Fanny McBride. The sight of her old friend brought a smile to her face and she turned round to Sarah and explained excitedly, 'Look, bend over, there's Mrs. McBride coming down the steps. I'll pull the curtain and you can wave to her.'

Mary Ann dared to pull Mrs. Flannagan's stiffly arranged curtains to one side, and she went even further, she dared to tap gently on the pane to attract Fanny's attention. And when Fanny, her eyes darting across the road, caught sight of Mary Ann, she waved her great arm in the air. Mary Ann now acting on the assumption 'In for a penny, in for a pound', ran to the couch and pushed the head towards the window ... and now Sarah waved. The two girls watched Fanny hesitate a moment at the bottom of the steps, undecided to risk the journey across the road to the portals of her enemy. But the habit of years was too strong. Mary Ann knew that Fanny was indeed sorry for Sarah, but she also knew that she still held Mrs. Flannagan in lip-curling disdain. But the sight of the old woman did them both good, for they laughed as they watched her wobbling away down the street to the corner shop. And when her figure had disappeared, Mary Ann said, 'Well, there's one thing you should be thankful for: you're in this room and not in Fanny's.' Yet as she said this she wondered if Sarah would not be better, in both health and spirits, were she in the untidy, smelly, lumber-filled room on the ground floor of Mulhattan's Hall.

Later that evening, as Mary Ann neared home, her depression deepened, which was unusual, for the mere sight of the farm had the power to bring a feeling of security to her and to lessen the day-to-day irritations, which were multiplying, she was finding, as she was growing older. But this evening she didn't want to reach home, she didn't want to face her mother, for she knew that she wouldn't be able to resist bringing up the question of ... the front room. It was funny about the front room. Her da had thought the front room was a grand idea for Michael and Sarah. Michael had thought the front room was a grand idea for himself and Sarah. She had thought the front room was a grand idea for the pair of them. Yet to her knowledge not one of them had mentioned the subject to her mother, and yet she knew that her mother was well aware of what they were all after. She also knew that the front room was her mother's pride. It was the only room in the house in which she had been able to let her ideas have scope. The front room was really hers. A place where she could invite people without making any excuses about the upset, or the untidiness. None of them left magazines, or books, or sweet papers lying about in the front room. It was an unspoken agreement that they cleared up their stuff each night before they left the room. The kitchen could look – as Lizzie sometimes said – like a paddencan, but never her front room.

And now Mary Ann knew the time had come when the room must be brought into the open. Not only to relieve the tension in the house, but the tension in Sarah. She was very worried about Sarah.

She had hardly got in the door before Lizzie said, 'How is she?' and she answered, 'Oh, she's very depressed, Ma. I'm worried.'

'Why? What is she depressed over? I mean more than usual.'

Mary Ann looked at her mother. She was sitting in the easy chair in her front room. She fitted into the room. The subdued colour of her dress, the calmness of her face – she had her eyes cast down – all seemed to be part of the atmosphere of the room. She was busy copying some recipes from a weekly magazine into her cookery book.

Mary Ann stood in front of her, their knees were so close they almost touched. She knew it was no use leading up to this subject. She was feeling so keenly about the matter at the moment that she would only make a mess of any strategic approach, so she said, straight out, 'Ma?'

Lizzie gave a little lift to her head and said, 'Well?'

'Sarah doesn't want to go and live in the bungalow.'

'No?' There was a sound running through the syllable as sharp and hard as the point end of a carving knife.

'It would be as bad there as it is in Burton Street. And she's nearly going off her head there. . . . Ma . . . Ma. . . . She wants to come and live with us.'

As Lizzie stared back into her daughter's face she had the strong desire to lift her hand and slap it. It would have to be her who would bring this thing into the open, this thing that had hung around them for weeks. Hidden under quick tempers and sharp retorts. Under sullen silences and pathetic looks. She had resisted them all. Because it wasn't as if Sarah was homeless, she was going to have a lovely bungalow built. She was going to marry Michael; yes, she was going to marry Michael. Was she not having her son? Wasn't that enough? But no ... she wanted ... they all wanted to take this room from her. There had been no suggestion of Sarah having one of the rooms upstairs, because that was an impossibility. No, the idea, which she knew was a flame behind the asbestos curtain of all their minds, was that she should give up this room to Sarah and Michael.

'Get out of my way.'

'But, Ma.'

'I said, get out of my way, I want to get up.'

When Mary Ann was slow in obeying, Lizzie, jerking herself to her feet, almost thrust her on to her back. The little table to the side of the chair, which had held the magazine and her notebook, jumped from the floor as if it had a life of its own. Lizzie put out no hand to steady it. She marched towards the door. But before opening it, she turned to Mary Ann and demanded, 'Did they pick you as spokesman for them all?'

'No! No, Ma. I haven't talked about it with anyone. It was just what Sarah said.'

'Are you sure?'

'Yes, Ma.'

Mary Ann was speaking the truth, she hadn't discussed it openly with her da and Michael, but she knew that from the time Michael had heartened Sarah with the thought that she was coming to live here, the idea had been prominent in all their minds.

Lizzie, turning from the door, made one step back into the room, and, looking intently at her daughter, she said in an almost threatening tone, 'Well, if it hasn't been discussed, don't you start now, do you hear me? I forbid you to say anything about it. '

'All right, Ma.' Mary Ann's voice was very low.

'And furthermore ... listen to me.'

'I'm listening, Ma.' Her voice was still low.

'Well, do then. And remember what I'm saying. Don't you

tell either your father, or Michael, that you mentioned this to me. . . . Do you understand?'

Yes, Mary Ann understood. If the matter wasn't brought into the open by either Michael or her da, the room was safe. In as quickly as it takes lightning to strike, a strange feeling assailed her, a fearful feeling. Out of nowhere came a hate for this room, and, more terrible still, a dislike of her mother. As she looked at Lizzie's tight, straight countenance, she knew she disliked her. 'Oh . . .!' She groaned aloud with the fear of this feeling, and turning away she cupped her face in her hands. Then, sitting down, she dropped her head into the corner of the chair. But she did not cry, she was too frozen with fear of this dreadful thing that had come upon her – she didn't like her mother.

After one long look at the back of Mary Ann's head, Lizzie turned sharply away and went out of the room and up the stairs. When she entered her own room she stood in the darkness with her back to the door. She knew that she had reached a crisis in her life, not a crisis brought about by the desertion of her husband for another woman, not a crisis brought about by Mike's drinking, as had often happened during the early years of their marriage, or yet by her son walking out on her and picking a girl that she did not like. Nor yet a crisis where her daughter had got herself into trouble, but a crisis caused by the fact that she wanted to hang on to her way of life. And her way of life was personified by her sitting-room. The sitting-room that everyone remarked on. The sitting-room that she loved, that she had made part of herself. For months now she had been warding off this moment, daring them by her silence to approach her and mention this room. And now she knew that the matter could no longer be shelved, because Mary Ann had dared, with her usual foolhardiness, to bring it into the open. If Sarah came here to live, the life of the house would be changed. It wasn't that she disliked Sarah, she liked her. She liked the girl very much, she could even say she liked her next to Mary Ann. She could say in all truth that she liked her better than any of the friends Mary Ann had picked up for herself at school, much better. And she knew, crippled though she was, that she was the right one for Michael. She also knew something else. . . . She stared into the blackness of the room, and in its depths she faced up to a fact that she had not permitted herself to look at these past weeks, although it had been thrusting itself at her almost daily from the direction of her son and her husband, and within the last few minutes it had stared out of the face of her daughter, the fact was that if she kept her room she would lose them all. She might live with them for years and years, but things would never be the same again. If Michael took Sarah to the bungalow he would never come back into this house as her son . . . her Michael. She had felt him drifting away from her lately, but she knew now that by making this sacrifice she could pin him to her for life. But there was another reason why she hadn't wanted Michael and Sarah to start their married life in this house. She must be fair to herself, it wasn't only the room. As much as she liked Sarah, she knew she could not bear to see another woman – a girl, in this case – ruling his life. Being all in all to him. Filling her place entirely. Only if she hadn't to witness it, would it be bearable. This had been more than half the reason for her conduct. But now the decision had to be faced. Did she want to lose Mike, too, through this business? Not that he would ever leave her. But he could go from her without leaving the house. . . . And, Mary Ann? . . . Yes, and Mary Ann. Look how she had glared at her before she had turned her face away into the chair. She had never seen her daughter look at her like that before . . . never.

Lizzie groped in the darkness towards the bed. She did not switch on the light, nor turn down the cover. But flinging herself on to the bed she thrust her face in the pillow and cried. . . .

An hour later, when Mike came in, he found Mary Ann in the kitchen. 'All alone?' he said.

'No, Da.'

'Where's your mother? In the front room?'

'No, she's upstairs, Da.'

Mike looked intently at his daughter before asking quietly, 'What's the matter?'

'Nothing, Da. I think she's got a bad head. I think she's lying down.'

'You think, you're not sure. Haven't you been up?'

'No, Da.'

'What's happened?' He took her by the shoulder and turned her towards him. As she looked back at him she said, 'Nothing, Da.'

'How long has your mother been upstairs?' Mike's voice was quiet and even.

'Just over an hour, I think.'

'And there's nothing the matter?'

'No, Da. . . . Do you want a drink?'

'Yes. Yes, I want a drink. But it isn't tea or cocoa.'

The old anxiety leapt within her to join the fear that had sprung on her in the front room. If her da went out in this mood he would likely come back drunk, and he hadn't been drunk for a long time. She said to him, in the little-girl voice she had used to coax him years ago, 'You're not going out now, Da, are you?'

'What do you think?'

'I wouldn't. I would have some tea, strong tea.'

'Aye . . . well.' He sat on the edge of the chair undecided. And as she stood before him the anxiety made her tremble, and he thrust out his arm and pulled her towards him, saying, 'All right, all right, come on, don't worry. Stop that.' He punched her gently in the chest. 'Where's that tea?'

Mary Ann made him a strong pot of tea. She cut him a shive of meat pie. She watched him as he ate, and when a few minutes later she watched him settle himself in the big chair towards the side of the stove, she felt sick. He wasn't showing any signs of going upstairs to see what was wrong with her mother. This in a way was worse than him getting drunk and coming back roaring out all the things that were troubling him. Her ma, she knew, would suffer more from this attitude than from the drink. She felt, as she had done years ago in Mulhattan's Hall, torn asunder with anguish for them. She could stand anything, anything as long as they were close. The feeling of dislike for her mother had fled as swiftly as it had come. All she wanted now was to see her ma and her da close once again, laughing and chaffing, and that meant loving. And they hadn't been like that for weeks.

115

CHAPTER SEVEN

DURING the weekend that followed the tense atmosphere of the house did not lessen, and at the beginning of the week Lizzie began to behave peculiarly. Rain, hail or snow, she washed on a Monday, but not this Monday. On this Monday she declared to her family that she was going to do no more heavy washing. She was going to send all the sheets, towels and pillow-cases to the bag-wash. She'd had enough of heavy washing to last a lifetime. It was as she served breakfast that she made this revolutionary statement.

Under ordinary circumstances there is no doubt that the family would have shot comments at her. Why? Hadn't she said, time and again, that the laundries poisoned the clothes, they were never the same again if sent to the laundry? But this morning they did not bombard her with whys, and if she thought their reactions were peculiar she made no comment.

There was really very little she could comment on, for neither Mary Ann nor Michael said anything. And Mike, merely raising his glance from his plate, remarked, 'You feeling like that? Well, it's Monday mornin'.'

That was all.

On Monday evening, when she stated she was going into Newcastle the following day to do some shopping, Mary Ann was the only one who reacted. Without a great deal of enthusiasm she said, 'Do you want me to meet you?'

'No, I don't think so,' said Lizzie, in a tone that could be considered airy. 'I'll see how I feel, but I might go to the pictures in the afternoon.'

Mike was doing his accounts at the edge of the kitchen table – it was warmer in the kitchen than in the office – and he brought his head round to look at Lizzie, but Lizzie was bending over the stove. And as his eyes returned to his work they met Mary Ann's for a second, and widened slightly. Still he did not say anything.

But Mary Ann knew that, like herself, he had been surprised. Her mother never went to the pictures, she didn't care for the pictures. They had talked about getting television ages ago, but she had said, 'I don't care for the pictures, so I don't suppose I'll care for that.' And now she had stated she was going to spend the afternoon at the pictures. . . .

By Friday of that week Lizzie had been out on her own three times, and it came as a surprise to no one except perhaps herself, when Mike stated, in a casual, even off-hand manner, which however did not disguise that his statement was one of retaliation, 'I think I'll have a day out the morrow meself. I'm long overdue for a trip.'

Michael's eyes darted towards his father, but Mary Ann did not look at him. She knew what the trip forbode, and she thought sadly to herself, 'Well, me ma has asked for it this time. She may never have done before, but she's asked for it this time.'

Lizzie had been on her way to the scullery with a tray of dishes as Mike spoke, and when she reached the table she slowly put the tray down, but without releasing her hold on it she bent forward over it and bit tightly on her lip. That was all for the moment.

Mike went out to do his round, and Michael, as usual after changing, got on his bike and rode to Jarrow and Sarah, and no sooner had the door closed on him than Lizzie's cold, calm front dropped away. Coming to Mary Ann, where she sat before the fire, working assiduously at her shorthand, she said quickly, 'Leave that a minute and listen to me. Your da will be back at any time. . . . Put it down, I say.' She flicked the book from Mary Ann's hand, and this caused Mary Ann's face to tighten.

'Don't look like that. I'm telling you don't look at me like that. And listen to me. . . . If your father goes out tomorrow you must go with him.'

'He won't want me with him.'

'I don't care if he wants you with him or not. . . . Look.' Suddenly Lizzie knelt down by Mary Ann's side, and as she caught hold of her daughter's hand her whole expression changed. Mary Ann was now looking at her old ma, the ma she knew and loved. And when she saw the tears come into Lizzie's eyes her face and body relaxed, and the resentment she was feeling at the moment against her mother died away. She asked under her breath, 'What is it, Ma? What's the matter?'

'Nothing, nothing. I only want you to do this for me. Please do this for me, keep with him tomorrow. He mustn't get anything into him tomorrow. Will you do it? You can. You know you can.'

'But if he says I haven't got to go with him. If he says no, what about it then?'

Lizzie turned her eyes away and looked towards the fire, and after a moment she pulled herself to her feet and said in a dead tone, 'Well, if he won't let you go with him, I'll . . .' Her voice trailed away. 'I'll only have to tell him. . . .'

'Tell him what?' Mary Ann was on her feet.

Lizzie shook her head. 'Oh, it doesn't matter . . . it doesn't matter. I just didn't want him to break out tomorrow, that's all. Go on, get on with your work, it doesn't matter.'

Mary Ann stared at Lizzie as she went towards the scullery again. What was the matter with her mother? What was up anyway? Where had she been those other times this week? On Monday she had gone to the pictures. But she was out on Wednesday, and yesterday again. and she looked all worked up, and she sounded worked up. Mary Ann went back to her seat, and as she picked up her notebook she looked down at the last words she had written in shorthand. They read, 'Me da says he's going out tomorrow. He sounds just like he used to years ago when he was going on the beer. . . . Will things never straighten out?' She looked up from the book. Would things never straighten out?

There was a wind blowing over the fields. It was like a gigantic scythe whipping across the frozen earth. It bit into Mary Ann's ankles causing her to comment, 'I wish I'd put my boots on.'

Mike, walking by her side up the road towards the bus stop, did not pick up her remark, and it was the third such she had made about the weather since leaving the house. But when she slipped on an icy patch in the road his hand came out swiftly and steadied her, and as he released her he said, 'Your mother told you to come along of me, didn't she?'

'No, Da.'

'All right, don't tell me if you don't want to. But I know me own know. After last night she was frightened I was goin' to get bottled, and she had reason, for that's just what I intended to do.'

'No, Da.'

Mary Ann was looking up at him, but Mike kept his eyes ahead as he asked abruptly, 'Do you know where your ma's been this week?'

'No, Da.'

His eyes were hard on her and there was a a sharpness in his tone as he said, 'Now look, Mary Ann. This could be serious. I might do just what she fears, and in spite of you go and get a skin full. I feel like it. By God! I do at this minute. So if you know what she's been up to on these jaunts, tell me.'

'But I don't, Da.' Of one accord they drew to a halt, and Mary Ann looked at him as she went on, 'I only know she's upset about something, sort of worked up.' Her eyes flicked away. 'She did say to me to come with you today. For some reason or other ... well, she doesn't want you to do anything. . . .' Her voice trailed off.

Mike continued to look down on her for a moment, then with a deep intake of breath he walked on, and she had to hurry her step to keep up with him.

Mike did not speak again until they reached the cross-roads and then he said, as if to himself, 'If the old fellow were here I'd feel there was something hatching, but I can't blame him for this.'

Mary Ann, picking up his words, said, 'No, Da, you can't. And talking of him, I'm scared of him coming back an' all, for there's going to be trouble.'

A moment ago she'd had no intention of telling him about Tony, but it now appeared like a heaven-sent diversion, a subject that would interest him and keep him, at least for a while, from thinking, and not kindly, of her mother.

'Trouble?'

'Yes, about Tony. . . . He told me yesterday that he's going
. . .' She lowered her head and finished in a soft-toned rush,
'He's going to marry Mrs. Schofield, da.'

Mike was silent so long that she looked up at him.

'He told you that himself?'

'Yes, Da.'

'Well, my God!' Mike pushed his trilby back from his
brow. 'That'll be news that'll knock the old man over. Although it's really no surprise, not to me, it isn't, but it will be
to him, because he hasn't got the vestige of an inkling. I
know that. . . . And what about you?' His head came down
to her. 'How did you feel when he shot that at you?'

Mary Ann raised her eyebrows, then turned her gaze away
over the fields as she said, 'A bit odd for a moment.'

'You're still keen on Corny though?'

'Yes, Da.'

'If there hadn't been Corny would you've had Tony?'

She brought her eyes back to him again. 'That's what
Tony asked me. How can I say? I don't know. I like Tony, I
always have.'

'Do you think your mother knows and this is what's been
upsetting her?'

'No, da. No. He told me first, I feel sure of that.'

'Well, there's one thing certain.' Mike drew in another
long breath. 'When your mother does know it's not going to
make her any happier. She didn't take much notice of that
tale your grannie brought that Sunday, about seeing them
together. She remarked at the time on Mrs. Schofield being
so much older than him and she dismissed the idea as rid-
iculous, because she wanted to go on thinking about the nice
cushy future all planned out for you. For, like the old fellow,
she had set her heart on this business and believed in the tag
that time would tell. But you know, when he first mentioned
it she went off the deep end. Can you believe that? She was
actually shocked. Ah well, time has told, hasn't it?' He put
his hand out and touched her cheek. 'Life's funny. But don't
worry. Tony wasn't for you. He's a fine fellow, but not for
you. He's not your type of man . . . don't worry.'

'But I'm not worrying about that, Da. Not about Tony

and me, but I am worrying about Mr. Lord coming back. You remember the last time him and Tony went at it?'

Again Mike took in a deep breath before saying, 'We'll wait until he does come and see what happens then. I think the best thing that you and me can do is to both get drunk ... eh?' He was bending down towards her, and they both laughed now. With a sudden impulsive movement she tucked her hand into his arm, and for no other reason but that she was with her da and he wasn't going to go on the beer, she felt a momentary wave of happiness.

As was usual on his visits to the city, Mike did some business for the farm. Then he and Mary Ann had lunch together. Following this, he pleased her mightily by taking her to the pictures.

It was turned four o'clock and nearly dark when the bus dropped them at the crossroads again. They were quiet now as they went down the road, and neither of them spoke until, through the dusk, the farm came in sight, when Mary Ann exclaimed, 'Look, da. Is that our Michael on the road?'

Mike screwed up his eyes. 'Aye, it is. I wonder what's up. He's waitin' ... he seems as if he's on the look-out for us. ...'

Before Mike had finished speaking, Michael came towards them at a run, and Mary Ann's heart began to pound with painful intensity. Something had happened to her ma. She knew it had. That was the feeling that had been with her all day. In spite of the joy of her father's company, and the brief happiness she had experienced this morning, there had been a heaviness around her, and Mike endorsed this feeling in himself when he muttered under his breath, 'I've been waitin' for this.'

But when Michael's face loomed up through the dusk and he came panting to their side, both their expressions took on a similar glint to his own, for Mary Ann was smiling, and Mike's eyebrows were raised in pleasant inquiry.

It was Mike who spoke first, saying, 'It can't be the sweep, the results won't be through yet. ... What are you looking so happy about?'

'It's me ma.' Michael, in this moment of high excitement,

had dropped what was to him the familiar use of mother. 'You'll never believe it. But come on . . . come on, hurry up. I've been on the look-out for you on and off for the last couple of hours. Where've you been?'

'To the pictures. But what is it?' Mary Ann tried to catch hold of his coat as they now hurried on. 'What's me ma done?'

'Wait and see.' Michael was one step ahead of them, practically at a trot.

'Here, hold your hand a minute.' Mike gripped his son's arm. 'What's happened? It's something nice for a change anyway to make you look like that.'

'Just you wait and see . . . just wait and see. No, don't go in the back way.' He turned and pulled at Mary Ann as she was about to enter the farm gate. 'Come on in the front.'

'With our slushy boots on? Do you want us to get murdered?' Mike was still following Michael, and Michael threw over his shoulder, 'You won't get murdered this time.'

When they reached the front door, he stopped and, looking from one to the other, he said, 'Shut your eyes.'

'Shut me eyes!' Mike pulled his chin into the side of his neck, and slanted his eyes at his son. 'What's the game?'

'Go on, Da. Shut your eyes.'

Mary Ann didn't need a double bidding to shut her eyes. She screwed them up, anticipating as she did so a happiness streaked with wonder. It must be something wonderful that Michael had to show them because his face was portraying a look that she had never seen on it before. It radiated a feeling of deep, deep happiness.

After opening the door she felt Michael grip her hands, and her da joggled her as they tried to get through the framework together. She wanted to giggle, but it was not the moment for giggling, she knew that. When she felt Michael turning them in the direction of the front room she sensed immediately what she would see. Yet the surprise was so great that she was for the moment struck speechless. She was looking at what had been her ma's room. Now, as if a giant hand had swept the house, mixing up the furniture, she was gazing wide-eyed at a complete bed-sitting-room, and there, sitting propped up in bed, looking almost like her old self, was Sarah.

Michael, standing near the head of the bed gripping Sarah's hand, looked at them, saying softly, 'Would you believe it?'

'No, no, I wouldn't.' Mike came slowly across the room, and when he was standing at the foot of the bed he looked down at Sarah and said, with what might have been a break in his voice, 'Hello, lass ... you got here then.' It sounded as if he knew she had been coming. So much so that Michael exclaimed in a surprised whisper, 'You didn't know, did you, Father?'

'No, I didn't know. Not an inkling.'

'Nor me.' Michael gave a series of quick shakes to his head. 'It's amazing.'

Mary Ann came and stood by Michael's side, and putting her hand out she touched Sarah's face, and there was no disguising the cracking of her voice as she said, 'This is what me ma's been up to all week, isn't it?'

Sarah nodded. She was unable to speak.

Mike now said, 'I'll be seeing you, lass,' and turning quietly from the bed, went out of the room.

Sarah, looking from Michael towards Mary Ann, brought out brokenly, 'I'll love her all me life.'

It was too much emotion for Mary Ann to cope with without openly breaking down, and she too went hastily from the room, thinking as she made her way towards the kitchen, 'An' I will an' all.' In moments of great stress she always dropped into the old vernacular.

As she pushed open the kitchen door it was to see her mother held tight in her da's arm, and to hear him saying over and over again, 'Oh! Liz. Liz.' And as her mother raised her head quickly from his shoulder, he finished, 'You won't regret it, we'll all see to that.'

Lizzie braced herself against Mary Ann's rushing onslaught. It was indeed as if they had all slipped back three or four years. And as Lizzie's arms went round her daughter, she said, 'There now, there now, stop it, and let me get on.'

'Oh, Ma, I think you're wonderful.'

Lizzie made no open comment on this but a section of her

mind, speaking with a touch of sadness, said: 'All my married life I've done what one or the other wanted and they never thought to say I was wonderful, until now.' The feeling she thought she had conquered during the early part of the week returned, and for a moment she felt the bitterness rise in her again. She had created a beautiful room – it was the symbol of her personal success – worthy in its taste of the finest house, and then they had succeeded, with their innuendoes of silence and suggestion, to bulldoze the ultimatum at her . . . the room or us. . . . Either you let Sarah have the room or you keep it . . . just to yourself, for we'll have none of it.

'But how did you manage it?' Mike was following her round like a kitten – a better description would have been a huge cat – purring on her, and when his arm, coming swiftly out and round her waist, almost lifted her off her feet as he pulled her to him again, the action seemed to slam the door shut on her self-pity. She had been right. Oh, yes, she knew she had been right. Sarah was happy and would likely get better much quicker here. And although she had only been in the house a matter of three hours, her gratitude had been so touching that it didn't seem to matter any more about the room. There would be times, she told herself, being a level-headed woman, when she would want her room to herself, but they would be few and far between. The main thing was she had her family with her again going her way. How, she wondered now, had she ever let them go so far from her? She must have been mad. She pushed off Mike's arm, saying, 'And you stop it, an' all. I've got to think of the tea, nobody else seems to be going to bother.'

'But how did you do it, Liz? I want to hear.'

'I went out three times this week, didn't I?'

'You did, Mrs. Shaughnessy!' He nodded his head deeply at her.

'I went off jaunting to the pictures!'

'You did, Mrs. Shaughnessy.' His head was moving slower and deeper now, and Mary Ann began to laugh. The laugh was high and thin. It spun upwards in a spiral of sound ending almost on a squeak, and the next minute Mary Ann had her head resting in the crook of her elbow on top of the sideboard and Mike was saying, 'Ah, there now, there now, give over. It's no time for crying.' With his one good arm he swung her up and carried her like a child towards the chair, then, sitting down, dumped her on his knee, and as he stroked the back of her head he muttered into her hair, 'You're always the one for enjoyment, aren't you? It's like old times; when anything nice happened you always had to bubble.' Mike looked to where Lizzie was now flicking the cloth across the table and their gaze met and held. They were both thinking back to the ending of many of their rows and disagreements, and they couldn't think of one where Mary Ann had not howled her eyes out with happiness. Or was it just relief?

'Now that's all right, Mr. Flannagan.' Mike laid his heavy hand on the small man's shoulder. 'She would have been coming into the family soon in any case.'

'Yes, yes, I know that. They would have got married, yes, I know that, Mr. Shaughnessy.' Mr. Flannagan had always addressed Mike as Mr. Shaughnessy. From that far-away day of the peace tea, when the little man had rebelled openly against his wife's tyranny and had marched down the street with Mike to get blind drunk for the first time in many years. From that day, whenever he had spoken to him since, he had always given Mike his full title, and Mike had returned the compliment.

Mike liked the little bloke, and in a way admired him, for he had showed his missus he was no worm, although she had treated him as one for years.

'That room was so pokey.' Mr. Flannagan moved his head from side to side. 'I'd think about her at odd times of the day stuck in there and her loving the open air, but here it's so wide looking, so free. And the view from that window does your heart good. I'm not being hoodwinked by what you're sayin', Mr. Shaughnessy. It's the goodness of yourself and your wife's heart that have brought this about. And if she gets better, I mean if she gets her legs back, then it'll be thanks to the pair of you.'

'Now, now, let's forget it. What about a little wet on the side . . . I've no hard.' He winked at the smaller man. 'It's not allowed in the house, except at Christmas, and births and deaths, and we haven't had any of them for a long while.' They both laughed. 'Of course, beer's a different thing. Liz tells me that the beer hasn't been brewed yet that could make me drunk!' Their laughter rose, then Mike, jerking his head towards the front room, said, 'Hark to 'em. They're going at it in there, aren't they?'

'It sounds like a party. It does that Mr. Shaughnessy. And listen there a minute ... I believe I can hear her laughing above the rest.' The her referred to his wife, and Mr. Flannagan's face was definitely stretched with amazement. There came a deep twinkle into his eye now as he looked up at Mike. 'The age of miracles isn't passed, is it, Mr. Shaughnessy?' Mike's head was going back to let out a bellow of laughter when he checked it, saying, 'I think that's someone knocking, but I can't hear for the noise.'

He handed Mr. Flannagan a glass of beer, then went hurriedly through the scullery towards the back door, and when he opened it he exclaimed in almost startled surprise, 'Good God!'

'No, just me, Shaughnessy. I always turn up like the proverbial bad penny.'

'You're ... you're welcome, sir.'

'Yes, but you didn't expect me, you never do. May I come in?'

'Yes, sir. By all means.' Mike pulled the door wide.

'Oh, you've got company?' The sound of the laughter penetrated to the scullery, and Mike answered, 'Only the family, and Sarah and her parents.'

'Sarah?' Mr. Lord nodded at Mike. 'She's here then? Oh, that's good, she's getting out and about, I'm very pleased to hear that.'

Mike did not at this moment go into any particulars. The old boy wasn't going to like it when he heard that Michael was turning down the bungalow. He mightn't be greatly distressed about it, but nevertheless he didn't like any of his suggestions to be flaunted, and it would be in that light he would take this business.

In the kitchen, Mike said, 'This is Sarah's father. This is Mr. Lord, Mr. Flannagan.'

'Good evening.'

'Good evening, sir.'

Mr. Lord did not know Mr. Flannagan, but Mr. Flannagan knew Mr. Lord. He received his pay packet from him every week, for he worked in his yard. It was funny when you came to think about it, Mr. Flannagan's mind told him, but if things worked out the way Mrs. Flannagan said they were going to, Mr. Lord here and himself would, in a way, be connected. . . . Very distantly, admitted, but still connected. Life was indeed funny, Mr. Flannagan commented.

'You're Sarah's father?'

'Yes, I am, sir; I am that, sir.'

'Very nice girl, very nice. A great pity about this business. But still, wonderful things are done these days. . . . We'll see, we'll see.'

'Did you have a good trip, sir?' Mike was speaking now.

'Yes, Shaughnessy. A very, very good trip. I enjoyed every moment of it. I only wish I could have made it longer.'

Mike was thinking . . . 'Well, why didn't you then, things go on just the same,' when Mr. Lord said, 'Is Tony here?'

'Tony? No, sir.'

'Do you know where he is?'

'No. No, I don't, sir. He doesn't usually tell me where he's going.' Mike gave a small smile.

'He hasn't been out with Mary Ann today?'

Mike's eyes dropped away. 'No, no, not today. I took Mary Ann into Newcastle. . . . Won't you sit down a minute?' He turned the chair towards the old man, then added generously, 'I'll tell Mary Ann you're here. She'll be pleased to see you.'

'Thank you, Shaughnessy. I'll be pleased to see her, too. Yes, yes, I will indeed. Thank you.'

Mike left the kitchen and went into the front room, and held up a sharp warning finger to stop the laughter and chattering. Making sure that the door was closed behind him before he spoke, he said under his breath, 'He's come home. The old boy.'

'What, Mr. Lord?' He looked towards Lizzie, who had risen to her feet.

'But I thought Tony said another week or so,' Michael put in.

Mike now nodded at Michael as he whispered, 'Well, you know him.'

Mary Ann hadn't moved from her position on the side of the bed near Sarah. Part of her wanted to dash into the kitchen and throw her arms around the old man's neck in welcome, but there was a larger part that was filled with anxious fear. It was just like him, as Tony said, to do the unpredictable. They had all been so happy ... happy and laughing. It had been like old times. She had felt during the last hour or so that life was going to run smoothly again. She had forgotten for the moment what Tony had told her about him and Mrs. Schofield. She had forgotten what that would mean to the old man who had just come back. Her da was looking at her and speaking again, still in a whisper, 'Come on. Get off that.' He pointed to the bed. 'He wants to see you.'

'What's the matter with you?' Lizzie's voice was soft but sharp. 'Don't go in looking like that. He'll think he's as welcome as a snake in paradise.'

Lizzie did not often make these quips, and there was a low rumble of suppressed laughter. Mary Ann did not laugh. She pulled herself off the bed and went slowly round the foot, excusing herself as she stepped over Mrs. Flannagan's feet, and made her way towards her da who was now opening the door. There was nothing to laugh about, nothing to smile about any more. They weren't to know that perhaps in a short time – the distance was determined on how long it would take Mr. Lord and Tony to come together – he would be dead. He could not stand shocks, great shocks, at his age, with his heart in the bad state it was already.

When she reached Mike, he stopped her passing him by saying quickly, 'Hold your hand a minute till I bring Mr. Flannagan in here, it'll be better that way.... Stay a minute.'

Within a matter of seconds Mike came from the kitchen accompanied by Mr. Flannagan, and nodding to Mary Ann he held the kitchen door open for her, and she went in to greet Mr. Lord.

'What's the matter with you?' said Lizzie some time later, as they piled sandwiches on to plates ready for transporting into the front room.

'Nothing,' said Mary Ann.

'Now don't be silly . . . nothing. You know there is something. You were all right until Mr. Lord put in an appearance.' She stopped her arranging of the sandwiches, and, turning Mary Ann towards her, she said, 'You haven't been up to anything, have you?'

'Me, Ma?'

'Yes, you. And don't look so wide-eyed.' Lizzie was smiling now. Smiling down on her daughter. She was relaxed and happy, it was as if she'd had a drink, like at Christmas. But the strongest drink she had taken tonight was coffee.

Mary Ann could have told her mother what was troubling her, but she did not want to spoil this night, and if she said to her, 'Tony is going to marry Mrs. Schofield,' the night would indeed be spoilt for her. She would have to know sooner or later, but not tonight, because she was happy in the sacrifice she had made. Everybody was full of praise for her, and all their gratitude flowed round her in a heart-warming wave. She could not spoil it.

'Well then, if you've been up to nothing' – Lizzie moved her head gently – 'stop looking like that. To say the least, you don't seem very glad to see him back. And as usual he's been more than kind. Fancy him thinking about a camera for Michael, and such a camera. And a projector to go with it. The two must have cost sixty pounds if they cost a penny. And he's going to get a television for Sarah. You know, he couldn't be kinder.'

She lifted up three plates now, and balancing two on one hand and one in the other, she went towards the hall, saying, 'I'm looking forward to seeing his American pictures. You know he's a marvellous old man really, going around taking pictures at his age. You remember the ones from his last holiday. . . . Oh, that's them now.' She half turned. 'They've got back. Bring the coffee.'

Mary Ann picked up the tray with the percolator and milk jug, and turned from the sound of her father's and Mr. Lord's voices coming from the scullery.

Mary Ann, at this moment, was not interested in seeing the pictures of where Mr. Lord had been. She was feeling very down and apprehensive. She wished that Mr. and Mrs. Flannagan would go home, and the house was quiet and they were all in bed. She wanted to think, and you couldn't think in this chattering racket. . . .

The big chair was pulled up to the side of Sarah's bed and Mr. Lord directed to it.

Michael had arranged a portable screen at the far end of the room and fixed the table for the projector. This took a little time as he had to arrange a number of books to bring it to the required height. And then all was ready.

'We'll have the lights out now,' said Mr. Lord. Then with a little lightness that for him amounted to high gaiety, he said, 'The show is about to begin.' There was a murmur of laughter before silence took over in the room. Silence but for the warm burr of the projector.

There were six magazines of slides, and Michael, after slipping in the first set, worked the handle that clicked each picture into focus on the screen, and on each one Mr. Lord commented. This was the aeroplane with which he did the trip to New York. That was the hotel in which he stayed. . . . Oh, yes, that Negro had been a porter in the hotel and had proved himself very helpful. On and on it went, thirty-six pictures in the first magazine, thirty-six pictures in the second magazine. And when Michael was about to slip in the third set, Mr. Lord stopped him by saying, 'We won't have that one as arranged, Michael, let me have the end one next. . . . Yes, the end one.'

There was a few minutes of anticipatory silence while Michael made the changeover, then came the first click. Hardly had the picture lit up the screen but there burst from everyone in the room, perhaps with the exception of Mrs. Flannagan and Mr. Lord, one name . . . Corny! For it was Corny. A full-length picture of Corny in a red sweater, tight cream jeans, and a grin on his face that almost split it in two.

Mary Ann's hands were cupping her face, pressing her cheeks in and her lips out. Her eyes were riveted on the screen. Corny was looking straight at her, smiling his wide grin. Michael did not click away Corny's face for some minutes. When he did, she recovered her breath and turned with the sound of a laugh in her voice as she cried to the old man, 'You said you wouldn't be able to see him. . . . You said it was too far . . . thousands of miles down the country. . . . Oh, Mr. Lord! . . .'

'Wait a moment, wait a moment.' He checked her impetuous thanks with a quick pat on her knee. 'There are many, many more. Wait a moment.'

The click came again, and there was Corny once more. His figure was shorter now. He was in a sort of gigantic showroom, where cars stretched, it appeared, for miles. It seemed to hold all the cars in the world, and there was Corny standing by one of them, pointing out something to a man.

Mr. Lord's voice penetrated Mary Ann's mind now saying, 'He sold that car to that client. He's doing very well in that department, although he's only been there a month. Yes, he's doing very well indeed. We'll have the next one, Michael.'

They had the next one, and the next, and the next. Corny with this car, and that car. Corny in a great glass office. Corny sitting at the wheel of a car. Then the pictures changed abruptly. First, there was a picture of a house. It was a beautiful house with an open garden. There were two cars standing in the roadway, each looked as big as two English cars put together. There was a number of people sitting on the lawn of the house having tea, and Corny was one of them.

The next picture was of a tennis court. Corny was playing tennis. Mary Ann's eyes narrowed at the stationary figure on the screen, the racket held ready for a back-hand drive. She had never imagined Corny playing tennis. The picture changed again. And there was the blue sea, it was very, very blue, and the edge was trimmed with a high frothy breaker. On the beach there were a number of people, and Corny was among them. They were having a picnic.

'They are a great family for picnics.' Mr. Lord's voice broke in on Mary Ann's thoughts again. 'They're always eating out of doors. They have taken to Cornelius and like him very much. America has done him good. He seems to have opened out quite a lot . . . not so tongue-tied as I remember him ... at least, that's a mistake, I wouldn't say tongue-tied, brusque would be a better term. Yes ... he is not so brusque as he used to be.'

Mary Ann's fingers were holding the neck of her jumper now. She was looking at Corny in the water. His head was close to that of a girl, the girl she had seen in the front garden of the house. And also on the same side of the net on the tennis court. Although then she had her back to the camera, Mary Ann knew it was the same girl, for she had blonde hair, and although it was tied back it still reached below her waist. Suddenly she hated that hair. Her own hair, although a lovely dark chestnut with a deep shine, only came below her shoulders. She not only hated the fair hair, she hated its owner, but more so in this moment she hated Corny Boyle. And she thought of him as Corny Boyle, not just the familiar Corny.

'He seems to be having the time of his life.' This was Mrs. Flannagan's voice coming out of the darkness.

'Yes, I think he is.' Mr. Lord's voice was pleasant, and he seemed to be speaking to Mrs. Flannagan alone. 'At least he is getting a broader view of life. His years in America will certainly not be wasted.'

His years. . . . Mary Ann gulped and tried to make it noiseless.

The machine clicked again, and there was Corny playing his beloved instrument. Elbows up, head back, it was as if he was standing in the room before them. But he wasn't in the room, he was standing on the steps of that house, and there, squatting all round, were that family again. Only there seemed to be more of them this time, for protruding from the edge of the picture were numerous arms and legs. It looked like another party.

'This was one of their usual get-togethers. Corny and his playing are in great demand.'

There was no answer to Mr. Lord's remark.

The machine clicked yet again, sharply this time, and there was Corny in a close-up, sitting on the top of a gate, and next to him was the girl with the long fair hair. She was very bonny, beautiful they would call her out there ... and Corny and her had their arms round each other.

It was the end of that particular magazine and no one made any comment whatever until Mr. Lord spoke, and directly to Sarah now. 'Would you like to see more pictures, Sarah?'

It was a few seconds before Sarah said, 'Yes. Yes, I would ... please.' But there was no enthusiasm in her voice. Sarah was now one of the family and through her own feelings for Michael she could gauge at this moment how Mary Ann felt, and she knew, as surely as did Mary Ann, that the pictures of Corny had been shown for a purpose.

The set of pictures now flicking on and off the screen were dealing with the scenery, and as Mr. Flannagan said in a respectful tone, 'Aye, it's a grand-lookin' country. I've always had an idea I'd like to go there,' Mary Ann slid quietly from her chair and went out of the room, and no one said, 'Where are you going?'

But it was only a matter of minutes before Mike joined her in the kitchen. He came straight to her where she was standing looking down into the fire. She wasn't crying, but she nearly did when Mike put his arm around her shoulders and, pulling her tightly to his side, said, 'The old swine. He's a bloody scheming old swine, and I've got to say it.'

Mary Ann said nothing. And Mike went on, 'Take no notice of pictures like that. Ten to one he was told to pose for them. Things are done like that, you know. Come on, they'll say. Come on, huddle up together there, I'm going to take your picture. . . . You know what it's like, don't you? We've done it ourselves in the garden. You remember when Michael took me and Mrs. Schofield and we were laughing our heads off, remember that tea-time? Well, anybody seeing that would get the wrong idea, wouldn't they?'

Still Mary Ann did not answer. She had been hating Mr. Lord, she was still hating him. She knew, and her da knew, that he had deliberately brought these snaps to show her that Corny was no longer remembering the North or anyone in it ... was no longer remembering her. And the name of Mrs. Schofield did not for a moment soften her feelings towards the old man. But as though Mike had picked up her thinking, he said after a moment's silence, 'I could have one great big bloody row with him at this minute if it wasn't for the fact that he'll have enough to think about in a very short while when Tony spills the beans. . . . Look.' He turned her round, gripping her with his one hand. 'I tell you, take no notice of them pictures. You know the old fellow's always scheming. When he took them he didn't know that his plans were already down the drain. And if I know Corny Boyle, and I think I know him, he's not the kind of lad to be swept off his feet by a bunch of golden locks and two goo-goo eyes.' Mike gave a little laugh. 'She had goo-goo eyes, hadn't she? Not forgetting a big sloppy mouth. Come on . . . come on, laugh at it. What do you bet? I bet Corny's back here within the next few months.'

Within the next few months, her da had said. Within the next few months, not this month, or next. The year was nearly up, and next month it would be Christmas again, and Corny had said he would give it a year. But when he said that he hadn't realized the temptation of promotion, of big money, of a car . . . if he wanted one . . . of a girl with long blonde hair whose eyes weren't goo-goo, nor whose mouth was not big and sloppy. Mary Ann didn't hide the fact from herself that the girl with the long blonde hair was beautiful, by any standards she was beautiful.

'Look, come on back into the room, and don't let him see it's affected you. Keep the old boy guessing, that's the best way with him. Come on . . . laugh, smile.' He stretched her mouth gently with his middle finger and thumb, and when she didn't respond, he said urgently, 'Listen to me. Apart from what you feel, what we both feel about this, for it's made me as mad as a hatter, we don't want to spoil this day for your mother, do we? . . . and Sarah. Because Sarah is as near content now as she'll get until she's on her legs again. We don't want to do anything to bust up this day, eh? Come on.'

Side by side they went out of the kitchen, across the hall and quietly into the room again to hear the end of Mrs. Flannagan's comment, 'He's a very lucky young man.' Which told them that there had been more pictures of Corny.

'I'll have to put the light on a minute, this one's stuck,' said Michael.

As the light went up in the room, and caused them all to

blink, Mary Ann found that Mr. Lord was looking at her, but his eyes were not blinking. With their penetrating blueness they peered out at her from the wrinkled lids, and there was a question in their depth and Mary Ann, looking back at him, found she could not play up to her father's request and smile. And the old man, reading the hurt he had dealt her, looked sad for a moment. But only for a moment.

They were all late going to bed. Mary Ann heard the clock strike twelve as her father came up the stairs and made his way to his room. She had been lying for the last half-hour staring at the sloping ceiling, her eyes dry and burning. She hadn't cried and she told herself she wasn't going to. She was angry not only with Mr. Lord, she was angry with Corny Boyle. She did not believe what her da had said, that Corny had been pushed into posing for these pictures. He might have been the first time, but there had been a dozen or more of him with those people ... and that girl was always near him. If he wanted to stay in America then he could; nothing apparently she could say or do could stop him now. He was too far away for her to have any impression on him. But she hated him for wanting to stay in America.

As the muttered, companionable sound of her da, talking to her ma, came to her from their room across the landing, she was enveloped in a wave of self-pity. Of a sudden she felt utterly alone, quite lost, friendless. She had neither Corny Boyle nor Tony. The term 'falling between two stools' was certainly right in her case. The burning in her eyes became moist, and now she no longer tried to prevent the hot tears flooding down her face. Turning swiftly, she buried her head in the pillow.

She must have cried for about half an hour, for she felt weary and sick when she turned on to her back again, and continued, through blinking wet lids, to look towards the ceiling. It was at the point where sleep was about to carry her away from her misery that the sound of the telephone bell jangled through the house.

Mary Ann brought her head up from the pillow and listened. She expected to hear the door of her parents' room being pulled open. After some seconds, when the telephone bell, ringing again, seeming determined to disturb the quiet of the house, she threw back the bedclothes and, getting out of bed, pulled on her dressing-gown. She was on the landing when Michael's door opened, and she whispered across to him, 'It's the phone.'

As they went softly, and hurriedly, down the stairs together Michael whispered back at her, 'I'll bet something's happened to me grannie.'

Mary Ann felt not a trace of sympathy at the thought of anything happening to her grannie, and whispered back, 'She would pick this time of the night. It's just like her.'

So sure were they both that they would hear some news of Mrs. McMullen that, after switching on the hall light, they exchanged knowing glances as Michael lifted the mouth-piece from the stand on the hall table.

'Hello?'

The voice that came over the phone was no stranger's telling them that their grannie had been taken ill, but the voice of Mr. Lord. He was saying, 'Oh, is that you, Michael? I thought it might be your father.'

Again they exchanged glances.

'Is anything the matter, Mr. Lord?'

'No, no, nothing I hope . . . I just wanted to inquire if your father knew where Tony was going this evening . . . or last evening. It is now after one o'clock and he's not in.'

Again the exchange of glances.

'Your father is not awake, I suppose?'

'No, no, Mr. Lord, or he would have been down. I suppose he's in a deep sleep, and my mother too, they had rather a hectic day.' Michael said nothing about his own hectic day, and the excitement that was still depriving him of sleep. He said now, 'Very likely Tony's gone to a dance.'

'To my knowledge, he doesn't go to dances.'

Michael's eyebrows went up as his eyes slanted towards Mary Ann's again, and his lips pressed themselves into a tight line and his expression interpreted the words coming over the wire.

'Would Mary Ann know where he was likely to be?'

Mary Ann bit on her lip and shook her head at Michael.

'I don't think so, Mr. Lord.'

'Haven't they been going out on a Saturday as usual?'

Again Mary Ann motioned towards Michael, nodding her head this time.

'Yes . . . yes, I think so, Mr. Lord.'

'You think so? You're not sure?' The voice was loud and the words clipped, and Mary Ann took more of her lower lip into her mouth.

'Did Tony not tell Ben how late he might be, Mr. Lord?'

'As far as I can gather, no. From the information I have screwed from Ben, it would appear that he hasn't even seen my grandson since I left the house three weeks ago. I have long suspected Ben to be an idiot, now I have proof of it.'

From this heated remark, Mary Ann knew that Ben was within ear-shot of the old man. Poor Ben. He'd likely got it in the neck because he hadn't been able to tell Mr. Lord where Tony was. Very likely if he knew about Mrs. Schofield he still wouldn't have told on Tony. The main reason being not so much to protect Tony from the old man's wrath, but to protect his master from the consequences of that wrath.

'I shouldn't worry, Mr. Lord. He's likely gone to a dinner or something.'

There followed a pause so long it would have indicated that Mr. Lord had left the phone but for the fact that there hadn't been the usual click at the other end of the line. The old man's voice came now, thick and muffled, saying curtly, 'Thank you. I'm sorry to have got you out of bed. Thank you.' Now came the click. And Michael put the receiver back on to its rest.

'Lord! There'll be a shindy. I wonder what Tony's up to. He doesn't dance, does he?'

Mary Ann did not give a reply to this but said, 'We'd better look in on Sarah and tell her it's all right.' Michael nodded and moved towards the front-room door, and after opening it gently and putting his head round, he said, 'You awake, Sarah?'

He closed the door quietly before turning to Mary Ann. 'She's dead to the world. Relief, I suppose.' And going towards the stairs again he whispered, 'I wonder what

Tony's up to. Likely he's got in at a party or something. But I didn't think parties were in his line.'

'He's with Mrs. Schofield.'

'What!' Michael stopped dead on the stairs. 'How do you make that out?'

'They're going to be married.' There was a trace of bitterness in Mary Ann's tone.

'Him and Mrs. Schofield. You're kiddin'?'

'No, I'm not kidding.'

'How long have you known this?'

'Since Friday.'

'I didn't even know he was seeing her.'

'Well, you and me ma and Mr. Lord must be the only three people on the Tyne who didn't know about it.'

Michael watched Mary Ann ascend the stairs in front of him. Then, moving slowly, he followed her. For a moment he felt a deep brotherly concern for her. She was a tantalizing, aggravating little madam at times, but she was also an engaging little madam. And she was kind. Look at her with Sarah. And she had indeed been given enough tonight to try the temper of the best, with those pictures of Corny and that blonde. And this, on top of knowing that Tony was going to marry Mrs. Schofield. ... Mrs. Schofield, of all people. She seemed old enough to be his mother. Well, perhaps not quite, but too old for him.

On the landing he paused as Mary Ann's door closed on her, then his eyes were drawn towards his mother's room. Lord, this was going to be a blow for her. She had set her heart on Tony for Mary Ann as much as the old man had done. There was a balloon going to burst shortly.

Mary Ann, sitting on the edge of her bed, tried not to think of where Tony was at this present moment. He could not have married Mrs. Schofield, as the decree had not yet been made absolute, but there was no other place she could think of where he could be, except with her. The young Mary Ann told herself he was wicked, wicked. And she was answered by the Mary Ann against whom life had been thrust wholesalely these past few months, saying, 'Be your age, it happens ... it happens every day. Is he any different?'

Yes, Tony was different. He should be different. Like Corny. Corny was different. . . . He should be different. It appeared to her that because she liked both Corny and Tony, they should be different. When her mind, still clinging to the black and white theory of her upbringing, asked her why people did bad things, she said to herself, and impatiently now, 'Oh, go to sleep and forget it.'

But she couldn't go to sleep and forget it. It must have been around four o'clock in the morning that her fitful dozing overbalanced into sleep. Then it seemed as if she was only in this beautiful oblivion for a matter of seconds when a hand dragged her upwards out of it. She woke to her father's voice, saying, 'Mary Ann!' and his hand gently rocking her shoulder.

'Yes, Da?' She was sitting straight up blinking at him.

'Don't look so worried, it's all right. There's nothing wrong.' He bent towards her. 'I had to get up a short while ago, I heard Prudence bellowing her head off. She got her horns fixed in between those boards again, and when I was out I saw the light on up in the house, downstairs, and I was just wondering what was wrong when I caught sight of the old man walking up the hill. I could see him plainly . . . the moon's full.'

'What time is it?'

'About twenty past five now, but this was before five, I've just had a word with Michael. He's had a sleepless night it appears, too much excitement over Sarah I think in that quarter, but he tells me that the old man rang about one o'clock. Tony wasn't in then, and it looks as if he's still not in. I've got a feeling that I should go up and have a word with him. What do you think?'

'You mean tell him about Tony and – and Mrs. Schofield?'

'What do you think?'

Mary Ann looked down at the rumpled bedclothes, and she pulled her legs up under her and shook her head before answering, 'I don't know. When Tony does come in there'll be a dreadful row, because now, having to explain . . . well, he'll likely blurt it out.'

'Yes, that's what I was thinking. I was thinking an'

all it wouldn't be a bad idea if it was to come from you.'

'Me, Da! Me tell him about them?'

'Yes. I don't think the shock would be half as great. You see, Tony will lose his temper, but you won't, not on this occasion.' He smiled at her. 'And although the old man will be worked up he won't be aggravated, and by the time Tony does get in he'll likely have got the matter settled in his own mind. He won't be less furious. I'm not looking forward to seeing him when he hears the news from either you or Tony but I think it's likely to have less of a bad effect if you tell him.'

Mary Ann looked towards the window as she said, 'When, Da?'

'Well, what about now? Do you feel like getting up?'

'Yes, Da. I'll be down in five minutes.'

'Don't make a noise. I don't want your mother disturbed. She won't take this matter much lighter than the old man, you know.'

'I know, Da.'

Bending swiftly, Mike kissed Mary Ann on the side of the cheek. It was an unusual gesture. Their deep love and understanding for each other did not show itself in demonstration, other than the clasping of hands. And when the door had closed on her father, Mary Ann had a desire to start to cry all over again, even more heart-brokenly than she had done last night, but instead she grabbed angrily at each garment as she got into her clothes. . . .

Ben let them in, it was as if he had been waiting for them. 'He's in the drawing-room,' he said.

If the business of coming to the house at this hour wasn't odd enough, Mr. Lord too seemed to be expecting them, for he showed not the least surprise when Mike, gently pushing Mary Ann before him, went past Ben, who was holding open the door, and into the room.

Mary Ann looked towards Mr. Lord sitting in a chair to the side of the big open fireplace, with the fire roaring away up the chimney. And for all the heat of the room, she felt as cold as Mr. Lord looked.

'Sit down, Shaughnessy.'

Mr. Lord did not appear to notice Mary Ann as he addressed himself to Mike. 'Do you happen to know where my grandson spent the night? Don't tell me, please.' The old man lifted up a tired-looking hand. 'Don't tell me that you think he has been to a party, or a dance. He is no dancer, and not given to all-night parties. I happen to know the friends he has do not go in for all-night parties.'

'It's a pity, sir. Perhaps it would have been better if he had picked friends who did go in for all-night parties.' Mike did not end as he was thinking, 'You've made a rod for your own back.'

'What are you telling me, Shaughnessy? That he has gone off the rails and that it is my fault? ... And I think it would have been better had you come alone.' Mr. Lord was still ignoring Mary Ann's presence even as he spoke of her.

'I don't think so, sir. Mary Ann, we all seem to forget, is no longer a little girl, and this business concerns her more than any of us. Next to you, she, I should imagine, is the most concerned.' Mike knew he wasn't actually speaking the truth here. Next to the old man it would be Lizzie who would be most concerned about the failure of the plans for Mary Ann's future. And he ended, 'And as she's known what has been going on while all the rest of us were in the dark, I think it had better come from her.'

For the first time since she came into the room, Mr. Lord looked at Mary Ann. He looked so frail, so tired, that pity for him mounting in her obliterated all other feeling at the moment. Only his eyes indicated the vitality still in him.

'Well! What have you to tell me, Mary Ann?'

She did not know how to start. There seemed no way to lead up to this business. Even as she searched frantically in her mind, none came to her.

Mike gave her arm a gentle squeeze, saying, 'Go on, tell it in your own way.'

Someone began to talk. Mary Ann didn't feel it was her voice. It had a cracked sound, yet was unhesitant, and she heard it say, 'You like Mrs. Schofield, Mr. Lord?'

'Mrs. Schofield? Yes. Yes, I like Mrs. Schofield. What about her?'

'Only that Tony and Mrs. Schofield have been seeing a lot of each other this past year.'

Mr. Lord's face seemed to close. It had looked tight and drawn before, but now the wrinkled flesh converged towards the point of his nose and became white. The whiteness spread over the nostrils and around the blue-lipped mouth.

The voice that still didn't sound like her own, went on 'It was one Saturday when I went to see Janice ... Janice Schofield, and as we knocked on the door there was shouting, and we saw through the window Mr. Schofield hitting Mrs. Schofield. . . . It was from then.'

She watched the tremor pass over the old man's body, right from the lips, over his shoulders, down the legs right into the hand-made shoes. But whatever emotion Mr. Lord was feeling he was going to great lengths at this moment to control it. Now his lower jaw began to move slowly back and forward, and she could hear the sound of his dentures grinding against each other in passing. Her father's voice broke in quietly, 'These things happen, sir, unavoidably ... unaccountably ... for no reason whatever. People don't want them to happen, but they happen. . . . Mrs. Schofield's a nice woman.'

'Mrs. Schofield is a married woman.'

The words came from Mr. Lord's closed lips as if they were indented on a thin strip of steel.

'She got her divorce a few weeks ago, sir.'

'She is still a married woman.'

My God! Mike closed his eyes for a moment. The old man wasn't speaking from any religious bias. He had no God, not to Mike's knowledge anyway, yet in this day and age he could be narrow enough still to discredit divorce.

'Moreover she is a woman years his senior.'

'She doesn't look it, sir.'

'He won't marry her, I'll see to that.' With what seemed a great effort the old man pulled himself up in the chair until his spine was pressed tightly against the back.

'You can't stop him.' It was Mary Ann speaking now. 'He loves her. He loves her very much.'

'What are you talking about, child? What do you know about love?'

'I know that Tony loves Mrs. Schofield.' Mary Ann had stepped a small step away from Mike and towards Mr. Lord as she spoke. She could recognize her own voice now. She felt that the worst was over, he wasn't going to have a heart attack, not yet anyway. 'Mrs. Schofield's a nice woman. She'll be better for him than I would have been. Tony never loved me and I didn't love him, not in that way.'

'She's a silly, feather-brained woman.'

'Now, sir.' Mike was smiling. 'You know that isn't true. You know yourself you found a depth in her that couldn't be hidden by that airy-fairy manner. If I might suggest, sir, it would be a good thing if you would accept the situa—'

'Be quiet, Shaughnessy! I will accept no such situation.' Now Mr. Lord did look as if he could be on the point of a heart attack. His turkey-like neck was stretching out of his collar and his head was wagging with such speed that it looked as if it could spiral itself up and off. 'Accept the situation! I will tell you this much. He will come into this house just once more, and that to get the little that belongs to him, and that will be the end. I want to see him, or hear of him, no more. . . . Accept the situation! What do you think I am? He has been out all night. . . .' Mr Lord flicked his eyes towards Mary Ann then back to Mike. 'I want to speak to you alone for a few minutes.'

Mary Ann looked at her da, and when he gave a nod of his head she went slowly from the room and into the hall, there to see Ben standing.

'He's all right? He's not bad?'

'No.'

'He didn't have an attack of any sort?'

'Only temper, Ben.' Mary Ann touched Ben's sleeve. 'Don't worry, he's all right. At least until Tony comes. What will happen then. . . .' She shook her head.

'Is it true what you said in there about Master Tony and Mrs. Schofield?'

'Yes, Ben.'

'God above! I knew there was something on. I felt once or twice that he wanted to speak to me but was afraid to in case I told the Master. He needn't have worried. . . . I wouldn't be the one to kill him off.'

'Well, it hasn't killed him off, Ben. We can be thankful for that.'

'Yes, but as you said, not yet. Wait until the young one comes in. . . . I'll make some strong coffee and lace it.'

He turned like a busy old woman and shambled towards the kitchen, and Mary Ann went towards the long window that looked on to the garden. The curtains had not been drawn and she looked up into the still dark, deep, frost-laden sky. Well, part of it was over. She knew why Mr. Lord wanted her out of the room, he wanted to talk about Tony, and where he had been all night. He needn't have worried about shocking her. She knew Tony had been with Mrs. Schofield. Married or not, they had been together. As she turned from the window and walked across the hall towards the kitchen she felt old, very old. She seemed in this moment to know all about life, and it wasn't a nice feeling. She had thought that no matter what happened to her in her life, whatever sadness came into it, she would still have the desire to go on breathing . . . living. And oddly enough it wasn't the fact that she had lost Corny . . . and Tony, that made her for a moment lose this desire but the cause of her having been sent out of the room. This was what momentarily dampened the desire for existence. This thing that wasn't nice. This thing that you read about in the papers. This thing that the girls at the Typing School nattered over, and giggled over. This thing that made you turn on yourself at times and say, 'Be your age. Remember Janice Schofield had to get married because she was going to have a baby. And there are girls at the school who don't go home until four o'clock in the morning. And another is going with a man nearly fifty; and people think nothing of it.'

In the kitchen Ben was pouring a glass of brandy into a cup of black coffee. It was as he picked the cup up that they heard the car come into the courtyard, and at the moment Tony entered the kitchen Mike came in from the hallway.

Tony stood with the door in his hand looking from one to the other. Then in a voice that sounded remarkably like Mr. Lord's when about to mount his high horse, he said, 'He's back then?'

This wasn't a question, it was a statement, but Mike answered, 'Yes, last night, early evening.'

'Trust him.... And now I'm to be chastised like a naughty little boy for being out all night. Is that it, eh?'

'I think it's a bit more than that, Tony.' Mike's voice was low. 'Mary Ann, on my advice I might say, broke the news to him. I thought it would come easier on him from her than from you.'

Now there was a strong resemblance to Mr. Lord as Tony looked at Mike and said, 'You shouldn't have done that, Mike, that was my business.'

'Aye, it might have been, but I know what the pair of you are like when you get going. I didn't want you to have anything more on your conscience.' Mike's voice too had taken on a cold note. 'If he had collapsed on you I doubt whether you would have felt so determined to go through with this business of yours.'

'Nothing would have stopped me going through with ... this business of mine, as you call it. And it's because it happens to be my own business that I prefer to look after it.'

Mary Ann's eyes, dark and large, were flicking now between her father and Tony. Things were taking a tangent she had never imagined possible. Her da and Tony were on the verge of a row. Her da liked Tony, and Tony liked her da, but there was a bitterness between them now, she could feel it. Her da might subdue himself to Mr. Lord out of respect for the old man's age and because, deep down, he was grateful to him, but she was sure he did not have the same feeling towards Tony. Tony had come to the farm as a boy, a student, out to learn. That he was Mr. Lord's grandson made no difference, he was still an ordinary young fellow in her da's eyes. There were very few people whom her da would knuckle under to, and Tony was taking the wrong tack if he was going to try to put her da in his place. To deflect their attention from each other, she said sharply, 'I had made up my mind, Tony, to tell him in any case, because, what you seem to forget at the moment is that I am concerned in this affair. Not that I want to be. And I don't think I was minding anyone else's business but my own when I explained to him that his plans hadn't worked out. What's more, I didn't want to see him drop down dead when you blurted this—'

'Don't worry, Mary Ann.' The voice came from the half-closed door in front of which Mike was standing, and they all swung round as Mr. Lord came through into the kitchen. '. . . don't worry, I've no intention of dropping down dead.'

Mary Ann looked at the tight face. The skin had that awful bluish hue, right from the white hair line to where his neck disappeared into his collar.

The old man turned his gaze now from Mary Ann, and although his eyes were directed towards his grandson they did not look at him, but at some point above the top of his head, as he said, 'I'm not expecting any explanation from you, nor have I any intention of listening to one. I would be obliged if you would make your departure as quick as possible.'

Tony's chin was up and out, but nevertheless it was trembling. 'You needn't worry, this is one time I'll be pleased to obey you. But whether you want any explanation or not, I'm going to tell you that I haven't spent the night with Mrs. Schofield. She happens to be in London. You can confirm that if you like.'

'I'm not interested in your activities, nor in the people you choose to share them with.' Mr. Lord's eyes came down from the space above Tony's head, and looking at Ben he said, 'As soon as our visitors have gone you might lock up. I think we need a little rest.'

As his thin body turned stiffly towards the hall door again, his glance came to rest on Mike. His expression did not alter, nor yet his tone, as he said, 'Thank you, Shaughnessy.' He did not look at Mary Ann.

When the door had closed on him, Mary Ann, Mike and Ben turned towards Tony. Whereas Mr. Lord's face had been of a blue hue, Tony's was scarlet. He was shaking, and this was evident to them all when he turned to Mary Ann and there was deep bitterness in his voice as he said, 'You see, it'll take a lot to make him drop down dead. He's tough, and he glories in it. You have to live with him just to know how tough he is. He's—'

Ben's quivering lips were open to make a protest when

Mike put in sharply, 'Don't say anything you'll be sorry for later, Tony, because then you'll remember he's always been good to you ... I would say more than good. You can't blame him for wanting his own way. We all do. You particularly. And you've gone your way, so don't blame him.'

'You definitely know which side you're on, don't you?' Tony's voice was as furious as his glance.

Mike's tone threatened fire too, with the retort, 'Look here! I'm only being fair. You know my feeling about the old fellow, and I damn well toady to no one, so be careful. But if you want my opinion – and you don't – I'll say you've got off pretty lightly with this business. What did you expect him to do? Greet you and her with open arms?'

For a moment longer Tony returned Mike's glare, then with a swift movement his head drooped sideways and, his teeth digging into his lower lip, he stared at the floor. Then with a muttered, 'Oh, hell!' he thrust himself out of the room.

Mike walked to where Mary Ann stood near the table, and turning her about, he led her to the door, saying grimly, 'So long, Ben.'

'Good-bye, Mr. Shaughnessy.'

Mary Ann did not speak. She did not speak as they went down the hill and across the farmyard. Nor did she speak when she entered the kitchen, but she flung herself into a chair and, burying her face in her arms, burst into a storm of weeping.

As the sound of Tony's car breaknecking down the lane into the main road came to them, Lizzie pushed open the kitchen door, her eyes blinking with sleep, as she exclaimed, 'What on earth's the matter?'

'You'll know soon enough,' said Mike. 'But I think we'd all better have a strong cup of tea first.' On this, he lifted up the kettle from the hob and went into the scullery. And Lizzie, bending over Mary Ann, said, 'Stop it, stop that crying and tell me what's the matter now, and at this time in the morning. What is it?'

'Tony ... Tony's lea ... ving. He's going to marry Mrs. Schofield.'

Lizzie straightened her back. Her mouth was open and her gaze directed to where Mike was coming in from the scullery, but she could only stare at him, she could not speak.

CHAPTER EIGHT

The Typing School term had ended and Mary Ann had received a diploma for her speed at typing and a certificate for her shorthand. Moreover, she had written her first short story, but she knew that no magazine would print it, because it was much too sad, and too long. Also she realized, from what she had read about short-story writing, that it lacked two main essentials: a plot and a twist. Her story was just about people and the sad things they did. She could not write about the reverse side of life, for at the moment she could not see it.

There had been no word at all from Corny since Mr. Lord had come back. Mrs. McBride would undoubtedly have heard from him. But in spite of her promise to go and visit his grannie, Mary Ann had not been near Burton Street for some weeks. Mrs. McBride, she knew, would have been kind. She would likely have laughed the whole thing off, and the louder she laughed the more awful, Mary Ann knew, would have been. She couldn't risk it. Nor had Lizzie been near her old friend, but she had sent a parcel now and again and had received a card in Fanny's almost illegible handwriting to say, thank you. Neither of the women mentioned Corny . . . or Mary Ann.

So many things were adding to the sadness of life for Mary Ann at the present moment. Her mother, for instance. Her mother had taken the news of Tony much better than she had expected. At least, that was, at the time, that early morning in the kitchen. But as the days went on there seemed to settle on her the lassitude of defeat, and this quietness spoke of her disappointment louder than any words. Mary Ann thought that if it hadn't been for Sarah's presence in the house, which strangely enough had a brightening effect on them all, the place would have been more dismal than a cemetery.

If Mary Ann could have measured her own feelings, she would have found that her sadness, which was balanced between Corny and Mr. Lord, tipped not a little towards Mr. Lord. Although the shindy on that particular early morning had not caused him to have a heart attack, it seemed to have brought him up-to-date with his age, for suddenly he was a very old man. The vitality that had suggested youthful vigour was gone. So much so, that he had been into town only twice during the last month. As Mike had said macabrely, 'The house was like an open grave, with him lying in it just waiting to be covered up.'

Mary Ann left the warmth of the kitchen and the Christmas smell. She left Sarah sitting in her wheel-chair close up to the table, happily helping Lizzie with the Christmas cooking. Getting her hand in, as she laughingly said, for when she would have to do it herself. Sarah had become very close to Lizzie during these past few weeks and this had aroused just a tiny bit of jealousy in Mary Ann, although she saw that the urge to be close came from Sarah. Lizzie made no effusive return of affection, but Mary Ann knew that her mother was pleased with Sarah's gratitude; moreover, she liked Sarah. With the wisdom that was an integral part of her, Mary Ann realized, despite her own feelings, that this state of affairs was really all to the good, because Sarah was going to need her mother in the future, more than she herself would.

She pulled the coat collar around her ears as she went up the hill towards the house. It would snow before the morning, she could feel it. Like most northerners, she could smell snow coming.

Her breath was rising before her face in clouds when she entered Ben's kitchen. Ben was setting the tea-tray with old-fashioned silver that was polished to reflection standard. Mary Ann smiled at him as she took off her coat, saying, 'There'll be snow before morning.'

'We don't want that.'

Mary Ann looked towards the Aga cooker and said, 'Is the tea made? I'll take it in.'

'You'll do no such thing.' Ben hadn't even looked at her.

He was going about his duties as if she wasn't there. But that didn't effect her, for she knew he was always glad when she came up. One day lately she hadn't paid her usual visit and he had trudged all the way down the hill to find out why. He hadn't seemed satisfied that having a tooth out was sufficient reason for her not coming up to see his master. Ben, too, seemed to have aged in the past few weeks. He had always appeared to Mary Ann as a very old man, half as old again as Mr. Lord, but now the word ancient was more appropriate to him. She said impetuously, 'Don't be silly. I'll carry it in.'

'When I'm not able to carry the tea-tray in, then you can do so with pleasure. And I won't mind, for I won't be here.'

She gave in and said, 'How is he?'

'Just the same. Very cold. I doubt if that coal will see us over the holidays. We should have had another ton in.'

'Oh, there's plenty of wood down in the shed. I'll get Len to bring some up.'

She tapped on the drawing-room door and without waiting for an answer went into the room. In contrast to the outside atmosphere the room was stifling. There, before the fire, almost lost in the huge armchair, sat Mr. Lord. He turned his face towards her as she came across the room, but did not speak. She sat down in the chair at the other side of the fireplace. She did not say 'How are you?' or 'We'll have snow by the morning,' but she sighed and leant back in the depth of the chair. Then after a few moments she said, 'I've just finished a short story.'

He nodded his head at her. 'What about?' His voice was just a mumble.

'Oh, I don't know. . . .'

For a moment he seemed to come out of his cocoon, and a tiny spark of the old irritability was visible as he said, 'Don't say such silly things. You say you have written a story, so you are bound to know what it is about.'

She said, 'Well, I meant to say that it wasn't the right way to write a short story, there are too many people in it doing too many things.'

He said now with a show of interest that caused her to move in the chair, 'You must bring it and read it to me.'

'Oh, I couldn't do that.'

'Why? . . . Is it about me?'

'No. Oh, no.' Her denial was too emphatic, and he lifted his hand wearily as if to check any further protest. Now leaning his head back against the wing of the chair and closing his eyes he said, 'What would you like for Christmas?'

What would she like! She knew what she would like. He had taken from her the person she had liked best in the world, apart from her da, and he could give him back to her. For it was in his power to bring Corny tearing across the Atlantic. But she wouldn't want Corny that way, she wouldn't want Corny as a gift from Mr. Lord. She didn't want anyone who hadn't a mind of his own. She was going to answer him, 'I don't know,' when Ben entered the room following a tap of the door. But he was not carrying a tea-tray. He came right up to the side of his master's chair and, bending his already stooped back further down, he said gently, 'There's someone to see you, sir.'

'Who is it?' Mr. Lord had not opened his eyes.

'It's a lady, sir.'

'A lady! Which lady? What's her name?'

'She did not give me her name, sir.' This had been quite correct, there was no need for the visitor to give Ben her name. If he hadn't already known it, he would have surely guessed it.

Mr. Lord now opened his eyes, and his wrinkled lips flickered as he said, 'I don't have to tell you that I'm not seeing anyone, lady or gentlemen. Why have you . . .?'

There was a movement in the room, and as Mary Ann brought her head from the cover of the wing, she almost gasped to see Mrs. Schofield standing well inside the drawing-room. With a wriggle and a lift, she was on her feet, apprehension showing in every part of her.

Mr. Lord had his eyes on Mary Ann, and now he slowly moved his body in the chair, bringing it round so that he was looking squarely at Ben. Then his eyes, flicking to the side, came to rest on Mrs. Schofield, where they stayed a moment before returning to Ben. His voice was louder than Mary Ann had heard it for a long time when he said, 'I have no desire to see this lady, Ben. Kindly show her out.'

'I know you don't want to see me, Mr. Lord, but I must see you.' Mrs. Schofield's voice was low but her words came slow and distinct.

'You heard what I said, Ben.'

Ben turned away, but he did not go to the door and hold it open for Mrs. Schofield. He passed her and went out and closed the door after him, and the action brought a flow of blood to Mr. Lord's deathly complexion.

Mary Ann now brought a chair towards Mrs. Schofield, and Mrs. Schofield looked at her, and thanked her, as if she had brought her some precious gift.

'I do not wish you to sit down, madam.' Mr. Lord was not looking at Mrs. Schofield but directly ahead, and now Mary Ann, coming to the side of the chair, surprised even herself, with not only her tone, but her words as she said, 'Don't be so silly.'

Mr. Lord's Adam's apple moved up into the hollow under his chin, stayed there for a second, then slid down to the deeper hollow at the base of his neck.

Mary Ann said, 'I'm going now. . . . Listen to her . . . listen to Mrs. Schofield. There can be no harm in listening.'

'Sit down.'

'But I'm—'

'I said sit down.'

Mary Ann, turning from the chair, sent an apologetic glance towards Mrs. Schofield, then sat down.

After a moment of an uneasy silence she looked towards the older woman, and her first thought was, 'By, she's beautiful!' and then, 'She's not old.'

Mrs. Schofield was staring at the averted profile of the old man, and her lip was trembling, just the slightest as she began to speak.

'I – I haven't come to plead my cause. I am not going to marry your grandson, Mr. Lord.'

Mary Ann's eyebrows sprang upwards, drawing the contours of her face with them. She transferred her wide gaze to Mr. Lord, but his expression had not altered in the slightest.

'I – I intended to marry him when my divorce was made absolute, but since he left you I have realized that should I marry him I would have to combat you for the remainder of my life.'

Now there was a movement in the old man's face. For a moment Mary Ann felt he was going to turn his glance on Mrs. Schofield and it would have been one of inquiry. But when his nostrils stopped twitching he remained immobile.

'My married history will, I am sure, be of no concern to you, but I have been combating forces, seen and unseen, for the past seventeen years. And I am tired, Mr. Lord, very tired. I am tired of putting on a front. I have acquired a deep feeling for Tony, but it isn't strong enough to enable me to take up my life with him, knowing that you will be always there in the background of his mind, and whether he would believe it or not, he would be blaming me for having separated him from you. I have started by telling you this, but it isn't the only reason for my visit. Nor is it, I think, the real reason, for I didn't come with any hope that you would relent and give us your blessing. I came ... I came because Tony has had an offer from Brent and Hapwood. Since they heard about his break with you they have been after him. They have even offered him a place on the board, so badly do they want him.'

Even before Mrs. Schofield had finished speaking, Mr. Lord's body had turned towards her. Slowly, as if on an oiled pivot, he brought himself round to face her. And then he spoke. 'Hapwood,' he said under his breath. 'Hapwood? Why do you think they want him? Do you know why they want him? ... They want him because they imagine I will relent and leave him everything. There is nobody else I can leave the yard to, is there? And so I will relent ... Old Lord wouldn't leave his money to a Dogs' Home or Spastic Children. No of course he wouldn't. He's only got one kin and he's too fond of him not to relent. That's the idea, isn't it? And when I'm gone – which won't be long they hope – they will be able to amalgamate Lord's yard with their fiddling, little-finger-in-every-pie industry. Well, you can tell him and them that I have no intention whatever of relenting. So if they are going to employ him it better be for his work alone.'

There was a pause before Mrs. Schofield said, 'It may be difficult for you to believe, Mr. Lord, but I am convinced that Tony does not want your money. But he must live, he must work. He doesn't want to go to Brents, he – he wants to come back to you.'

Her voice had sunk to a whisper and Mr. Lord continued to stare at her for a long moment before saying, 'Then why, madam, may I ask, had he to send you as his advocate?'

'He didn't send me. He doesn't know I'm here. Nor would he admit to me that he wanted to come back. But I happen to know him.'

'Your acquaintance has ripened in a very short time.'

'I think you can live with some people for twenty years and know nothing at all about them. Well, there it is, Mr. Lord, if I drop out of his life will you have him back? Make – make the first gesture.'

'Make the first gesture!' Mr. Lord's eyes looked like small pale-blue beads. 'No, madam, I will make no gestures whatever. I didn't bring about this state of affairs, it was he who did that. Whatever gestures are to take place they must come from him. If he is sorry for deceiving me, and is man enough to say so, then I hope I will be man enough to listen.'

On this pompous statement Mary Ann closed her eyes. Tony was too much of his grandfather ever to admit openly that he was in the wrong. She could not envisage him coming to this house and saying, 'I am sorry, please forgive me.' But it was not so much Tony she was concerned about at the moment, it was Mrs. Schofield. She wanted to cry for Mrs. Schofield. With the impetuousness of her emotional make-up she wanted to fly the few steps to her and comfort her, to put her arms around her, and bring her head down to rest on her shoulder. She felt that if anyone needed comfort at this moment it was Mrs. Schofield. She was sitting there, looking so humble, sad, sweet and painfully humble. If she went to her she knew she would say, 'Oh, don't look like that, he won't thank you for it. He knows nothing of humility, you've got to stand up to him.'

In the next moment Mr. Lord brought her attention away from Mrs. Schofield, and, listening to him, it seemed that he had regained a spark of his old self, for picking up a point that

154

Mrs. Schofield had made earlier he said, 'You decided before you came here that you weren't going to marry my grandson?'

'Yes. Yes, I came to that decision.'

'Because you thought his conscience would be an irritant to you?'

'If you like to put it like that.' Her voice was so low her words were scarcely audible.

'Taking the supposition that he might some day return, what then?'

'I'll give you my word, I won't marry him.'

Mary Ann was sitting right on the edge of the chair. With intent concentration she was watching Mr. Lord. She could almost see his mind at work. Tony back in the fold, Mrs. Schofield's promise to which she would hold, making the way clear – Tony would be in the market for herself again. 'No. No.' The protest was so loud in her head that it burst from her mouth, startling both Mr. Lord and Mrs. Schofield. But it was to the old man that she addressed herself, and without any finesse. 'I'll never marry Tony. Don't think that if he were to come back things would go as you want, because if there had never been Corny I wouldn't have married Tony, because I don't like him enough to marry him. Nor he me. He never wanted to marry me, so don't get that into your head.'

'Mary Ann.'

Definitely it was the tone of the old Mr. Lord, the Mr. Lord who would brook little or no interference. But for the moment she was past caring. She was standing up now and their heads were on a level. She had regained her breath and her next words caused him to close his eyes, for she was speaking in the idiom that was natural to her, and claimed no connection with her convent education. 'Now look here, an' I'm tellin' you, if Tony comes back an' he doesn't marry Mrs. Schofield, then I'll leave home. I can, you know ... if I made up me mind. If there's a good enough reason me ma or da wouldn't stop me, I know that. Not if I went to live with Mrs. McBride, an' that's where I would go, an' ...'

'Be quiet!' Mr. Lord still had his eyes closed, and he repeated in what was nearly a growl, 'Be quiet!'

Mary Ann became quiet. The room became quiet. There

was no sound, not even of hissing from the fire, until a knock came on the door and, following it, Ben entered, pushing a trolley noiselessly over the thick carpet. As Mary Ann turned towards him she knew that he had been standing outside the door listening, and must have felt that this was the strategical point at which to make his entry.

Mr. Lord looked towards Ben and the moving trolley, but he made no comment. Slowly he turned his body away from both Mary Ann and Mrs. Schofield, and sinking back into the big chair he directed his gaze towards the fire.

Ben now moved the trolley close to the side of Mrs. Schofield's chair, and his action, and words, startled not only her, but Mary Ann, so much so that she waited for Mr. Lord's thunderous countenance to be turned on his servant and to hear his voice blasting him out of the room. For Ben said, 'Would you care to pour out, madam?'

Ben's voice was not low, nor was it loud. It was just clear enough to make sure that his master heard it, and in hearing, would know his servant's opinion on this delicate matter.

And Ben's opinion, Mary Ann knew, was conveyed to Mr. Lord as clearly as if he had shouted 'I'm for her.' And not only that, Mary Ann saw that Ben's deferential attitude, as he arranged cups to Mrs. Schofield's hand, also said clearly that she was a woman he wouldn't mind having about the house. Mrs. Schofield might not be able to read this from the old man's attentiveness but she could, and, what was more, Mr. Lord could.

When the door had closed on Ben, Mrs. Schofield looked appealingly at Mary Ann, then flicked her eyes towards the figure in the big wing chair. All Mary Ann did was to nod. It was an encouraging nod which said, Get on with it.

The cups rattled slightly as Mrs. Schofield poured out the tea. Mary Ann took Mr. Lord's cup, putting in the required amount of sugar, before placing it on the little table to the side of him.

It could not be said that any one of them enjoyed the tea, and no one partook of the hot buttered scones.

Mrs. Schofield had scarcely finished her tea before she gathered her gloves and bag towards her and, standing up abruptly, said, 'Good-bye, Mr. Lord.'

It was evident to Mary Ann that her quick departure had nonplussed him, for she saw his lower jaw working agitatedly. But he did not answer Mrs. Schofield until he heard the door open, and then moving only his head, he said, 'Madam.'

'Yes?' She had the door in her hand and she turned and looked at him.

'Thank you for coming.'

Mrs. Schofield made no answer to this, she merely inclined her head just the slightest, then went out and closed the door softly behind her.

Mary Ann could not see the door because the tears were full in her eyes. She could not even see Mr. Lord, but she spoke to him, saying quietly, 'She's nice. Tony will never get anyone nicer than her. You're being very wrong in stopping them.'

'I am not stopping them.'

'You can say that, but you know you are. She'll make Tony come back, she'll promise him this, that, and the other, so that he'll come back. As soon as he does, she'll go off where he can't find her.'

The tears cleared from her blinking eyes for a second as his voice came to her with the old cutting quality, saying, 'I would keep your romantic fiction for the books you intend to write.' For a moment she could have laughed, but only for a moment.

He said, now, 'Stop crying and come here.'

She went to him and stood by the arm of his chair, and his thin, mottled-skinned, bony fingers touched hers lightly as he said, 'Were you telling me the truth when you said that you didn't care enough for Tony to marry him?'

'Yes, the absolute truth. Nothing would make me marry Tony. You sent Corny away because you thought if I didn't see him, I would turn to Tony, didn't you?' She didn't wait for an answer but went on, 'You see, you cannot make people like people ... or love people, or turn liking into love. Tony and I ... well, we like each other, but that's all, we'd never be able to love each other. But he loves Mrs. Schofield, and if you don't let him have her, he'll likely marry somebody eventually who's entirely opposite to him and who'll drive him round the bend.' She just restrained herself from adding, 'Like you were when you married somebody who didn't suit you.'

'Mary Ann.' His voice cut in on her.

'Yes?'

'I'm very tired.' He withdrew his hand from hers and slumped back into the chair. Then looking at her, he said, 'Would you like to tell Ben I want him?'

This was dismissal, and she nodded at him. Then bending forward she laid her lips against the blue cheek. When she straightened up his eyes were closed again, and she put her fingers gently on to his brow and lifted to the side a wisp of thin white hair, saying, 'You'll sleep better tonight. I'll be over first thing in the morning.'

When she reached the hall Ben was waiting, and she said to him, 'He's tired, Ben.'

'I guess he would be.' He moved past her towards the drawing-room door, then turning his bent shoulders round towards her, and beckoning her with a finger as bony as his master's, he whispered, 'Here, a minute.' And when she came to his side his head nodded with each word, as he muttered, 'If you see Master Tony tell him Ben says he liked madam.' And then he gave her the reason for his swift and open championing of Mrs. Schofield. 'There's no telling, I might go before he does, and what then?'

'Oh, Ben! You're going to live a long time yet.' She smiled at him. 'But I'll tell him what you said, Ben. I know it will please him.'

But as she went out of the house she thought dully, 'How can I? I don't even know where he is, or even where Mrs. Schofield is staying.' And as she went down the hill she chided herself for her lack of inquisitiveness in this particular case by saying, 'You are a mutt. Why didn't you go after her and ask her?'

CHAPTER NINE

EARLY in the morning of Christmas Eve Mary Ann brought her mother to a dead stop as she was crossing the kitchen. She said to her, 'Ma, what am I going to do with me life?'

'What?' Lizzie had heard what her daughter had said. But this was Christmas Eve, and a mountain of work staring her in the face. It was no time to discuss life, particularly Mary Ann's life.

Mary Ann, aware that her mother had heard her remark, went on, 'I'll never be able to write, not to make anything of it. Everything I do reads like rubbish, and I don't want to go into an office . . . not stuck indoors all day.'

'Look,' said Lizzie slowly, 'it's Christmas, and me up to my eyes.'

'Well, I don't feel it's Christmas,' said Mary Ann bluntly.

'You mightn't,' said Lizzie. 'It may surprise you that I don't feel it's Christmas either. But there are other people to consider; and when you are grumbling about your future life just remember you've still got the use of your legs.'

'Oh, Ma, that isn't fair.'

Lizzie, coming towards her daughter, now said softly, 'Look, Mary Ann, you've got to snap out of this; what can't be cured must be endured.'

'It isn't only me, Ma.' Mary Ann was looking at her feet. 'It's everybody. Nobody seems right.'

'That's life, and you'll find you've got to accept it. You never used to go on like this. What's really the matter with you?'

Mary Ann lifted her head and stared back at her mother, until Lizzie turned away sharply, saying, 'Well, I've just got no time to bother with you and your fads.' But as she neared the hall door she looked over her shoulder, and said quietly and patiently, 'Why don't you go down and see Mrs. McBride. We can't get at the decorating until after tea, and Sarah is going to help with the last bit of baking this afternoon.'

'I'm not going to Mrs. McBride's.'

'Very well.' Lizzie closed her eyes and lowered her head in a deep abeyance, and the irritation was back in her voice as she said, 'Do what you want to, only don't go round with a face like that, because when you're like that, he's not far behind.'

Mary Ann looked at the closed door. It was true what her mother said. Her da too wasn't particularly joyful these days. Although he didn't say so, she felt that he was concerned about Mr. Lord, and not only him, but Tony. He had parted in anger from Tony, and her da wasn't the one to hold his anger. But he had been unable to do anything about it, because from the morning Tony left the house no one had seen or heard of him since.

With what she felt was righteous indignation, Mary Ann asked herself now how her mother expected her to go about grinning from ear to ear when everybody was at sixes and sevens. And anyway, if the rest of the family were falling on each other's necks, she would still feel the same. She had not had the scribe of a pen from Corny, and threaded through her longing, and hurt, was a strong feeling of bitterness against him. He could have written her, couldn't he, and told her he wasn't coming back, not left it to those pictures, which he knew Mr. Lord would show her. It was a cowardly way out, and she had no use for cowards of any sort. . . . But oh! oh, she wished. . . .

She heard the telephone ringing in the hall and her mother answering it. Then the kitchen door opened and Lizzie, her tone lowered and slightly puzzled, said, 'It's Ben, he says Mr. Lord's asking for you. . . . But you've just come down, haven't you?'

'Asking for me? Yes, Ma. I've just come down because he wasn't awake. Ben said he was dozing. He had been on the prowl about the house half the night again.'

'Well, he wants you, so you'd better go right away.'

'Did he say he was bad or anything?'

'No. No, he didn't sound worried. He just said that Mr. Lord wanted you.' Lizzie smiled now. 'Very likely he's going to give you your Christmas box.'

Mary Ann raised her eyebrows and widened her eyes as she shook her head. It was as if she had never heard of Christmas boxes. And truth to tell, she was not interested in Christmas boxes, not the ordinary ones anyway. She pulled on her coat and went out, and she didn't slide on the thin patches of ice covering the flagstones, along the path, nor yet scrape the sprinkling of frosted snow into a ball and pelt it into the air. The joy of breathing, of being alive, had slipped its hold; she felt very old. And she had once imagined that nothing could happen to her to make her want to die. How wrong could you get?

Ben said, 'Go up. He's still in bed.'

'Is he all right?'

'No different from what he was yesterday, or the day before, as I can see.'

She mounted the thick carpeted stairs, crossed the wide landing, and tapped on Mr. Lord's bedroom door, and was immediately bidden to enter. He was sitting, as she had so often seen him before, propped up in bed, his white night-shirt buttoned up to his chin, his face, like a blue-pencilled etching, above it.

She said immediately, 'Are you all right?'

'Yes. Yes, I'm all right. Sit down.'

'Did you have a good night?'

'I have had some sleep.'

'I think we'll have more snow, it's enough to freeze you.'

'We won't waste words talking about the weather. You're wondering why I sent for you.'

'Yes, I am.' She could be as blunt as himself.

'I'm very tired, Mary Ann.'

Although she was looking at him she jerked her body now more squarely to him. 'You're not feeling ... bad, or anything?'

'I'm no worse, or no better, than usual. I've just said that I am very tired. Tired of fighting, tired of wanting, tired of desiring, tired of hoping. I am very tired of life, Mary Ann.'

'Oh.' It was a small sound and again it came, 'Oh.' She knew how he felt but she said, 'Don't say that.' She reached out and grasped his hand between her own, and he looked down at them, and placing the long thin fingers of his right hand on top of hers he actually smiled as he asked, 'Are you happy, Mary Ann?'

She stared into the pale-blue eyes for a moment before saying, 'Not very.'

'I have been rather cruel to you. What I did, I did with the best intention in the world.... Selfish men always use that phrase, and I can't think of a better one to replace it. . . . Yes, I have been cruel to you.' His fingers tapped hers. 'And now I doubt whether I shall be able to rectify my mistake. You know what I mean?'

She knew what he meant. He had sent Corny to America. He had had him housed with a charming family, and the charming family had a daughter. Oh, she knew what he meant. But she said now soothingly, 'It's all right, it's all right. Don't worry.'

His fingers patted her hand again and he lay back on his pillows and closed his eyes, and after a space he said, 'You have a big heart, Mary Ann. It was bigger than your body when you were a child. It hasn't grown any less, that is why I love you.'

She nipped at her lip and blinked her eyes but kept looking at him. Never before had he said outright that he loved her. She had the desire to drop her head on to his knees, but she refrained because he wasn't finished, there was something more he wanted to say. And after a short space, during which he kept moistening his lips, he said it.

'I want to see my grandson, Mary Ann. I have waited for him coming, forgetting that he is so much a part of me he won't give in. If there had been only himself to consider perhaps he might have come back . . . But there . . . there . . . Will you tell him, Mary Ann?'

'Yes, oh yes.' The words had to leap over the lump wedging her gullet, and now she dared to say, 'And Mrs. Schofield?'

'With or without her.'

The words were so low she could scarcely catch them, but

she squeezed his hand tightly, and getting immediately to her feet she bent towards him, saying, 'I'll bring him.'

He did not open his eyes. She felt he dare not. He was not Mr. Lord at this moment, not THE MR. LORD. He was just an old man, a lonely old man, and he was weak as old men are weak.

She managed to pause in her rush through the kitchen and cry to Ben, 'He wants me to get Tony.'

'Thanks be to God.'

'Yes ... yes, thanks be to God.' She was out of the door and running down the hill – she actually slid on a stretch of ice – and her running did not stop until she came to the cowshed and heard Mike's voice calling to Michael at the far end. And then she herself called, 'Da! Da!'

'What is it?' Mike turned about and, seeing her bright face, added, 'Hello, what's happened this time?'

'He ... he wants to see Tony. He told me to fetch him ... and Mrs. Schofield ... and Mrs. Schofield, Da.'

'No!'

'Yes, yes, it's a fact. He said, Da' – she shook her head – 'he said he was tired.'

'Poor old boy.'

'What's this?' Michael came up and joined them, and Mary Ann said, 'He wants to see Tony. He wants me to go and fetch him. And Mrs. Schofield an' all.'

'No kidding?'

'No kidding, that's what he said.'

'Well, what's holding you?'

Mary Ann didn't move, the smile slid from her face. She looked from Mike to Michael then back to Mike again. Her first finger and thumb were jointly tapping at her teeth as she exclaimed on a high note, 'But, Da, where will I look? I've no idea where he is.'

'You've hit something now.' Mike nodded his head at her.

'You could try phoning places, that would be a start,' Michael said. 'Try some of the yards first, he's bound to have a job of some sort.'

'Can I use the office phone, Da?'

'Go ahead.'

Mike pushed her, and she ran out of the byre.

It could be a Dickens Christmas Eve. She did not like to think of Mr. Lord as a Scrooge, but part of her mind was commenting, 'It's funny what Christmas does to people.'

By five o'clock Mary Ann had not only made thirteen phone calls, she had been into Newcastle as well. Michael had been going in to pick up some goods from the station, and he had run her out to Mrs. Schofield's old home, only to find it completely empty. So empty that it looked as if it hadn't been inhabited for years. They even visited Mr. Lord's yard, but the chief clerk in the office could give them no help. He hadn't seen Mr. Brown for weeks, but he said that Mr. Connelly might be able to help them. Mr. Connelly was works manager, and they went out to his house, but without success. . . .

And now Mary Ann was tired, and Lizzie said to her, 'Sit down there and get your tea, you're not going out again unless you have something to eat. The next thing I know I'll have you in bed.'

It was Sarah who said, 'Have you thought of going to Father Owen?'

'Father Owen?' Mike screwed up his face. 'It isn't likely that Tony would go to the priest; he's not a Catholic, you know, Sarah.'

'I know that, but you did say that Mr. Lord and Father Owen used to be friends in their young days. It was just a thought, and Mary Ann seems to have been every place else.'

Mary Ann, jumping at this pleasant possibility, gulped at her tea and said, 'It's an idea, Sarah, there are very few people around that Father Owen doesn't know.'

'That might be in Jarrow and thereabouts' – Lizzie moved her head slowly – 'but don't forget Tony is more likely to be living in Newcastle.' She did not add 'because Mrs. Schofield will be there'.

'And don't you think Father Owen would have said something when he was up to see Mr. Lord last week?' Lizzie again was using her reason.

'No, Liz. I don't think he would have,' Mike put in. 'He knew how the old boy felt, and he wasn't likely to talk about Tony, not even to mention his name. He knew that one thing might lead to another, and before you could say Jack Robinson something would be said that would be better unsaid. For he's not without his share of temper, is Father Owen, and whatever some people might imagine to be the reverse, priests are not infallible.'

On this remark Lizzie's expression became prim, and she was just about to make some sharp comment when Mary Ann startled her by jumping up from the table, saying, 'Well, look, I'm going to see him anyway.'

'Sit down and have your tea first.'

'Oh, Ma, the time's getting on and he's been waiting all day. . . . Will you run me in, Michael?'

'Okay.'

'It will be a wild-goose chase, if you ask me.' Lizzie looked around at the tea – hardly anything had been touched – and Mike, following her gaze, leant towards her and, patting her on the shoulder, said, 'Don't worry, it'll all have disappeared afore the night's out. . . . Go on.' He turned towards Mary Ann and Michael, and pushed at them with his hand, saying, 'Get yourselves away. And don't come back without him.'

As Mary Ann ran to the hall once again to scramble into her coat, Lizzie exclaimed on an indignant sigh, 'I get sick to death of this family and the things they get up to . . . always something happening, Christmas Eve and everybody going mad.'

'You want the old boy to go on living, don't you? Or do you?'

'Mike! The things you say.'

'Well then, hold your whisht.'

Michael with head reverently bowed, spoke out of the corner of his mouth, saying, 'We'll be here all night, there's half Jarrow waiting to go in.'

Mary Ann turned her head slightly on her clasped hands and answered in a whisper, 'I'll go to confession and ask him there.'

Michael made no comment on this. Trust her to do something that other people wouldn't even dream about. Using the corner of his mouth again, he said, 'You'll be a good hour, I'll slip home and come in again.'

She made a slight motion of assent with her head, and when Michael left her side she too rose, and crossing over from the aisle that fronted the altar of the Holy Family, she went and joined the sombre throng waiting to go into Confession.

Father Owen sat in the candlelit gloom of his section of the confessional and waited. Mrs. Weir had bad feet, it always took her a long time to shuffle out of the box, and once outside she always meticulously closed the door after her. That it would be pulled open almost instantly seemingly did not occur to her, she must finish the job properly. So she obstructed the next penitent with her overflowing hips. As Father Owen listened to her fumbling with the door, he wondered, rather wearily, how many more were out there. He would like a little quiet and rest before midnight mass, and he was feeling cold. Either that boiler chimney was blocked up or Jimmy Snell had gone off again without banking down properly. It was either one or the other. Or perhaps it wasn't, it was more likely the system. He had felt the church cold more than once lately, and it wasn't all due to his old bones. He rested his head on the palm of his hand and wondered if in the beginning of the year he could encourage somebody to start off a subscription jaunt to get a new water system in. If only Father Bailey would come off his high horse about tombola, the thing would be as good as done. But there, he had a very pious bee in his bonnet. If only the bee didn't split hairs. What was the difference in tombola and running raffles at every function he could.... Oh there, what was the use. Anyway, sooner or later there would be a burst, and if it took place in the pipes under the grid the consequences could be both disastrous and amusing. He had an irreverent picture of one of a number of his more tiresome parishioners being sent heavenwards on a spurting jet of hot water.

'Please, Father, give me your blessing for I have sinned. It is three days since my last confession.'

In the name of God it was Mary Ann. Well! well! well! It was some time since she had been to him for confession. She took herself to Newcastle or Gateshead more often than not now, because they were nearer. Well! well! Christmas Eve and Mary Ann. He felt a spark of gaiety ascending up his cold body, but this was followed immediately by what could only be described as a long question mark which covered him from head to toe, and the question mark said, 'What brought her in? Something's wrong.' Three days since her last confession and here she was again! She was after something . . . oh, he knew Mary Ann.

'Is that you, Mary Ann?'

'Yes, Father.' It was a haloed whisper.

'How are you?'

'I'm not too bad, Father.'

Not too bad. He knew it, he knew there was something wrong. 'How's your da?'

'Oh, he's fine, Father.'

Well, that was the biggest obstacle out of the way. It was usually her da who brought her helter-skelter to the church. At least in the past it was Mike who could have been given the credit for her ardent piety. 'And your mother?'

'She's very well, Father.'

That disposed of the two main factors in her life. Michael and Sarah were all right, at least they were up to a few days ago when he had visited the farm. He hadn't seen Mary Ann on that occasion, in fact, he hadn't seen her for quite this long while. Was it her grannie? He said now, 'Don't tell me, Mary Ann, that you've come to confess to murdering your grannie.' Aw, it was Christmas Eve and the Good Lord would forgive him for a joke even in the confessional.

On her side of the box Mary Ann suppressed a giggle. And her lips were quite near the wire mesh as she whispered, 'No, Father, but it's very likely that some day I will.'

There was many a true word spoken in jest. He metaphorically crossed himself and said, 'Go on, my child. I will hear your confession.'

And Mary Ann had enough sins on her mind to make a confession, even though her conscience had been cleared three days previously. She laid aside her main reason for coming to see Father Owen and said, 'My heart is full of bitterness, Father, against someone, and I don't want it to be like that – I want to forgive. And there is Sarah, Father. There are times when I give way to jealousy. I like Sarah, Father, I like her very much. But my mother has become very fond of her and I get jealous. It is wrong of me but I can't help it. It would be different if—' She stopped, she couldn't go on and say, 'If I had anyone of my own.' Because she had someone of her own. Hadn't she her da? But that wasn't what she meant.

'Go on, my child.'

'I miss my morning prayers very often, Father, and I have started ...' There followed another long pause, and the priest prompted her, saying, 'Yes? yes?' 'I have started to criticize my religion, Father.'

There was silence behind the grid. She'd had no intention in the world of confessing that sin, it had just slipped out. And she didn't really criticize, she only tried to work things out in her own mind.

On the other side of the grid Father Owen suddenly knew he was an old man. He had known Mary Ann since she had first toddled up to the side altar and made her bargains with the Holy Family, and now she had reached the age when she was thinking for herself, and when you started thinking for yourself you couldn't help but criticize. It was a phase of life. He said to her gently, 'You are growing up, Mary Ann. Don't worry. Your religion will bear your criticism. A thing that cannot bear criticism is built on sand and will soon be washed away by the tongues of men. Come and have a talk with me sometime and tell me what you think. We'll have a long crack on the subject, eh?'

Oh, he was lovely was Father Owen, he was always lovely. He made things so easy.

'Make a good act of contrition.'

'Oh, my God, I am very sorry that I have sinned against thee, because thou art so good, and by the help of thy Holy Grace, I will not sin again.'

He said the absolution.

'Amen.'

'A happy Christmas, Mary Ann.'

'A happy Christmas, Father.'

'Father.' She could, in this moment, have cast off nine or ten years and be hissing her petitions through the grid once more.

'Yes, Mary Ann?'

'Do you remember Tony?'

'Do I rememember Tony? Of course, I remember Tony. Why?'

'Do you know where he is?'

Ah, so that was it. He said, 'No, I don't, Mary Ann. Why? Do you want to find him?'

'Mr. Lord has been asking for him.'

'Oh!' So he had been asking for him. When he saw him the other day the name of Tony was not mentioned between them. He had hoped it would be because he felt that Peter Lord's burden needed lightening if he were to go on living. He was a man without hope. He whispered now, 'I wish I could help you, Mary Ann, but I can't.'

'Thank you, Father.'

'Wait a minute.' Father Owen took his hand away from the side of his face that sheltered it from the penitent, and he brought his fingers over his lips as he thought, Young Lettice Schofield! He had known her father, Brian Trenchard, as a young man, and many were the times that Brian had dined him well. It was hard to think that she, whose life story had been filling the papers of late, was the same young Lettice he had teased when he was a guest in her father's house. He had seen little of her since her marriage, and it had come as shocking news to him the life she had led. For he felt she must have suffered nothing less than refined torture to keep up the façade of respectability. God knew that she was to be pitied, yet it was she who had caused the rift between Peter Lord and his grandson. Unintentionally perhaps, for he could not imagine there being any vice in Lettice. He had run into her quite unexpectedly about three weeks ago and they had talked about this and that without touching on anything personal. But he did remember now that she had mentioned that she was staying with her uncle, and if he remembered rightly Brian Trenchard had only one brother, and his name was Harold. He said now, 'Mrs. Schofield might help you. She was staying with her uncle. His name is Harold Trenchard. Look in the telephone directory and go on from there.'

'Thank you, Father. . . . Oh, thank you, Father.'

'God bless you, my child.'

'Good night, Father.'

'Good night. . . . A minute, Mary Ann. How many do you think are waiting?'

'I should say over twenty Father.'

Father Owen closed his eyes. Over twenty! 'And at Father Bailey's box?'

'About ten, Father.'

Father Owen sighed. 'Thank you. Good night.'

'Good night, Father.'

Self-consciously Mary Ann went down the aisle, past the patient penitents. They would, she thought, be thinking that she hadn't been to confession for a year, she had been in so long.

Kneeling before the crib she said her penance, one Our Father, and three Hail Marys. It was a stock penance of Father Owen's. She didn't know what other people got, but she had never got anything worse than that. Even when she had tried to empty the candle money box behind the altar. She looked at the Holy Family, not the real Holy Family that stood up on the altar, larger than life size, but the little Holy Family staged among the straw with the animals around them. And she prayed for each member of her family, and for Father Owen. And then, still being Mary Ann, she had to ask for something. She said, 'This being Christmas Eve, please help me to find Tony, and I'll—' She just stopped herself from making some outrageous promise in return for their guidance. In the past she had always promised them to stop hating her grannie, or to tell no more lies, or to resist getting one over on her enemy, Sarah Flannagan. This thought coming into her mind made her smile, and, looking up from the small statues towards the group that had been the focal point of her spiritual life, she knew that the power of God was wonderful, for there was in her heart now not the smallest trace of jealousy towards Sarah. In this moment when the sacrament of penance was washing her conscience she could even see the funny side of her grannie. This feeling wouldn't last, she knew it wouldn't, but while it did she thanked God. She did not mention the name of Corny Boyle to them. It would have been too difficult to explain about the part of her that didn't care, and the part of her that cared too much. And then about the part of her that was bitter and full of resentment. Oh, she couldn't go into all that.

And now she went out of the church, and there was Michael waiting in the sloping passage to greet her; as he had done once many years ago. He said, 'Where on earth have you been?'

'You know where I've been.'

'Well, you've taken long enough about it. I've nearly froze waiting for you. What did he say?'

'He doesn't know where Tony is, but he thinks Mrs. Schofield's staying with her uncle. ... I want a telephone directory.'

'Where for?'

'It'll be in Newcastle.'

'Oh, good Lord. We're not going tearing off there now, are we?'

'If there's a Harold Trenchard, we are.' She looked at him and smiled, and then with an unusual gesture she tucked her arm in his.

Mr. Harold Trenchard's name was in the telephone directory. Michael suggested, before dashing off to Newcastle, why not phone and find out if Mr. Trenchard were there. And this she did.

It was a woman's voice who answered the phone, and she said she was Mrs. Trenchard. Mary Ann politely made her inquiries, and the woman at the other end said, 'Who's speaking?'

'My name is Mary Ann Shaughnessy.'

'Oh, Mary Ann Shaughnessy. Oh yes, I've heard of you ... Well, Lettice ... Mrs. Schofield is not with us now.'

'Oh.'

'But I can give you her address.'

'Thank you. Thank you very much.' Mary Ann repeated the address and Michael wrote it down in his pocket book.

And then Mary Ann said, 'Good-bye and thank you.' And she added, 'A Merry Christmas.'

Mary Ann had hardly put down the phone before she started to gabble. 'Look, it's not in Newcastle, it's in Shields. She's in Shields, Sunderland Road!'

'Well, come on, don't stand gaping.' With brotherly courtesy Michael pushed her out of the box, and when she almost slipped on the frost on the pavement he grabbed at her, saying, 'That's it, break your neck. We only want that now.' They were both laughing when they got into the van.

Within a quarter of an hour they had reached Sunderland Road, and after some searching they found the house. There was a plate to the side of the door that held three cards, and the bottom one which said Flat 3 had the name Lettice Trenchard written on it. They rang the bell twice before there was any response, and then a man opened the door. Without waiting to question them he said, 'I thought I heard someone there. Is it the top flat you want, because the bell's out of order? But just go on up.'

'Thank you.' They went past him and up the two flights of stairs. And when they came opposite the door they exchanged glances before Mary Ann tapped gently.

When the door opened there stood Mrs. Schofield, her lips apart with surprise. No one spoke until Mary Ann, after what seemed a long moment, said quietly, 'Hello, Mrs. Schofield.'

Mrs. Schofield, after wetting her lips and looking from one to the other, smiled and said, 'Mary Ann!' Then she half-turned her head over her shoulder and looked behind her, before saying, 'Won't you come in?'

Mary Ann walked slowly past Mrs. Schofield into a tiny hall, and Mrs. Schofield said, 'Will I take your coat?'

'We won't be staying, Mrs. Schofield. We just came to ... to ask you something.'

'Well, you'll sit down for a while. Let me have your coat ... and yours, Michael.'

She took their coats and hung them on the hallstand. Then going towards one of the three doors leading out of the hall, she opened it. And when they entered the room, there, standing on the hearth-rug before a small fireplace, was Tony.

The sight of him was as much a surprise to Mary Ann as her and Michael's arrival had been to Mrs. Schofield. She hadn't really expected to find Tony here. Somehow, she thought Mrs. Schofield would have cut adrift from him in order to make it easier for him to return to Mr. Lord.

Mrs. Schofield must have sensed something of what Mary Ann was thinking, for after she had seated them she looked at her and said, 'You may not believe it but Tony has only been here a short while; a matter of minutes, in fact. I'm being discovered all in a bunch it would seem.'

Tony had not spoken to Mary Ann, and his greeting to Michael had been merely an abrupt nod of the head. Now all his attention was on Mrs. Schofield, and Mary Ann's attention was on him. He did not, she noticed, look his usual spruce self, anything but, in fact – he looked rather ill. Her sympathy aroused, she said now, 'Well, hello, Tony.' And when he turned towards her he gave her a smile as he answered, 'Hello, Mary Ann.' Then looking towards Michael he added hastily, 'How's it going, Michael?'

'Oh, not so bad, Tony. How's it with you?'

'Oh fine. . . .'

'It isn't fine, don't tell lies.' Both Mrs. Schofield's glance and voice were soft as she looked at Tony. Then glancing between Mary Ann and Michael, she said, 'He's been ill, he's had flu. I knew nothing about it.'

'Have you been on your own?' Mary Ann's tone was full of concern as she gazed at him, and now he replied in a slightly mocking tone, 'Yes, entirely, but I don't want you to cry about it.'

'Who's going to cry about it?' Mary Ann's chin jerked up, and on this they all laughed. The tension was broken, and Mary Ann, becoming her natural self, exclaimed as she looked him straight in the eye, 'You're a fool.'

'I wouldn't for the moment dream of contradicting you. Now tell me, what have you come for? What are you after?'

'Well, if you're going to use that tone, I've a good mind not to open my mouth.'

'That'll be the day.'

This retort came almost simultaneously from Tony and Michael, and again there was laughter.

'Take no notice of them, Mary Ann. . . . Come here.' Mrs. Schofield was holding out her hand to Tony. 'Come and sit down.'

As Mary Ann watched Tony, with willing docility do as he was bid, she thought, and not without a slight pang, 'She could do anything with him, anything.'

'Tell us what brought you, Mary Ann.' Mrs. Schofield was now looking at her, and Mary Ann answered her as if Tony was not sitting beside her, saying, 'Mr. Lord wants him back. He asked me to fetch him. . . .'

'On conditions that I—'

Mary Ann, turning sharply on Tony, cut him off with, 'Oh no conditions attached whatever! You don't give me time to finish.' Her voice dropped. 'He's very low and tired . . . and lonely, and he said to tell you to come back, with or without . . .' She turned her eyes from him now to Mrs. Schofield as she ended, 'With or without you. But I do believe he would rather it were with you.'

There followed an embarrassing silence, during which they all seemed to be staring at each other, until Mrs. Schofield whispered, 'Oh, Mary Ann.' Her face began to twitch and she lowered her head and bit hard on her lip.

When Tony's arms went about her and he drew her tightly into his embrace as if quite oblivious of either Michael or herself, Mary Ann experienced embarrassment that brought her to her feet, and she blurted to no one in particular, 'We'd better be getting back. If you like, we can all go together.'

Again Mrs. Schofield said, 'Oh, Mary Ann.' Then pulling herself away from Tony's clasp and looking up through wet eyes, she exclaimed on a broken laugh, 'That's all I seem able to say . . . Oh, Mary Ann. But I must add: Thank you. Thank you, my dear.'

'And me too, Mary Ann. That's all I can say too: Thank you.' Tony was on his feet now looking down on her. 'You were always the one for getting things done, for getting your own way. And from the bottom of my heart I can say at this moment, I'm glad you're made like that. Because – because I want to see him. It's been pretty awful these last few weeks. . . .' When Mary Ann, finding it impossible for once to say anything, remained mute, Tony turned abruptly from her and, looking at Michael, said in a lighter tone, 'How's Mike?'

'Oh, the same as usual, you know.'

'Yes. But I don't suppose he'll be the same with me though. . . . I'll have to do a bit of apologizing in that quarter.'

'Oh, forget it. I'm sure he has, he's not the one to remember rows, he's had too many of them.'

'Well, come on, get your coat on.' Tony had turned to Mrs. Schofield, but now she looked back at him and shook her head, saying, 'No, you go alone. I'll come tomorrow. You can come and fetch me.'

'I'm not going without you.'

'Now don't be silly, Tony.'

'He's right, it's Christmas Eve and we're not going to leave you here.' Mary Ann bounced her head. 'And if you won't come now we'll just sit down and wait until you change your mind, won't we, Michael?'

'We will that.'

Mrs. Schofield looked from one to the other, then she turned swiftly from them and went into the bedroom.

Tony went into the hall and collected their coats, and as he handed Mary Ann hers, he said under his breath, 'I woke up this morning feeling like death and wishing it would come quickly. I was in digs, awful digs, and I thought: Oh, my God, Christmas Eve. . . . But I never dreamt it would turn out like this.' A quiet smile spread over his white features as he ended, 'It wouldn't take much to make me believe that your . . . Holy Family had been at work, Mary Ann.'

'You can laugh.' Her voice was prim. 'But if it hadn't been for Father Owen, we wouldn't be here would we, Michael? So you can say that the Holy Family had a hand in it.'

'I'm not laughing, Mary Ann, far from it. I don't feel like it at this moment. Oh, no, I'm not laughing, not when I've just been handed two good reasons for living. And the Holy Family apart . . . thank you, Mary Ann.'

When Tony put out his hand and gently touched her cheek she had a sudden desire to howl her eyes out there and then, for the excitement was over, the good deed had been accomplished. Tony had Mrs. Schofield, Mr. Lord would have Tony. Sarah had Michael, and her ma had her da. And who was there for her? Nobody. She hated Corny Boyle.

CHAPTER TEN

'WELL!' Mike let out a long-drawn breath that expanded his chest and pressed his ribs against his shirt. 'It's been a night and a half.'

Lizzie, making no pretence to stifle the yawn, said, 'Night? It's day again. It's half-past one on Christmas Morning. Come on, let's get upstairs or I'll sleep until dinner-time tomorrow.' She turned towards Mike who was now standing staring pensively at the two bulging stockings hanging from the brass rail. On Christmas Eve two stockings had always hung in front of the fireplace, no matter where they lived or how little money they had. But this year they were not Mary Ann's and Michael's, they were Mary Ann's and Sarah's, Michael having thankfully relinquished the childish habit kept up by Lizzie.

Mike had his hand in his pocket and his shoulders were hunched, and after looking at him for a moment longer in silence she said softly, 'What is it now?'

'Oh, I was just thinking.' He raised his head and looked across the high mantelpiece which was covered with a galaxy of Christmas cards, then up to the strings looped to the picture rail which were carrying the overflow, and he remarked, 'Everybody happy but her.'

'Now, now. Oh, don't let's start that, not at this time.'

Mike turned slowly towards her, and putting his hand out he softly lifted her chin, and his voice held a deep and gentle note as he said, 'You're the best in the world, Liz, and I know it, but there are times when I think you've got a hard spot in you towards her.'

'Oh, Mike, that isn't right, and it's unfair of you to say it. Just because I don't go around dribbling, it doesn't say that I don't feel for her. I do.'

'Yes, perhaps you do. I'm sorry.' His fingers rubbed against her soft flesh.

Lizzie was very tired. Her eyes began to smart and her voice broke as she said, 'You shouldn't have said that to me, Mike. Not at this time. Bringing up things like that at an hour when we should all be in bed.'

'Well, it was in me mind, and you know me. I said I'm sorry, and I am. But I'd mortgage me life at this minute to see her happy. She's run off her feet all day to put things right for the old man and Tony, and she's as happy about Mrs. Schofield as if she was you. And then the night, at supper, did you see her face when Sarah named the wedding day?' He now slipped his arm around Lizzie's shoulder as he said, 'Our girl is very human, Liz. She's all emotion, all feelings, and she's seventeen and a half and she hasn't got a lad. You know, I feel in two minds about Corny Boyle at this minute. If he was standing afore me now, I don't know whether I'd punch him on the jaw or shake him by the hand. . . . What would you do, Liz?'

Mike had shot the last question at Lizzie, and he felt her start under his hand. And then she said, 'You think I didn't like Corny. It wasn't that at all. Corny was a nice enough lad. Being part of Fanny he was bound to have good in him. I had nothing against Corny, not as a lad. But somehow I wanted somebody different for her, somebody who could give her things. It is understandable, isn't it?' She turned her head and looked up at him.

'Aye, Liz, I suppose it is. Her mother didn't do very well for herself, did she?'

'Aw, Mike.' She dropped her head now against the strong muscles of his neck. 'What do you want me to say?'

'Nothing, nothing.'

'Well, I can tell you this.' Her voice was smothered against him. 'If I had to pick again this minute I would make the same choice.' As his arm pressed her tighter to him she straightened up, saying, 'Come on, we'd better get up, and quietly, or we'll be wakening the house.'

When he released her she did not move away from him, but looking into his weathered, ruggedly handsome face, she said simply, 'I love you, Mike.'

'An' I love you.' Slowly now their heads came together, and the kiss they exchanged was gentle.

'Happy Christmas, Liz.'

'Happy Christmas, Mike.'

Their arms around each other, they went out of the room, Lizzie switching off the light as they went through the door.

It was as they went, still linked together, to mount the stairs, that the unmistakable sound of a motor-bike being pulled up in the road outside the house brought them to a halt.

'That's a motor-bike, and stopping here.' Lizzie was whispering.

Mike's ear was cocked. 'Likely somebody looking for Len and didn't see the cottages.'

'They're not having a do, are they?'

'I didn't think so, not till the New Year.'

Simultaneously, they turned from the foot of the stairs and went into the hall again. And although they were both expecting a knock, they were visibly startled when the rat-tat came on the door.

Mike went forward, leaving Lizzie in the centre of the hall, and when he opened the door the exclamation he let out was high. 'Well, my God!'

Lizzie repeated this phrase to herself when Mike, moving aside, said, 'Look, Liz. Look what the wind's blown in.'

As Corny Boyle stepped slowly into the hall, Lizzie gaped at him with open mouth, and her gaping was caused by a number of reasons, not the least was that here stood a different Corny Boyle from the lad she knew. Here, enveloped in a great coat, his big head actually on a level with Mike's, was a man, not the boy she remembered.

Corny Boyle cast his glance between them as he said quietly, 'I'm sorry I'm so late, but I'm glad I caught you up, I thought I might. I was held up here and there, or I'd have been over sooner.'

'Well! well! well!' Mike was gazing at Corny. He too was surprised at the change he saw in him. It was only a few minutes since he had said that if he were confronted by this lad he wouldn't know whether to shake him by the hand or punch him on the jaw. But he knew now what to do, for his hand went out as he said airily, 'Don't worry your head about the time, the day's young. I'm right glad to see you, Corny. You're a better sight than Santa Claus. . . . Mary Ann!' This last was a bellow up the stairs.

'Mike! You'll have the house awake.' Lizzie's lids were blinking rapidly.

'And why not?'

'MARY ANN! Do you hear? MARY ANN!' His voice was even louder this time.

'Are they all in bed?' Corny looked at Lizzie, and Lizzie, not quite sure of her feeling at this moment, almost answered, 'What do you expect, going on two o'clock in the morning?' But she managed to be gracious and say, 'Well, they haven't been up all that long, but we have Mrs. Schofield with us. You remember Mrs. Schofield?'

Corny's smile was the old wide remembered grin, and he nodded his head as he said, 'I should say I do. Is she staying over Christmas?'

'Yes.' Lizzie paused and then added, 'Yes, she's staying with us over Christmas.' It was evident that Corny knew nothing about Mrs. Schofield's affair. Lizzie still thought of the situation as an affair but Corny disillusioned her the next moment by saying, 'Is Tony with her?'

Lizzie's eyebrows moved just the slightest. 'No, not here, he's up at the house with Mr. Lord.'

'Mary Ann! . . .' Mike was at the beginning of another bellow when Michael appeared at the top of the stairs. He was pulling his dressing-gown on as he exclaimed, 'What is it? What are you bawling for?'

'I'm not bawling for you, anyway. Give a rap on her door or else I'll be up there.'

But there was no need now to give a rap on Mary Ann's door, for even as Mike spoke she came on to the landing, and looking down the stairs, she too asked, 'What is it?'

'What do you think?' Mike had pushed Corny towards the wall out of her line of sight, and his face was one large grin as he looked up at her saying, 'What would you like in your stockin'?'

If Mary Ann hadn't been sure that she had left her da

solid and sober in the kitchen somewhere about an hour ago, she would have sworn he was tight.

Michael had gone down the stairs, and was now standing in the hall under the pressure of Mike's hand, which warned him to make no comment on what his eyes were seeing, and then Mary Ann came within three stairs of the bottom and she looked from her da to Michael standing side by side, then behind them to her mother. Following this her eyes lifted to the side and saw, standing near the wall between the kitchen door and the sitting-room, a man who looked like Corny Boyle. Her fingers went to the top button of her dressing-gown and pulled on it so sharply that she gulped.

'Hello.' The man that looked like Corny Boyle had stepped away from the wall and was speaking to her. She felt slightly dizzy. All the faces rolled together, and before they separated her da's voice came to her saying, 'Well, open your mouth. Here he's come all the way from America on a motor-bike.' Mike laughed at his own joke and went on, 'And you can only stand and stare. Didn't you ask Santa for something in your stockin'? . . . Well . . .'

'Be quiet, Mike.' Lizzie now took the situation in hand. 'Come on into Sarah's room. She's bound to be awake and it's warmer in there.' Lizzie pushed open the door exclaiming, 'Are you awake, Sarah?'

'I'd have to be dead, Mam, not to hear the cafupple.'

'It's Corny.' Lizzie was talking into the room.

'Yes, I've guessed as much.'

During this Michael had moved past his mother into the sitting-room, and Mary Ann had moved down the stairs and was now standing opposite Corny Boyle.

Corny Boyle . . . Corny Boyle. . . . But a different Corny Boyle. This was not the boy she remembered, he was almost a stranger. So much so that she felt she didn't know him.

'Well, this is a nice welcome. What's the matter, have you lost your tongue?'

Mary Ann jerked her head from Corny and looked at her da. She stared at him for a moment before turning towards Corny again. And now she did speak. 'Did Mr. Lord send for you?' she said.

'No, he didn't. Nobody sent for me. I COME on me own.'

The answer had come so quickly it startled her, and for the first time in the last surprise-filled minutes she recognized in this unfamiliar man the boy she knew.

A laugh now came from the sitting-room, and Michael's voice cried, 'They've started.'

At this Corny too laughed and, turning completely away from Mary Ann, said to Mike, 'It's as if I'd never been away, isn't it? Oh, Mr. Shaughnessy, you don't know what it's like, this feeling of being back.'

Mary Ann, still looking at him, but at his back now, was thinking two things. He had come on his own after all. That was one. And the other, that although he looked different, and sounded different, for he didn't talk like he used to, he still called her da Mr. Shaughnessy. As she allowed her da to push her into the sitting-room, she remembered that for years she had tried to make Corny speak differently, with little success. Yet here he had been gone just over a year, and besides looking like anybody else but Corny Boyle, he was speaking like anybody else but Corny Boyle. There was only one explanation ... somebody had worked on him. This thought pulled her round to look at him as he went across to Sarah and took hold of her outstretched hands. Nothing could make him beautiful, nor handsome, yet he looked ... She searched for a word, and might have found it, but Mike's voice cut across her thinking as he yelled up the stairs again, 'Mrs. Schofield!'

'Oh, Mike, have you took leave of your senses?' Lizzie was dashing out of the room, and Mike answered her, 'We can't leave her up there and all this going on.'

It only seemed a matter of seconds before Mrs. Schofield's voice came from the landing, saying, 'Nothing could stop me coming down. I heard who it was. Oh, I am glad.'

In the sitting-room, Mary Ann, seeming to stand apart as if watching a play being acted, saw Mrs. Schofield and Corny greeting each other, holding hands and laughing as if they had been lifelong friends.

'Where is it?' Mrs. Schofield made a pretence of looking behind him.

'Where's what? ... Oh, I've left it in me grip, but I'll bring it over tomorrow and serenade you.'

Indeed here was a different Corny. His grip ... and he would serenade Mrs. Schofield. The other Corny would never have talked like that. If this time yesterday someone had said to her, 'How would you feel if Corny were suddenly to drop out of the sky and into the house, how would you feel?' she would have drawn a long breath and clasped her hands together, and answered truthfully, 'Oh, wonderful. It would be the most wonderful thing on earth that could happen.' And now here he was, larger than life, and she was quite numb. She was even asking herself at this point: Had she ever been mad about Corny Boyle? The Corny Boyle that she had known ... and loved ... was a reticent person; brusque, Mr. Lord had said. But Mr. Lord had also said that America was bringing him out ... America had certainly brought him out, you could say that again. Sarah turned Mary Ann's attention away from her questioning thoughts by saying, 'Oh, Mary Ann, isn't this wonderful! I'm so happy for you.'

She was holding Sarah's hand now, and looking down into her great dark eyes. She was envying her again, jealous of her in a funny way. Sarah was happy ... she loved Michael, and Michael adored her. Somehow it didn't seem to matter about her legs. Sarah had said, 'Oh, I'm happy for you.' For what? Why was she feeling like this? Things weren't right.

Mike's eyes were tight on his daughter now, and the tie between them that had always been stronger than any umbilical cord transferred to him in some measure what the effect of Corny's appearance was having on her, and so he cried, 'Look! We want something to celebrate with. It's either got to be tea, or beer.'

'We'll make it tea.' This was Lizzie.

'Good enough. Hi! there, Mary Ann, get yourself into the kitchen and get busy.'

'I'll—'

The pressure of Mike's hand on Lizzie's arm cut off her words, and he cried again, 'Did you hear what I said? Get that kettle on, me girl. The sooner you get your hand in the better.'

Mary Ann, relinquishing her hold on Sarah's hand, went

round the bed and out of the room, without once looking in the direction of Corny. And when she closed the kitchen door behind her, she stood with her back to it and with the fingers of both her hands pressed over her mouth. She stood in this way for some seconds gazing, but unseeingly, at the stockings hanging from the rod, before going to the fire. The kettle was on the hob, but the fire had been banked down and would take too long to bring up again, so she took the kettle into the scullery and put it on the gas stove. Then she returned to the kitchen and put the cups on the tray, and after picking up the teapot she went into the scullery again. She was measuring out the tea when she heard the kitchen door open, and her hand became still as the footsteps came nearer. Then there he was, as she knew her da had planned. And when he spoke there was a faint resemblance to the old Corny by his straightforward approach to the subject.

'You don't seem overjoyed to see me.'

She turned and looked at him. 'Should I be?'

'Well, what do you think I'm here for?' His face was straight. 'It isn't like getting a bus from Jarrow, popping over from America!'

'No, no, it isn't.'

'Why didn't you go and see me grannie?'

'Why should I?' She rounded on him now, her tone sharp. 'You know, Corny Boyle, you've got a cheek. I never hear a word from you for months, and you expect me to be sitting waiting for you coming ... to drop in, as me da says, like Santa Claus!'

'You know that I don't like writin' letters, I'm no hand at them.'

'There's lots of things I don't like doing that I've got to do. . . . Anyway, you were going to come back when the year was up, but you didn't. And you didn't even write to tell me that. No ... you had to send some fancy photographs through Mr Lord.'

'I didn't send any fancy photographs through Mr. Lord. What are you gettin' at?'

'Well' – she shook her head slowly as she gazed at him – 'surely you haven't got a double in America, and Mr. Lord was taking the wrong Corny Boyle at picnics, parties, swimming and tennis.'

'No. It wasn't a double. I'm the same bloke. People live like that out there. Everybody mixes up together, it's a different world. It took me some time to get used to it, but—'

'But when you did, you lapped it up, didn't you?'

Corny's head had dropped slightly to the side, and now the corner of his mouth came up and there spread across his face the grin she remembered. But she could have slapped it off when in the next moment he said, 'I was beginning to worry, I thought you had stopped likin' me ... coo! I was sweatin'.'

'You needn't start any of your glib American chat here. Not on me. You can keep that for – for—'

'Good-looking girls with blonde hair?'

Her lips came together, her chin went up, and her eyes flashed danger at him. But apparently he was not unduly disturbed, for his grin widened, and he dared to go on and say in a voice that was almost a drawl, 'They called her Priscilla, but she wasn't a bit like her name. And she was tall, taller than most girls, five foot eight, and one of the best lookers over there, I should say.... But it was no use....' The smile suddenly slid from his face and he went on, rapidly now, 'Everybody was nice, more than nice. They had my life planned until I was ninety, and the more cushions they kept padding around me, the more I was seeing you. I told meself that I could live with you until I was ninety; even if we fought every day I could still live with you.... But those over there....' He shook his head slowly. 'I couldn't make them out. I couldn't explain if I tried, I only know why they have two or three wives. But even then I might have stayed, because although I told you I'd be back when the year was up, I'd no intention of comin'. I knew what your mother wanted for you, I knew what Mr. Lord wanted for you. I could never, not in a month of Sundays, hope to compete against Tony and what he stood for. And as me grannie said, it was better to leave the way open to you, there'd be less recrimination in later years if it was your own choice. Then she wrote me a letter, me grannie, not a fortnight since. She said that you hadn't been near the door but she had heard that there was an affair going on between Tony and' – his voice dropped – 'Mrs Schofield. That Mrs. Schofield was divorced and Tony had left old Mr. Lord. Well, that decided me. I couldn't come on the minute, I had to work a bit of notice. But I finished yesterday, or was it the day afore. Anyway, I didn't arrive in Howdon until ten o'clock last night. Well, there it is, Miss Mary Ann Shaughnessy, so what about it? Your mother isn't pleased I've come back, I know that, but what about you?'

'Oh, Corny! . . . Corny!'

As his arms came out and lifted her off her feet she cried again, 'Oh, Corny!'

They had kissed before, fumbling, shy, self-conscious kissing. This was different. Corny was no longer a gauche lad, and Mary Ann was no longer a little girl. When he released her they stood, their arms holding tight, staring into each other's eyes for a long while. And then he said thickly, in a voice that sounded oddly like Mike's, 'I've fetched you a Christmas box.' And putting his hand into his pocket he brought out a small box and handed it to her.

She knew before she opened it what to expect. But the sight of her first ring swamped her with joy. He said, 'Do you like it? I got it through the Customs. It was Christmas Eve and they were kind to me.' She raised her eyes from the ring. 'It's wonderful, Corny, wonderful.' Swiftly she put her arms round his neck again and once more they were lost in each other.

When next she looked at the ring she started to sniff, and said, 'I'd better make this tea. They're all waiting.'

'There's no hurry. Your da's a very astute man, Mary Ann.'

'Me da's a lovely man.' She looked up at him. 'I'm glad you like him, and he likes you.'

'I feel he does. I wish your ma did though.' He was once again speaking in the tongue of the old Corny, and as he ran his fingers through her hair she replied in the idiom of the real Mary Ann, 'Ee! I must mash the tea, leave over.' And they both laughed together.

In the kitchen she pointed to the tray of cups saying,

'Fetch it in.' And then she went before him into the room.

The conversation stopped as soon as the door opened. All eyes were turned on her, and as Corny put down the tray next to Lizzie, Mary Ann held out the box before her mother and said, 'Look. Corny's brought me a Christmas box.'

'Oh, isn't that beautiful!' The exclamations came from both Mrs. Schofield and Sarah. Michael said nothing, nor did Mike. And Lizzie just looked at the ring that Mary Ann was holding in front of her. Then she almost ricked her back, so quickly did she twist about when Corny made a casual-sounding remark, as he turned from the table. 'We're going to be married next year,' was what he had said.

'Well, my God!' said Mike, on a deep note.

'Fast work,' said Michael.

'Oh, how lovely, Mary Ann,' said Sarah.

'Congratulations, my dear.' This was Mrs. Schofield.

Lizzie said nothing, she just gaped. And Mary Ann gaped too, she gaped at the audacity of this big fellow who was again behaving unlike Corny Boyle. And without thinking about the rest of them she cried at him, 'What do you mean, next year? You haven't even asked me.'

'No?' Corny was looking straight at her, the quizzical lift was at the corner of his mouth again. 'I'm just tellin' you now. I'll ask you the morrow, or later on the day, that is.'

The bellow that Mike let out filled the room, and set them all off laughing, all except Lizzie. Lizzie was still gaping. Married next year, indeed! Married! Mary Ann? She was still ... The word child was ripped from her mind. No, she would never be a child again. She would soon be eighteen. In another year she would be nineteen. ... But married. She turned again, as Corny spoke and directly to her now, looking her straight in the eye as he said, 'If her mother will have me in the family?'

What could she say? What could she do? There was only one thing she was thankful for at present: this Corny Boyle was different from the Corny Boyle that went to America. Certainly the year abroad had not been wasted. And after all, she supposed, the main thing was that Mary Ann should be happy. She must remember the hell on earth her own mother had caused her when she married Mike. She mustn't be a pattern of her mother. She'd faced up to the problem of Sarah and that had turned out a hundred per cent to the good. Well, if this worked out properly, perhaps it would have the same result. She prayed to God it would anyway. She smiled now at Corny as she answered him, 'I can't see that you've left me much say in the matter, Corny. But there's one thing very evident. You would never have learnt to be such a fast worker had you stayed in England.'

'I don't know so much about being a fast worker.' Corny was slightly red in the face now, but showing a relieved grin. 'It was that way or going on shilly-shallying for weeks. It's no use talking to her.' He thumbed in the direction of Mary Ann. 'She'd only argue, you know what she's like.'

In her own mind Lizzie confirmed her previous statement. Yes, indeed, Corny Boyle had learned a lot in America. The person whom it was no use talking to and who would argue, had not been Mary Ann ... but herself. She had to admire him for his adroitness. In a way she felt pleased.

Mike was roaring, and as he hugged Mary Ann to him he cried down at her, 'Well, me lass, you've met your match this time.' And then he turned to Mrs. Schofield, who was seated at his side, and drawing her into the family, said, 'What's your opinion of all this?'

Mrs. Schofield, looking between Corny and Mary Ann, said softly, 'I think it will be a wonderful match. I hope they have all the happiness they both deserve.' She looked at Mary Ann and said, 'Do you remember your thirteenth birthday?'

Mary Ann nodded. Tears were misting her vision and she had no words to fit this occasion. Mrs. Schofield now looked towards Corny and said, 'Do you remember it?'

'Could I ever forget it? Me and me shrunken suit!' He extended his long arms to demonstrate how his coat cuffs had at one time receded.

'Oh, I don't mean that. Don't be silly. I meant you and your cornet. You remember how you played, and we all sat on the lawn and sang. Oh, I've thought about that day often, and often. And that song: "He stands at the corner".'

'Oh, aye.' Mike's head went back. 'He stands at the corner and whistles me out. By! It's a long time since we sang that one. Come on ... come on, all of you. Come on, all together. Come on, Liz.' He grabbed her hand and held it in a comforting grip. 'Come on now. One, two, three.

> *He stands at the corner*
> *And whistles me out,*
> *With his hands in his pockets*
> *And his shirt hanging out.*
> *But still I love him—*
> *Can't deny it—*
> *I'll be with him*
> *Wherever he goes.'*

Mary Ann was singing. She was looking at Corny and his eyes were hard on her. There were only the two of them in the entire world, and they were singing to each other. And when the chorus was finished for a second time the last line echoed loud in the large territory of her heart.

> I'll be with him wherever he goes,
> I'll be with him wherever he goes,
> I'll be with him wherever he goes,
> I'll be with him ... WHEREVER HE GOES.

Yes, Corny was the one for her and she would be with him – come hail or shine.

THE INVITATION

When the Gallachers received an invitation from the Duke of
Moorshire to attend his musical evening, Maggie was overwhelmed. Naturally, she did not see the invitation as the rock on
which she was to perish; nor was she prepared for the reactions
of her family. However, Maggie herself was to be the prime
mover of the downfall of the family she loved too dearly . . .

0 552 09035 2   35p

THE MENAGERIE

The Broadhursts were a mining family and, they appeared to be
happy, united, and loyal.
  But it was only Jinny – wife, mother, sister – who held the
Broadhursts together with a pride and strength that prevented
their fears and hates from overwhelming them. There was Jack,
her younger son; Lottie, her sister who was not quite . . . normal;
and Larry, the bright one, her favourite, who was obsessed with
the memory of the girl who had jilted him and who would
sacrifice anyone, family and friends alike, if he could only see
Pam Turnbull again . . .

0 552 08653 3   30p

THE LONG CORRIDOR

To outsiders the life of Dr. Paul Higgins appeared to be a con-
tented one. He seemed to have everything a man could want. But
the façade that Paul and Bett Higgins presented to the world
concealed a welter of hate that grew worse with the passing years.
  Between Paul and Bett stood the barrier of the past – of secrets
that, were they known, could affect everyone about them . . .

0 552 08493 X   25p

A SELECTION OF FINE READING
AVAILABLE IN CORGI BOOKS

War

☐ 552 09282 7   THE MAN WHO HIT THE SCHARNHORST (illustrated)
John Austin 35p

☐ 552 09283 5   TO SEA IN A SIEVE   *Peter Bull* 30p

☐ 552 09308 4   THE JUNGLE IS NEUTRAL   *F. Spencer Chapman* 50p

☐ 552 09246 0   MAUTHAUSEN: HISTORY OF A DEATH CAMP (illustrated)
Evelyn le Chêne 40p

☐ 552 08874 9   SS GENERAL   *Sven Hassel* 35p

☐ 552 09178 2   REIGN OF HELL   *Sven Hassel* 35p

☐ 552 08986 9   DUEL OF EAGLES (illustrated)   *Peter Townsend* 50p

☐ 552 09307 6   THE LONG DAY'S DYING   *Alan White* 30p

☐ 552 09260 6   FINALE AT FLENSBURG (illustrated)   *Charles Whiting* 35p

Western

☐ 552 09147 2   IN THE DAYS OF VICTORIO (illustrated)   *Eve Ball* 40p

☐ 552 08813 7   SUDDEN AT BAY   *Frederick H. Christian* 25p

☐ 552 09095 6   APACHE   *Will Levington Comfort* 30p

☐ 552 09115 8   TWO MILES FROM THE BORDER No. 70   *J. T. Edson* 25p

☐ 552 09227 4   YOU'RE IN COMMAND NOW, MR. FOG No. 71
J. T. Edson 30p

☐ 552 09298 3   THE BIG GUN No. 72   *J. T. Edson* 30p

☐ 552 09191 X   TREASURE MOUNTAIN   *Louis L'Amour* 30p

☐ 552 09264 9   THE FERGUSON RIFLE   *Louis L'Amour* 30p

☐ 552 09355 6   UNDER THE SWEETWATER RIM   *Louis L'Amour* 30p

☐ 552 90287 8   KILLING FOR THE LAW No. 21   *Louis Masterson* 25p

☐ 552 09311 4   THE KEAN LAND   *Jack Schaefer* 30p

Crime

☐ 552 09296 7   LET'S KILL UNCLE LIONEL   *John Creasey* 30p

☐ 552 09297 5   CALL FOR THE BARON   *John Creasey* 30p

☐ 552 09286 X   MURDER MOST FOUL   *John Creasey* 30p

☐ 552 09310 6   CAGE UNTIL TAME   *Laurence Henderson* 35p

☐ 552 09206 1   THE EXECUTIONER: NIGHTMARE IN NEW YORK
Don Pendleton 30p

☐ 552 09262 2   THE EXECUTIONER: CHICAGO WIPEOUT *Don Pendleton* 35p

☐ 552 09111 1   THE ERECTION SET   *Mickey Spillane* 40p

☐ 552 09072 7   SHAFT'S BIG SCORE   *Ernest Tidyman* 30p

☐ 552 09273 8   SHAFT HAS A BALL   *Ernest Tidyman* 30p

☐ 552 09309 2   SHAFT AMONG THE JEWS   *Ernest Tidyman* 35p

All these books are available at your bookshop or newsagent: or can be ordered direct from the publisher. Just tick the titles you want and fill in the form below.

CORGI BOOKS, Cash Sales Department, P.O. Box 11, Falmouth, Cornwall.
Please send cheque or postal order, no currency, and allow 7p per book to cover the cost of postage and packing in the U.K. (5p if more than one copy) 7p per book overseas.

NAME ....

ADDRESS ....

(SEPT 73) ....